"You are not eating, m'lord."

"Here, try this," Ingrith said, picking up a portion of pork dripping with red sauce with her fingertips and placing it at his lips.

He opened obediently, like the boyling she seemed to regard him, but the sensation that shot from her fingertips at his lips was anything but boyish. Without thinking, he grabbed her wrist when she was about to withdraw and licked the remaining sauce off her fingertips, one at a time.

"M'lord!" she exclaimed.

He knew exactly what she meant, whether she recognized it for what it was, or not. Just that tactile abrasion of his tongue on her soft skin caused him to want so much more.

She jerked her hand away. "What do you think?"

"Of your skin? A little sweet," he concluded. Then grinned at her. "Wouldst like to lick *my* fingertips?"

The Viking Takes A Knight

Sandra Hill

AVON

An Imprint of HarperCollinsPublishers

AVON BOOKS
An Imprint of HarperCollins*Publishers*
10 East 53rd Street
New York, New York 10022-5299

Copyright © 2010 by Sandra Hill
ISBN 978-0-06-167350-4
www.avonromance.com

First Avon Books paperback printing: September 2010

Avon Trademark Reg. U.S. Pat. Off. and in Other Countries, Marca Registrada, Hecho en U.S.A.
HarperCollins® is a registered trademark of HarperCollins Publishers.

Printed in the U.S.A.

10 9 8 7 6 5 4 3 2 1

This book is dedicated to my four sons, Beau, Rob, Matt, and Daniel. They've got Viking in their blood, rogue in their rascally brains, a comedic vein that would put SNL to shame, and enough alpha to drive a mother mad.

Instead of there having been a book titled Truly, Madly Viking, *there should have been one titled* Truly, Madly Viking Mom. *No kidding, every gray hair on my head (not that you'll ever see them), was put there by the four musketeers.*

Although none of them has ever read a word I've written (fear of learning Mom knows something about sex, I suppose), they have been supportive of my writing from the get-go. From spotting and reporting my books on store shelves (including that Maine bait-and-tackle shop), to setting up computer programs, to researching items, to talking up my books to friends and acquaintances, to general enthusiasm when I've won awards or made lists. Although the one who owns a pizza franchise for some reason refuses to put my books' covers on the delivery boxes. Jeesh! And each of them refused to dress as a Viking and wear a signboard at my book signings, not even for cash. Even so, they probably think they're going to inherit a million dollars some day from my writing. Ha, ha, ha!

They say there is a special place in heaven for mothers of sons. I believe it. But they bring joy and humor to this mother's life, as well.

So, this one is dedicated to you, guys. Maybe you'll even read it this time.

He said:
"My tongue, leaden with grief
Lies listless.
Naught will stir my soul.
No skaldic poem touches me,
My heart is heavy with woe.
So many tears! Such sadness!
All my thoughts are dark.
How can I breed joy from such blackness?
Rain in my sad heart
And rain drenching my lands . . ."

She said:
"I have braved sea waves
and fought serpent winds
through many countries to
make this visit to you . . ."

– A loose interpretation of *Egil's Saga,*
circa tenth century

The Viking Takes A Knight

CHAPTER ONE

C *lueless men get stung . . . every time . . .*

Honey was a lot like a woman. Sweet when you were in the mood, and sticky when you were sated.

John of Hawk's Lair grimaced at his own flowery musing. He was a warrior when called to service by his Saxon king, a good master to his various estates, but mostly just a reclusive student of . . . yes, honey.

He didn't realize that he'd spoken aloud until his visitor from the Norselands, Hamr Egilsson, made a snorting sound and said, "Hah! Forget about honey—when a man's sap is rising, a female nether nest is the only thing that will do."

Nether nest? Help me, Lord!

Hamr of Vestfold, the wildest Viking that ever rode a longship, dipped a fingertip in one of the dozens of small pottery jars that John was experimenting with, each marked with an identifying placard, such as "Clover" or "Cherry Blossom," and licked the honey appreciatively. Hamr was a nephew, thrice removed, of John's Norse stepfather, Lord Eirik of Ravenshire. Vikings considered even the thinnest blood connection family; John, though full Saxon, had been raised to do likewise.

John smacked his hand away. "Those are for research. Be careful you don't drop any on my notes."

While Lady Eadyth of Ravenshire, John's mother, was a beekeeper far-famed for her mead and time-keeping candles, John was more interested in the medicinal properties. His patience was wearing thin with his irksome guest, who was clearly getting restless after only three days here in the wilds of Northumbria. John doubted he would have his company much longer. Not that Hamr would be returning to his homeland anytime soon since he had been recently outlawed by a Vestfold Althing for trawling the wrong bed furs . . . those of a high chieftain's wife. Hopefully, it would be a short exile.

"Can you not go find a country to plunder, Hamr?"

"Done that."

"Pirate hunting?"

"Done that. In fact, I am thinking about becoming a pirate."

"Have you not fame enough as an outlaw? Must you add piracy to your sins?"

"Methinks I would be a good pirate. I would give piracy a respectable name."

"You would not know respectable if it hit you in your face." John inhaled for patience. "Swordplay then?"

"Done that."

"Visit a brothel?"

"Done that. And done that. And done that."

"Go exploring in the lands beyond Iceland?"

"Too cold."

"Join the Varangian guard in Byzantium."

"Too much work."

"Build a new longship."

"I have too many already. Rather, my father does."

John made a clucking sound of disgust.

"Lord Gravely, you are too somber by half and unimaginative," Hamr continued.

John frowned at the rascal for all his m'lording. John was entitled to wear the title of Lord of Gravely, which he disdained because of his deceased, evil, undoubtedly insane father. For that reason, he would never beget children of his own. The risk of the taint in his blood was too great. "Call me Hawk, or call me John, but do not call me Gravely," he warned.

Hamr crossed his eyes at John. Betimes the lackwit behaved like a youthling scarce out of swaddling clothes, even though he had passed the same thirty-one years as John.

Easing himself off the stool with a long sigh of boredom, Hamr finally started for the door, just before Graeme the Stableman knocked.

"Is there a problem, Graeme? One of the horses?"

Graeme twisted his cap in his hands. "Nay, the horses are fine. My manpart is not."

By the rood! What now?

Hamr's ears perked up and, instead of leaving, he turned to listen to the conversation.

"I know ye pay me and me wife to slather that honey on my manpart so we kin stop breedin' babes, but—"

"You can go now, Hamr," John said.

"Are you daft? This promises to be the most fun I've had since I got here." Hamr sat on his stool once again.

John was about to tell Graeme to come back later, but he blathered on, "By the saints! I was tuppin' Mary in one of the horse stalls las' night, and I'm still pickin' straw off my ballocks and in my crack. Mary says she has straw up her woman channel, and it itches somethin' awful."

Way more detail than John wanted or needed.

Hamr had a hand over his mouth. Laughing, no doubt.

"We both got flies swarmin' around our private

parts." Graeme was on a roll now. "What should we do, Lord Hawk?"

"You could take a bath," he suggested.

Graeme stared at him in horror. A bath a year was his routine, John guessed. Or twice a year, at best.

"I have an idea," Hamr said with a grin.

"Shut your teeth, fool," John advised. Then, to his stableman, "Do you want to quit the project, Graeme?" John had twelve couples of childbearing years involved in his experiments to prevent conception. One less would not be fatal to the study.

"Nay!" Graeme replied. "We need the coin."

"My idea . . . Does no one want to hear my idea?" Hamr was waving his hand to get their attention. "You could remove Mary's honey by licking her nether folds."

Graeme's expression bespoke his reluctance.

"And she could remove yours by sucking your cock."

Graeme's eyes lit up with delight. "Good idea!" he said. "I will tell Mary it is Lord Hawk's orders."

John groaned. But he had no time to bemoan his dilemma. Efrim the Woodsman arrived, holding a bloody rag to his left hand, which had been cut almost to the bone two months past. The wound still festered. "Maude, the scullery maid, said you used honey on her husband Harry's boil an' it healed jist fine."

Honey on a broken blister was one thing, a gaping wound quite another. Next, his people would expect him to cure leprosy with honey.

John washed Efrim's wound, then honey-salved it, emphasizing the importance of keeping an open sore clean and covered with unsoiled bindings.

"Thank ye very much, m'lord. I have no coin, but my Essie will send ye some of her special goat cheese."

Arguing that he did not need to be paid had gained John naught in the past; so, he just nodded. "I do appreciate good goat cheese." *I loathe goat cheese.*

"Do you do this all the time?" Hamr wanted to know once Efrim departed.

"I do not claim to be a healer, but, yea, a fair number of people come to me as a last resort when all else fails."

"And they pay for your services with cheese?"

"And eggs, fish, venison, live chickens, a pig, wool, manure . . . yea, manure for the gardens. Even a barrel of eels."

Hamr rolled his eyes. "Mayhap you could hint that a big-breasted woman with wanton ways would not be unwelcome payment."

John decided the best course was to ignore the lackwit.

That night a lone rider entered the keep gates.

A man of about fifty years with a grizzled white beard and long hair in the Viking style, and a patch over one eye. *Oh, Good Lord!* It was Bolthor, the world's worst skald, who quickly told John that he had been sent by his mother to keep him company. A mother he was going to throttle if she did not stop interfering in his life.

John knew from past experience that come nightfall there was going to be a poem about honey licking and miracle cures.

And there was.

That night in John's great hall, where the fare was plain due to the recent death of the longtime Hawk's Lair cook, a glaze came over Bolthor's one eye . . . a sure sign that he was overcome by the verse mood. Without much ado, Bolthor announced, "This is the saga of John of Hawk's Lair. I call it 'Hawk's Honey.'" It mattered not that John groaned and pleaded with Bolthor not to recite his saga aloud, or that Hamr laughed so hard he fell off his seat. Bolthor considered it his gods' given duty to spread his poetic wisdom.

In the land of the Saxons,
A lackwit knight was born.
Day and night he spent
Mooning over honey.
But alas and alack,

As time went on,
He did not realize that
Ice was growing on his heart.
Even worse, cobwebs were growing
On his manpart.
And the most important honey
Was missing from his life.
Mayhap honey is a bane betimes.
Mayhap man needs a bit of sour
To offset the sweet.
Mayhap the hawk should fly
Instead of resting on his feathery arse.

While everyone else laughed and clapped their hands with appreciation, John was heard to murmur, "Mayhap someone ought to stuff a codpiece in a certain skald's mouth."

CHAPTER TWO

&

To market, to market, to buy a . . . chauvinist pig?
Ingrith Sigrundottir walked through the busy streets of Jorvik with five young orphans trailing behind her.

To Ubbi, her elderly "guard," she whispered, "I feel like a goose with its goslings."

"Best ye not be waddlin', m'lady. Many a lustsome man here in the city might take it as an invitation."

"Ubbi! I'm almost thirty-one years old. Way past the time when men grow lustsome and drooling at my comeliness."

"Age is naught when the sap rises in a man," Ubbi said, "but ye are not to worry. I will protect you."

Which was ludicrous, really. Ubbi . . . seventy if he was a day . . . was no taller than ten-year-old Godwyn, who preceded him. If anyone waddled, it was him on his short bowed legs. The little man carried a lance in his gnarled right hand, but it was more for a walking stick. *No matter!* Ingrith was well-armed with sharp daggers at her belt and ankle, and she knew how to use them.

Truth to tell, Ingrith was still an attractive woman. It was her no-nonsense personality, rather than her appearance, that repelled most men, who preferred biddable women. She was happiest when she was organizing a kitchen and all the cooking, some said like a military commander. And she satisfied her maternal urges by caring for the orphans at Rainstead, an orphanage located outside Jorvik.

With blonde hair braided and wrapped into a tight coronet atop her head, Ingrith did her best to hide her tall, embarrassingly voluptuous figure with a modest, long-sleeved *gunna* under a calf-length, open-sided apron. She wore her usual prim expression on her face.

"As fer that,"—Ubbi was still blathering on whilst she had been woolgathering—"that Saxon commander, Leo of Loncaster, is certainly smitten with you."

Ingrith made a grimace of distaste at the reminder of the soldier, who persisted, despite her continual rebuffs. Lately, although she did not see him often, he had become vile in his attentions.

"Could we proceed?" Ingrith urged, suddenly nervous.

It was not that the market town was dangerous, especially during daylight hours, but it was crowded. And there were evil men who preyed on young children for the sex-slave trade. Those same men resented the children's shelter, which offered refuge to what they considered a commodity. In addition, the city was home to numerous thieves able to slip a pouch of coins from people's belts without them noticing. Godwyn had perfected that particular talent before being "rescued."

Jorvik, at the confluence of the Foss and Ouse Rivers, which led out to the North Sea, was once the site of the Roman city Eburacum, or what the Saxons still called Eoforwic. It had been held as the capital of Northumbria by Vikings off and on over the past two centuries, most recently as ten years ago when the Norse king Eric Bloodaxe had been driven away. For the time being, Saxon earls ruled in King Edgar's place, and the *clomp-clomp* of the garrison soldiers' boots could be heard as they patrolled the streets in groups.

"Stay close. Hold hands," she warned as they approached the minster steps, where two young monks were tossing out hunks of bread to the destitute who crowded there every morning.

"Why are the monks' heads bald only on the top?" five-year-old Breaca asked.

" 'Tis called a tonsure," Ubbi explained.

"A ton-*sore*? Oh, do they have sores on their heads, like Aelfric's flea bites? Listen to the bells. 'Tis like angel music. Remember the story about St. Michael the Archangel?" Betimes, Breaca chattered away like a magpie.

"I would like to see an angel some day." Seven-year-old Arthur sighed, and the other children nodded.

"I would not want to be a priest," Godwyn asserted. "They cannot tup girls."

"Godwyn!" Ingrith exclaimed.

"What? 'Tis true."

"The boyling has a point," Ubbi agreed with a chortle but still tapped Godwyn on the shoulder with his lance.

"What is a tup?" Emma asked.

"That is when—" Godwyn started to say.

But Ingrith cut him short with another "Godwyn!"

He ducked his head sheepishly, but he would probably be regaling the other children later with misinformation.

Motioning with her hand, Ingrith encouraged them all to move on behind her.

The city, which housed ten thousand people inside its walls, was laid out in an orderly grid of streets, best known as gates in the Norse language, such as Petergate, Stonegate, and Goodramgate. The Coppergate section, where they headed now, hosted dozens and dozens of craftsmen, merchants, and traders, many of whom lived in small, horizontally timbered or wattle-and-daub houses with neat front yards where tents and tables were set up to sell their services and wares. The children's heads swung left and right, mouths agape, as they took in all the sights. Jewelers, black-smiths, tanners, shoemakers, glassblowers, seam-stresses, lace makers, wood-carvers, knife and scissor sharpeners, barbers, potters, silver- and goldsmiths, weavers, candle makers, and so many more, including those women practicing the art of *orfrois* with gold and silver thread on bands of silk. Sometimes a damsel would weave strands of her own hair onto the patterns as a special gift for a lover.

In truth, the goods offered appealed to one and all, from ells of cloth in fat bolts as well as ready-made garments of samite silk, fine Northumbria wool, linen, and rough homespun. Horseshoes, swords and knives. Arm rings and amulets. Thimbles of all sizes and materials. Live animals: cows, goats, horses, and pigs. Poultry and eggs. Relics from the Holy Land . . . some of them out-landish, such as the Virgin Mary's toenails. Many varieties of fresh fish, including oysters and mus-sels. Newly butchered meats, still dripping blood. Rich cheeses, both hard and soft. Honeycombs, mead, and candles. Fresian wines.

The raucous noises were not unpleasing to the ear, whether they be merchants calling out their goods, the braying, bleats, and grunts of animals, conversations of passersby, the bells of the minster, or conversations in a dozen different languages. The smells, though . . . ah, some of the smells were enough to gag a rat, like the leather booth they were approaching, with its tannery in back. Then, too, there were the slave auction platforms down by the waterfront, which Ingrith always avoided.

"What kin I do fer ye, mistress?" the bootmaker asked.

"I need shoes for each of these children . . . leather ankle boots. Also, several lengths of leather thongs for laces."

"Fine children ye have, too, mistress," the bootmaker said, rubbing his hands together with anticipation of the coins he would soon have. "They look jist like you."

She laughed at that observation, especially since Kavil was a Nubian, with ebony skin.

Kavil caught her eye and smiled back at her, a smile that did not reach his liquid brown eyes. It never did.

What a dear boy he was! Too pretty by half, and for that reason had been misused by sodomites to whom his slave master had rented him out. His spirit and his body had been broken when they'd first found him. After a year, he was still not totally healed.

From there, the entire group stopped at various booths, buying spices from far lands, a new cauldron, carved horn spoons, and straining cloths for making cheese. For the thirty children from ages one to fourteen currently at the orphanage, they had two cows for milk and butter, as well as chickens that produced a large number of eggs, a goat, and several sheep. Still, there were essentials they needed to purchase. Fortunately the orphanage was well funded by generous benefactors.

A pottery booth drew her attention now. Behind the table was a petite woman with lustrous black hair and blue eyes. Although older than Ingrith, she was beyond beautiful.

"Are you interested in some pots today, m'lady?" The woman smiled.

"Yea, I am."

"My name is Joanna. Feel free to examine my wares." With a sweeping hand, she indicated her items for sale, both on a long table, and on shelves behind her. Presumably she lived in the neat timbered house in back. Ingrith could see a kiln on the side. "If these are not to your liking, I can provide you with any size or shape of container you want."

"Hmmm." There were redware pots of all sizes and shapes, glazed and unglazed. Jugs, too. The most interesting were those that had been decorated before firing with flowers and other designs. "Years ago, I was in Jorvik. As I recall, there used to be a red-haired man in this spot."

"That would be my husband, Gerald, who was a master potter. He died three years ago."

"My sympathies. You are fortunate to have found another supplier for your wares."

"That would be me," she revealed, lifting her chin with pride. "Gerald taught me the craft, but it was my idea to add the decorations."

"They're lovely."

Joanna blushed prettily. "Thank you, m'lady."

"I need some of this size to store soft cheeses, like *skyrr*." She pointed to two of the plain ones with wide mouths and lids. "And that one over there would make a wonderful gift for my sister Drifa. She loves flowers." It was an urn, decorated with twining roses.

After she paid for her goods with a halved silver coin, and while the woman wrapped her purchases in worn, rough cloth, Ingrith carried on a conversation for the sake of politeness. "Do you a thriving business here?"

Joanna shrugged. "The stall on market days is busy, but I must close over the winter. I have steady orders from some customers, though, like a beekeeper in one of the northern shires who finds that size over there perfect for holding whole honeycombs."

"Would that be Lady Eadyth of Ravenshire?"

Joanna's blue eyes brightened. "Yea. Do you know her?"

"My family is well acquainted with hers."

Joanna continued to wrap the pots, then seemed to hesitate before asking, "Do you know Lady Eadyth's son John?"

John? She refers to him by his given name? "Do you mean Hawk? John of Hawk's Lair?"

Joanna's face bloomed crimson with embarrassment. It could only mean that she knew John intimately. Was she his mistress? Ingrith had heard that men often sought widows for their mistresses, especially those not of the upper classes. Viking men took extra wives or concubines. Was that the case with John? *Oh, good gods! Why should I care?*

Joanna picked up a tiny glazed clay pot the size of her fist and caressed the edges in a loving fashion. "Lord Gravely"—she used his formal name now, having realized her error in calling him John—"buys numerous pots of this size for his experiments with honey."

Well, that may be one reason you know him, but you are either enamored with the rogue, or you are sharing his bed furs.

There I go again! Musing on affairs that are none of my business.

"This size pot would be nice for table salt, or for storing spices. I like to experiment with different seasonings in my cooking," Ingrith explained. "Could I have six of them?"

After completing her transaction, she smiled at Joanna and said, "Give my regards to Hawk when you see him next."

"Oh, nay. I do not . . . He does not—"

Ingrith waved a hand dismissively. "Thank you for my new pots. I will recommend you to my friends and family."

With those words, she began to gather the children together for a return to the orphanage, despite their protests that they wanted to watch the musical birds in gilded cages. As she made her way through the crowd, she could not stop thinking about Hawk . . . John, as she was more wont to call him . . . and Joanna. Did he love the beautiful woman, or was she a convenient mistress?

And Ingrith wondered if she would ever find a love of her own. At her age, probably not.

CHAPTER THREE

❧

And so the trouble begins . . .

Ingrith had gone only a few steps when she was stopped in her tracks by Commander Loncaster, who was glowering.

"Where is he?"

"Who?"

"You know good and well who. That royal bastard Henry. I have it on good authority that you gave the bratling refuge . . . after I specifically ordered you to send for me at first sight of the boy."

"I vaguely recall that conversation. 'Twas the day I slapped your roving hands from my bottom." And, yea, she knew young Henry. The deathbed wish of Henry's mother was that her five-year-old child be offered protection at Rainstead.

Ingrith gazed up at the commander as she tried to decide how to proceed. She had to admit that he really was a handsome man, with clean white teeth and even features. He was big. Very big. All over. Although he had never done her physical harm, she suspected he could be cruel and vindictive. A man not to cross.

He grinned of a sudden. "You cannot recall my warning about the boy, but you recall my hands on your rump?"

She barely restrained herself from smacking the arrogant smirk off his face. "Tell me again . . . why do you seek the boy?"

"Not I. King Edgar wishes to see him. It appears he is one of the royal by-blows."

"King Edgar will recognize him as his blood?" That was news to her.

"I doubt it, lest he has butter yellow hair and pale-as-a-mist blue eyes."

Exactly! "Then why . . . oh, I understand." Many a royal personage destroyed any heirs to the kingship that might jeopardize the legitimate lineage. The Viking Eric Bloodaxe, for example, was said to have killed a dozen of his brothers, all sons of the virile King Harald. "Tell me, commander, if King Edgar told you to kill the boy, would you?"

He shrugged. His silence was telling. "I will be coming to the orphanage to look over your charges. Expect me within three days."

Ingrith shivered inside. Not only would he find Henry, whose hair and eyes would attest to his relation to King Edgar, but there were several comely girls who had reason to fear soldiers, despite their young ages.

"I might be able to stay a day or two if a certain woman would be . . . agreeable." Leo ran a fingertip over her sleeve along her arm from shoulder to wrist. There was a message in his gesture, given as it was in such a public place. "I am weary with the wait for you, m'lady." Was that a threat in his soft-spoken words or his meandering hand that now rested on her hip, under her apron? *Agreeable*, meaning that she agreed to couple with him?

"Commander, I am—"

"Call me Leo."

"Leo, I am nobly born. A princess." Betimes, Ingrith found it convenient to mention her title. "My father would send a *hird* of warriors to kill any man who beds me without wedding vows."

"Well, then, I might just offer for you, I suppose." He smiled as if that were a great compliment and squeezed her hip and a portion of her buttock with his big hand. His pincer-like grasp would probably leave a bruise. "And do not be telling me that I am too far below your station. At your advanced age, you cannot be choosy."

If he thought to win her graces with such words, he was sadly mistaken. "At my *advanced age*," she asserted, "I am able to make my own decisions. Mayhap you should direct your attentions elsewhere. A woman not so old as I."

He laughed and squeezed her again, more on her buttock than her hip now. "You are mine."

Oh, the nerve of the man! "I have *never* indicated

that I am yours." Ingrith spoke with more forth-rightness than she usually did in his presence, but his insulting words defied diplomacy.

"M'lady, do not exceed yourself," he warned. "The fact that I've marked you as my woman does not give you license to malign me, whether it be through wedlock or otherwise." With those words, and before she could protest, he lifted her by the waist and took her to the side of a building, where he propped her against the wall, feet dangling off the ground.

As his men laughed behind them, calling out lewd jeers, he began to lower his head. She tried pushing against his massive, leather-vested chest, to no avail, then shrieked, "You are such a pig! Put me down at once, or I will—"

Her words were cut off as he chuckled, "Oink, oink!" and slammed his lips over hers, prying them open with a nip at her lower lip, then thrusting his tongue deep into her mouth. She needed to gag, but she could not breathe. The roaring in her ears presaged that she would soon faint, something she never did.

Then suddenly he jerked back with the exclamation, "What the bloody hell?"

It was Ubbi, striking at Loncaster's back with the wooden part of his lance. The children were rushing toward her from one direction, and a half dozen of Leo's men were coming at them from the other direction. Meanwhile, Leo had lifted Ubbi by the scruff of his neck and was shaking him like a limp rag.

"Nay, nay, put him down." She pulled at Loncaster's tunic. "He was only protecting me."

"From kisses?" Loncaster snarled at her. "Striking a soldier in the king's guard is a hanging offense."

"Please, Leo, I beg you. Put him down, and I will . . . I will welcome your visit to Rainstead."

He paused. "Hah! I want a hell of a lot more than a 'Greetings, Leo' from you."

"I understand," she said in a low voice only he could hear.

He dropped Ubbi to the ground, then eyed her icily. "Prepare yourself then, wench." He said *wench* with deliberate insult. "My appetite is huge and not easily sated."

On those ominous words, Loncaster joined his soldiers, and they ambled off, laughing at some ribald man-jest.

The children were sobbing, except for Godwyn, who looked fierce enough to do battle, as he helped a shame-faced Ubbi to his feet.

"Oh, Ubbi, we are in such trouble!"

"We?"

"Everyone at Rainstead. We must close down the orphanage for a while."

"Beggin' yer pardon, mistress, but we cannot just shove thirty children out ta fend fer themselves. Mayhap you could go home to the Norselands fer a short time, or to visit one of yer sisters in Northumbria."

"I would, except I'm not the only problem facing Rainstead. You are aware that King Edgar wants Henry . . . for some nefarious purpose, I fear. Now he grows more insistent. Plus, you know that the young girls we harbor were indentured to that brothel. More than that, the Saxon soldiers under King Edgar need little excuse to ravage anything associated with Vikings, and Rainstead is clearly a Norse-founded orphanage in Saxon lands."

"'Tis true. We operate by sufferance from the Saxons, but they have left us alone . . . thus far."

"Before I brought Rainstead to their attention." Ingrith pondered for a moment. "We could close Rainstead for a short while 'til the danger passes." She tapped her chin thoughtfully. "There are four adults at Rainstead, including the two of us, and thirty children. Each of us could take seven or more children and seek sanctuary in different places in the region."

"How long would we have to be gone?"

"I do not know. King Edgar usually spends the winter months at Winchester. It makes sense that Leo, as chief *hirdsman* in the king's guard, would travel with the king."

Ubbi groaned. "That is six months from now."

They drew straws that night to decide who went where. Ingrith would be going to Briarstead, a Norse-held estate in Northumbria.

Thus it was that by daybreak the next day, the other women had already left with their charges. Ingrith donned a man's *braies* and overtunic, her upbraided hair tucked under a floppy hat, as she prepared to drive a wagonload of orphans out of Jorvik heading north. With her were Godwyn, Kavil, Arthur, Breaca, and Signe, along with two of the fourteen-year-old sisters who had been indentured from age ten to a brothel before being rescued, and Henry, bless his royal heart, who now had green hair thanks to her failed attempt to dye his hair brown. And Ubbi, her self-proclaimed protector.

"You are the most pitiful-looking boy," Ubbi declared to Ingrith. "Mayhap you should practice spitting and scratching yerself if anyone stops you along the way."

"Ye could belch, too," Godwyn offered. "I could teach you how." He let loose with a loud belch to demonstrate. "I could also teach you how to break wind."

"Nay. Thank you just the same," she said quickly. But Ingrith's plans changed when she stopped at Ravenshire later that day on her way to Briarstead. Lord and Lady Ravenshire gave them welcome, but Ingrith was informed that no one was in residence at Briarstead at the moment, Toste Ivarsson and his wife, Helga, being in the Norselands, visiting family.

"Not to worry," Lady Eadyth assured Ingrith once they settled down for the evening meal.

"You must go to Hawk's Lair, which is not so far away. My son John will enjoy your company."

Ingrith was not so sure about that, considering the beautiful Joanna, and considering the sly look in Lady Eadyth's eyes.

"John can always use more help with his honey experiments, and it will save one of our men having to deliver more bees to him, as I had planned. This is a new breed of bees I ordered from the Arab lands. Besides, Hawk's Lair recently lost its longtime cook. Mayhap you could help train a new one." Lady Eadyth blinked at her with seeming innocence.

It all sounded logical, and Ingrith wanted to be helpful.

Why then, did she have this niggling reservation, as if something momentous was about to happen?

"It was meant to be," Lady Eadyth concluded.

All Ingrith could say was, "Gods help me!"

CHAPTER FOUR

❧

You did WHAT with my honey?
    John had taken his two guests to the far reaches of his estate, along with a small *hird* of his men, to hunt for boar. The real reason was to ease Hamr's boredom—*boar for boredom, he jested to himself, a clear sign of his shattering nerves.* And he hoped to tire out Bolthor so he would be too weary to make up any more ridiculous poems and—*please, God*—go home.

That did not happen.

In fact, John was thinking seriously about lopping off both of their tongues. Did they never stop talking? Jabber, jabber, jabber. Hamr had almost gotten them all killed when he made a lewd suggestion to one of the huntsmen's wives who came along to cook their meal over an open fire, a open fire which, incidentally, was made so large by the two lackwits that John had feared his entire forest would go up in flames.

And they never saw one single boar. The wild

pigs, and every other animal with any sense, had probably run for cover when they heard all the chatter.

All John wanted was peace and quiet.

As they ambled back to the keep on their horses, his *hirdsmen* having gone up ahead, Hamr remarked to Bolthor, "So, you married late in life, did you? And you have a wife and flock of children?"

"I do. I do. Katherine, my heartling. One child betwixt us we have, and four stepchildren from her first three marriages."

"Uh . . . shouldn't you be home taking care of your family?" John inquired, then quickly added, "Sorry. I did not mean to give offense."

Bolthor shrugged. "No offense taken. We have a thriving poultry business at Wickshire Manor, as you may have heard. Holy Thor, we must have the most lusty roosters and fertile hens in the world, because, I tell you, there are chickens everywhere. Hundreds of the buggers. And chicken shit! Phew! Not to mention the fact that I am somehow the one designated to cut off their heads, gut, and defeather them in preparation for market. What Norseman worth his salt raises chickens instead of going a-Viking, I ask you?"

John and Hamr exchanged grins.

"So that is why you are able to come visiting?" John asked with as much politeness as he could muster. Vikings prided themselves on their hospitality, and John had been raised by a Viking step-father.

"Actually, it is not." Bolthor sighed deeply. "I wrote a praise-poem about Katherine's breasts—"

"Oh, Good Lord!" John exclaimed. He did not want to hurt Bolthor's feelings, but *Good Lord!*

"I love it!" Hamr reached over and clapped Bolthor on the shoulder. "Proceed."

"It was a fine saga. Leastways, I thought so. But Katherine was so angry, I swear there was smoke coming out of her ears. I do not understand. Katherine has very nice bosoms. It was a compliment. Wouldst like to hear it?"

"No!" John said.

"Absolutely," said Hamr.

That was all the encouragement the skald needed. "This is the poem I call 'Ode to Katherine's Breasts.'"

John groaned.

Once was a lady from Wickshire,
With a bosom you had to admire.
Plump and rosy with a bit of bounce.
Caused many a man for her favors to pounce.
Big udders on women are surely a necessity
To give suckle to babes so pretty
And give a man something to hold on to in bedsport.

John was too stunned to speak.
But not Hamr. "Well done, Bolthor."

They were almost back to the keep by then, thank God!

"Looks like you have visitors," Hamr pointed out. "With a bunch of children. Could they be your family, Bolthor?"

Bolthor squinted his one good eye, then shook his head. "Nay. Not mine."

From this rise, they could see inside the palisades of his keep, as well as the surrounding fields. John was appalled at what he beheld.

There were two young girls rolling around in the wildflower patch he had specifically planted for one colony of his bees.

Two little boys, one of them with ungodly green hair, were chasing that ornery bearded goat Wilfred, one of many unwelcome gifts from his mother. Wilfred would no doubt soon butt their bottoms if they kept goading him.

A boy the size of a bucket was leaning over the edge of the inner well.

And there were two boylings, one of them a black-skinned Nubian, approaching one of the conical bee hives of twisted straw he had placed in strategic spots about his estate, this one closest to the keep. Hundreds of thousands of bees resided at Hawk's Lair under his cultivation. It was no playing field for children. They would surely be stung if they touched any of them, or even if they got any closer.

And a gnome! An honest-to-God gnome was driving a wagon across his back courtyard.

His horse clomped loudly as he galloped over the wooden drawbridge to the inner bailey, where he quickly dismounted, then demanded of Graeme the Stableman, "Who in the name of all the saints is responsible for these bratlings?"

Graeme stuttered, "Mistress . . . I mean, Lady . . . um, oh, nay!" Before he rushed off to grab a mite of a boy using a stick to poke a stallion in a nearby stall, Graeme pointed toward the wide-open double doors of his keep.

John stomped inside, through his great hall, through his downstairs solar, creating a path amongst his gawking people, toward the kitchen, where the most wonderful smells wafted out. Fresh bread, roasted meat, and stewed apples would be his guess. Probably a new cook had been found.

But that mattered not at the present. What mattered was finding out which troublemaker had the gall to invade his home and create such chaos.

He came to a screeching halt at the entrance to the kitchen. Bending over the oven to the side of a blazing hearth fire, where there appeared to be a small animal, probably a lamb, covered with some kind of red sauce on a spit, was a tall figure in slim *braies* and belted tunic. It was a woman. He knew that by the long blonde hair that was escaping from a single braid down her back to her waist, and by the heart-shaped arse deliciously outlined by the taut fabric of her breeches.

His mind went blank. His anger stalled. His heart raced, pumping blood to that other important organ, the one that apparently liked heart-shaped arses and was starved for attention.

Just then, a squeak from one of the scullery maids must have alerted the villainous woman, who turned with surprise, her eyes shining like the light-colored sapphire he'd seen once in an Eastern market. She smiled at him as if it was an everyday occurrence that she came into his home, uninvited, with a herd of children.

He knew her, of course. It was Ingrith. Princess Ingrith, truth be told. One of King Thorvald's daughters. Not that John was coming to all these conclusions logically or at once. His brain was still frozen at the sight of a wellborn woman in boy's clothing acting as queen, or rather princess, of his kitchen.

"Hawk!" She beamed happily, setting down a tray of oatcakes on the wooden table. "Good tidings, John!"

It is good to see you, too. Especially the view from behind. And the one from the front is not so bad, either. "Lady Ingrith! What a pleasant surprise!" *Not!*

Without a by-your-leave, the lady walked up and gave him a greeting-hug. She smelled of barley flour and woman . . . and . . . *oh, my God,* honey.

Setting her back with hands on her upper arms, he asked, hesitantly, "Why do you smell like honey?"

"'Tis the oatcakes. I have a special recipe that calls for lots and lots of honey. Would you like to try one?" She carefully picked up one of the warm oatcakes with a piece of cloth and offered it to him.

Ignoring her proffered treat, he inquired with as much calmness as he could muster, "Where did you get the honey, m'lady?"

"Uh . . . from the honey shed."

His eyes crossed with frustration. He breathed in and out, fisting his hands at his sides. *Do not shake the witless woman. Do not kick the witless woman in her heart-shaped arse. Do not think about how she looks under those man-garments.* "Any honey to be used for cooking is stored in the cold cellar."

"Oh."

That was all she said. Oh. As if that excused her heinous act.

"And all those children running about, ruining my bee fields, disturbing the hives, in danger of falling in a well, or being attacked by a goat . . . are they your children, Lady Ingrith?"

"Nay. I am not married."

He just stared at her.

She gave him a look that pretty much said, *What a dunderhead!*

Which he was. He had met her several times in recent years and she had no children then. How could he imagine that she had produced them in such short order?

"They are orphans from Rainstead. Are they not adorable?"

He said a foul word under his breath. "How many children?"

"Eight."

"Eight!" He cursed again. "And the gnome?"

"Huh? Oh, you mean Ubbi. He is not a gnome. He is my bodyguard."

He rolled his eyes.

"Uh-oh! Your mother told me that you would welcome us . . . me and the orphans, but I sense that you are not happy to see us."

"I get a rash around children," he blurted out . . . and could have kicked himself. What a stupid thing to say!

For a moment she stared at him as if he had lost his mind. Then she continued, "And your mother said that you are in need of a cook, or someone to train a new cook."

My mother! I should have known!

"There are some new types of bees from the Arab lands in swarms over there that your mother asked me to deliver to you. Your thanks are not necessary." Her biting wit did not amuse him.

Frowning, he glanced over to the far wall, where several oblong crates with screened sides were stacked. "Thank you," he muttered ungraciously.

"I am a wonderful cook," she said of a sudden.

As if good food is worth the trouble you bring!

"You will see."

Nay, I will not.

"Just you wait."

I would rather not.

"I will tell Godwyn to gather up the children and make them behave. You will not even notice we are here."

I doubt that. He decided to try a different tactic. "It is not proper for you to be working in a kitchen, like a scullery maid."

"I love to cook and experiment with different foods and sauces and spices. You place value on your honey studies, why not my food studies?"

That certainly turned the tables on him. But not for long. "I do not mean to be rude, but why are you here and how long do you intend to stay?"

Ingrith's face, already heated from the ovens, turned brighter. She really was a good-looking woman, despite her age, and height, and brassy nerve. Her figure was nothing less than spectacular, as blatantly displayed in her male attire.

Not that any of that mattered.

Much.

"We are here for a short while to avoid a Saxon soldier who is hell-bent on luring me to his bed furs."

I would not mind luring you there myself.

Nay, nay, nay! I did not think that.

I wonder if she is beyond childbearing years.

Probably not. She is almost the same as me. Thirty-

one. Women still have children at that advanced age, do they not?

Good heavens! I cannot possibly be thinking of swiving a Viking princess without giving offense to a Norse king, an army, my mother and stepfather, not to mention her gnome bodyguard.

But wait, her eyes were shifting from right to left, as if evading some truth.

His eyes narrowed.

She was lying, or not telling him the entire truth.

"Your seduction, you say. That does not explain why all these orphans are here. And why not go to one of your sisters?"

Ingrith's chin went up. "Loncaster would look for me there, first off."

"Loncaster? Commander of the king's garrison at Jorvik?"

She nodded bleakly.

"Could you have chosen a more high-ranking man? Loncaster is not known as the Saxon Butcher for nothing. He would rather drink sword dew than ale, so bloodthirsty is he."

Now she really bristled. "I did not choose him, believe you me."

He could not help but grin at her indignation. By the saints, the woman was incredibly attractive in her anger. Like a blonde Valkyrie, she was.

"You find humor in my plight? I had not expected such unkindness in Lady Eadyth's son."

"Guilting again, m'lady."

"We will depart at once. I am so sorry to have disturbed you." The expression of disdain on her face belied her apology.

"Where will you go?" Even he knew how bad that sounded and regretted his hasty words almost immediately.

"I have no idea, but then it is of no concern to you, you . . . you lout." Going to the outer door leading to the back courtyard, she yelled, loud enough to make John's ears bleed, "Godwyn, gather the children. We must leave immediately. And Ubbi, rehitch the horses to the wagon. Kavil, ask the stableman to saddle the other horses."

"Do not be ridiculous," John said, definitely feeling guilty now. Her ploy, if that was what it was, had worked. "You do not need to leave right away."

"How generous of you! Many thanks, but we do not stay where we are not welcome."

"I never said you were not welcome."

She arched her brows at him.

"I was just surprised," he said defensively, then added with more vigor, "I do not like my honey studies tampered with."

"Let us make an agreement then. I will not interfere with your honey work, and you will not interfere in my kitchen."

Her kitchen? He did not like the sound of that. "Ahem!"

Just then he noticed Hamr and Bolthor propping up the door frame, grinning like idiots. He threw up his hands in surrender, then stomped over, pushing them aside, heading for his great hall and about a tun of ale. Halfway there, he stopped and went back. Poking a finger in Bolthor's chest, he said, "If you dare concoct some bloody damn saga about me and an invasion by a beautiful woman and a tribe of little people, I swear you will be in the stew pot afore morning."

"Beautiful?" Ingrith stared at him, wide-eyed. "Me?"

He spun on his heel and could not decide whether to go for the mead in his hall, or go to his bedchamber and bury his head under the furs for a sennight or two.

That was when he heard Bolthor say in an overloud whisper to Hamr, "I was thinking more about an Ode to Heart-Shaped Arses."

John, for one, would not be attending dinner that night if that was on the menu.

On the other hand . . .

A woman's work is never done . . .

Ingrith endeavored with everything she did that day to please the irksome lord of Hawk's Lair, to no avail. By the time the evening meal was ready to be served, she could have fallen asleep on her feet in the bustling kitchen.

Ubbi was threatening to slit the throat of the

"ungrateful troll" if he complained once more. To which John had threatened to hang the "bothersome gnome" from the rafters if he did not get out of his way. Hamr, the outlaw Viking, just stood back enjoying the chaos. And Bolthor, the one-eyed giant, was composing saga after saga about the doings at Hawk's Lair, which would no doubt embarrass one and all, if their titles were any indication. "When Hawks Stutter." "The Princess and the Hawk." "Ode to Woman-Honey," whatever that meant. "When Norse Ladies Go A-Viking."

Hawk's Lair was a small keep, with only a hundred *housecarls* guarding its borders and another fifty servants or field cotters. She had fed, with ease, five hundred and more at her father's estate in the Norselands. Apparently, most of John's *hersirs* and *hirds* of soldiers were housed at Gravely, his deceased father's estate, which was a day's ride away.

The children had already bathed, for once not protesting, in the wonderful hot spring channeled into a bathing house. They were hopefully asleep, having already eaten. The boys were in a clean stable stall, and the girls in sleep closets along the back end of the great hall.

Now, as she sat supervising, platters and bowls of food were being carried by servants from the kitchen into the great hall, not to mention pottery pitchers of ale and mead and milk. Ingrith had worked her fingers to the bone preparing a meal to please the most particular palate. She doubted she would get any thanks from the scowling Hawk, however. He had made his displeasure over their presence in his keep more than obvious, not just on their initial meeting, either.

She had never met a more infuriating man. He could show the most extreme displeasure with just the arch of one eyebrow. Without ever saying they were unwelcome, he made it obvious how inconvenient their presence was. She would have told him in no uncertain terms what he could do with his backhanded welcome if the children's safety was not at risk.

As it was, Ubbi had finally been banished to the cow barn for having kicked John in the shins. Twice. For perceived verbal offenses against Ingrith.

The whole situation was a mess.

She had not the energy to rise and make her way to the small sleeping bower that had been set aside for her on the second floor. But then she recalled the hot spring bathing house where she could ease her sore muscles. Luckily, when she got to the women's section, it was empty, everyone either being at dinner, or serving dinner.

It was heaven, as she had known it would be, her father having a similar natural resource at Stoneheim. A long time later, after bathing and then soaking herself until her skin wrinkled, she felt better. As she began to emerge, she heard a loud male voice from outside, shouting, "Where is she? I swear, if she's hiding from me, best she beware. I am not amused." It sounded like John. Who else?

The door to the bathing hut swung open before Ingrith had a chance to react. Having just stepped out of the pool, facing the entrance, she froze in place.

A stunned lord of Hawk's Lair, speechless for once, kicked the door shut behind him with a booted foot. "You . . . you . . ." he sputtered.

Realizing belatedly that she was naked . . . *Holy Thor! How could I have forgotten something so important?* . . . she turned abruptly and reached for a drying cloth. Then, she glanced back over her shoulder to see why John was so quiet.

He was staring at her bare backside. Gawking, more like.

CHAPTER FIVE

❧

Oh, baby!

Boiling with chagrin, John yanked open the door to the bathing house . . . and almost had a fainting fit at what he beheld.

Ingrith had just walked up the steps from the small pool, her body dripping with water, and she was bare-as-a-babe naked. In all her glory. And glorious, she was, too. And . . . *Thank you, God!* . . . not at all like a baby.

She was tall for a woman, but unlike most women of her height, she was not slender, no doubt due to her excessive cooking. Oh, she was not fat, either. She was soft . . . and rounded. Voluptuous, that was the best word to describe her. From her high, full breasts to her small waist and flaring hips. Her tiny nipples and aureoles were of the palest rose hue, almost flesh-colored, blending into the breasts themselves.

All this he noticed in the mere moment before she collected herself and swung around to grab for a drying cloth.

Now he was presented with her glorious backside.

With his heart pounding like a warhorse, he watched as she bent over to pick up a drying cloth.

Was he becoming a pervert now?

Bloody hell, he could no more have *not watched* than pluck out his eyeballs.

"It really is heart-shaped," he remarked before he could bite his traitorous tongue.

"Whaaat?" She swung around to face him again, this time covered somewhat with a piece of cloth that scarce hid her breasts and thatch of golden curls, a darker shade than her blonde head hair, which was piled atop her head.

Amazing the details a man could notice when given a bare glimpse of a female's intimate parts!

"Why are you looking at me?"

"Do you jest?"

She made a clucking sound of disgust. "What are you doing here in the women's pool?" she demanded, then shouted, "Get out!"

"I'll wait for you outside until you are clothed," he said with as much dignity as he could muster, embarrassed as he was to realize that it had not even occurred to him that he was entering the section reserved for women. In his defense, he added, " 'Tis your fault I am here."

"Aaarrgh!"

That was woman language for "You are driving me barmy."

Well, she was driving him barmy, too, he thought

as he closed the door and heard a hard object hit the door behind him. Probably a bar of soap.

Mere moments later she came storming out, fully dressed in a long-sleeved, faded red *gunna*. "What? What is so important that you had to invade the private women's quarters? Who are you looking for?"

"You."

"Me?"

"Yes, you. You wily witch! Are you trying to guilt me into letting you stay here? Because, God knows, your actions are having the opposite effect."

"What in bloody hell are you yapping about? You could at least let me finish bathing afore accosting me."

"I did not accost you. Believe you me, if I were accosting, you would know it." *Have I lost my lack-brained mind?* "And, by the by, dost think foul language befits a lady of your standing?"

She said a word that was even more foul.

"For shame, Ingrith!" Oddly, John found he was enjoying himself. *Must be my brain is melting from lack of sex.*

"Oh, please! You have said far worse."

"I am a man." *If you only knew!*

"And that makes a difference . . . how?"

If you only knew! "Do not try to distract me with this pointless prattle." *I wonder if her nipples are still hard. They were moments ago.*

She inhaled and exhaled for patience. "What is the problem, John?"

The problem is that I haven't had a woman in months. The problem is you have a tempting body. The problem is I want to bed you. The problem is that I cannot.

"Stop looking at me like that."

"How?"

"Like you are seeing me naked."

He smiled then, a slow smile that accompanied a head-to-toe survey. "The image is imbedded in my brain. I cannot will it away."

She folded her arms across her chest, which, if she only knew, drew attention to their plumpness. And, by the rood, her damp gown was clinging in some very interesting places.

"Everyone is waiting for you to be seated so that the evening meal can start."

"What?" she nigh shrieked. "The food will be cold."

He shrugged.

"Why is my presence necessary?"

"Because every blessed person in the entire keep is chastising me for my treatment of you. The latest complaint being that I am working you to death and now starving you."

"And they do not even know that you invaded my private bath. Tsk-tsk-tsk! Wait 'til they add that to their list of your transgressions."

He ignored her snide remark. "They say I have

forced you to perform menial labor as payment for hospitality here. They say I have treated you with disrespect." She started to bring up the private bath invasion again, but he continued before she could speak. "They say you are no doubt weeping in your pillow because I begrudged you some honey. They say—"

"They say. They say. What do you care what *they* say?"

"Well, for one thing, Bolthor is composing a poem about it, as we speak."

"Bolthor? The skald?"

He nodded. "The world's worst skald." He grabbed her hand and began to drag her through the corridor toward the great hall.

"Wait! I cannot come to dinner like this. My *gunna* is damp from my bath."

"I noticed."

"What?"

"Never mind."

"At least let me get an apron."

Now he knew why Viking women wore those long, open-sided aprons. They were hiding treasures from their menfolks. On the other hand, he would not mind seeing Ingrith in one of those aprons . . . with naught underneath. Now there was another image to imbed in his lustsome brain.

With a snort of self-disgust, he said, "Your attire will have to do for now. The food will indeed be spoiled if we have to wait that long." He dragged her even harder now. In fact, he put one hand on her upper arm and the other at the back of her waist, propelling her forward.

"You are being a brute."

He stopped suddenly and pulled her to a halt beside him. They were just outside the great hall, where the buzz of conversation was heavy. He was pleased to see that his men, and some women, had already started eating . . . and were enjoying the meal immensely.

"You are right, Ingrith. I have been brutish. Let us start over."

She nodded. "I understand that we descended on your keep without invitation and that our presence here is . . . inconvenient."

Inconvenient? That was as good an explanation as any. "I tend to be reclusive," he attempted to explain. "And I do treasure my honey studies."

She put a hand on his forearm, which he could swear caused a tingle that traveled up his arm, down his chest, to parts best known to men as their best parts. So distracted was he that at first he did not realize she was speaking.

". . . and so I will do my best to find another place for us to stay until the danger passes. In the meantime, I promise that I and the children will stay out of your way."

"Oh, Ingrith! What a churl you must think me! You may stay as long as you want."

She beamed at him as if he'd handed her a pot

of gold . . . or in her case, a pot of rare kitchen spices.

He immediately wished he had not issued such a sweeping welcome, but what was done was done.

As they passed through an aisle leading to the dais, various of John's men called out to Ingrith.

"M'lady, the *nekkesan* is tasty," Cyril, his chief archer, said.

"Huh?" John looked at her.

"Turkey-neck pudding," she translated.

Gilbert, a groomsman, remarked, "The poached pike with mustard sauce is the best I have ever had."

Hah! Gilbert wouldn't know poach from roach.

He looked at Ingrith again.

"You are glaring."

He mentally wiped the furrows from his brow. "What are all these different dishes? Are we having a feast? A visiting dignitary? Perchance a saint's birthing day?"

"Nay! This is the way I cook every day."

He groaned.

"You are not to worry. It will cost no more than your usual fare. I will not deplete your larder."

"That is not what I am worried about. 'Tis spoiling my people, you are. They will ne'er accept another cook."

She blushed, and he suspected that she had no intention of finding a new cook for a good while yet.

Once they were seated at the high table with

Bolthor on one side of them and Hamr on the other, he stared, stupefied, as she named each of the dishes placed before them.

Pork with raspberry sauce. That must be what he'd seen earlier on the spit. But there was also *maymenye ryalle* . . . spiced pork in a nutted wine puree, Ingrith explained. Gingered carp. Almond eel soup. *Henne dorre*, or golden cardamom chicken.

Not to mention a sallat of wild endive, leeks, shredded cabbage, carrots, apples, and honey served in an aspic.

I wonder where she got the honey this time. He did not dare raise a ruckus over the honey again, considering the effect of his first tirade. "I had no idea we had so many different spices here at Hawk's Lair," he commented instead.

"You don't. I brought my own with me." She made that announcement in a way that required a compliment.

"How wonderful!"

She slanted her eyes at him. "Are you being sarcastic?"

"Who? Me? Of course not." He paused. "Mayhap a little."

Then there were the vegetables: creamed parsnips, horseradish, cucumbers in vinegar, herbed beets, cabbage with pork marrow, and *amyndoun seaw*, a vegetable gruel.

"I hate cabbage," he said. *Another halfwitted remark!*

"Then do not eat the cabbage," she advised patiently, as if he were a thickheaded boyling.

And for sweets: the oatcakes he'd seen her baking earlier, plus bilberry tarts, stewed pears, and gilliflower pudding.

Saints save me! Dinner will last for hours. God only knew how many hours afore the trestle tables could be dismantled and folks retire to their sleep benches. He enjoyed the occasional feast, but if she planned such an array every night . . . well, he might very well begin fasting.

However, no one seemed to mind, except him. There was a vast amount of smacking of lips, and oohs and aahs of delight. At the rate they were going, there would be no food left over for the morning breaking fast.

"You are not eating, m'lord," she commented.

He stared down at the trencher they shared, which she had piled with a little of all the dishes.

"Here, try this," she said, picking up a portion of pork dripping with red sauce with her fingertips and placing it at his lips.

He opened obediently, like the boyling she seemed to regard him as, but the sensation that shot from her fingertips at his lips down to his manpart was anything but boyish. Without thinking, he grabbed her wrist when she was about to withdraw and licked the remaining sauce off her fingertips, one at a time.

"M'lord!" she exclaimed.

He knew exactly what she meant, whether she recognized it for what it was, or not. Just that tactile abrasion of his rough tongue on her soft skin caused him to want so much more. Truly, his finger licking had caused desire to lick like a firestorm through his body. Trying to hide his arousal, he remarked, "I notice you m'lord me only when you choose. Other times I am Hawk or John. Make up your mind."

"M'lord," she emphasized. "*What* are you doing?"

"Acting as your finger bowl?" He gave one last lick that encompassed her palm as well. But what he really wanted to lick was . . .

She jerked her hand away. "What do you think?"

"Huh?"

"The taste?"

"Of your skin?"

"Nay, not of my skin. The raspberry sauce on the pork. Dost think it is too sweet?"

He took another piece off the trencher and chewed it slowly. "A little sweet," he concluded. Then grinned at her. "Wouldst like to lick *my* fingertips?"

"Why would I want to do that?"

A virgin . . . she must be a virgin. At her age! Poor thing!

"Tell me about your beekeeping, John," she urged then. "What is it that fascinates you so?"

"I don't know if it is fascination with the bees.

More like the honey and what can be done with it. I am not the first person to discover the medicinal properties. Even the ancient Romans knew that it could help heal wounds, cure coughs, that kind of thing. But I believe there are other uses it could have, such as . . ." He stopped and stared at her. "I am boring you. My apologies, m'lady. I get carried away betimes."

"You were not boring me. It is refreshing to hear of a man being passionate about something other than . . . well, passion." She grinned at him.

Passion was not a word he needed to hear from her lips at this point. Time to change the subject. "Tell me, Ingrith," he began, picking at the food in front of him with both his knife and a wooden spoon. "Why have you never wed?"

She rolled her eyes.

"What?"

"Everyone asks that of women once they reach a certain age. Do they ask the same of men? I think not."

"Actually, they do. Especially my mother."

She smiled at him, and—*Heavenly Hosts!*—he felt another lurch low down in his belly. What was happening to him? He had met Ingrith in the past and never experienced this overwhelming attraction.

"You are an attractive woman, Ingrith. It is a logical question."

"Mayhap. I have not wed because the right man never asked me to."

"Is there one 'right man' in particular who missed his chance with you?"

"How kind you are with your wording! I meant that I could not imagine spending the rest of my life with any of the oafs who offered for me. I want to love the man I marry."

"You still expect to wed?"

"Nay, I do not. I am fast approaching thirty-one years, well beyond the prime time for a woman."

"Are you still of breeding years?" he asked with sudden hope.

"Of course," she said with affront. "I am not that long in the teeth."

His hopes deflated.

"But that does not mean I will be having any of my own," she added.

"Is that why you work at the orphanage?"

"Partly. The main reason I came to Britain was to escape my father's ludicrous matchmaking efforts."

"Ludicrous?"

"In recent years, a sad array of men he presented to me and Drifa, my only remaining unwed sister. Olaf Wart-Nose. Vikar the Vicious. Hakon the Horse, who was rumored to have two phalluses, though I cannot countenance the truth of that boast and do not want to think how that would benefit any woman in the bedsport."

"I could think of several benefits," Hamr said from Ingrith's other side. "Wouldst like me to explain?"

"Nay!" he and Ingrith exclaimed at the same time.

He could not believe that a noblewoman would bring up such a subject in mixed company. In truth, her coarse tongue both fascinated and repelled him.

"Then there is the godly handsome Finn Finehair," Ingrith continued, "who would be acceptable except he is so vain he adorns his forked beard and the war braids framing his face with colored beads and feathers. Like a peacock, he is."

"My stepfather often speaks of a far-famed Norseman who insisted that he be buried upside down when he died," John related, "so the world would kiss his arse."

Ingrith smiled but at the same time shook her head, no doubt at his crudity. "The worst was Eyvor from the Danish lands. He was the champion of head-butting contests in all the Norselands. Not surprisingly, he drooled a lot and often appeared dazed."

Ingrith's sense of humor surprised and pleased John.

"I know Finn Finehair," Hamr interjected. "Dost know that he combs his chest hairs and trims the short hairs surrounding his manpart?"

"Shhh," John cautioned Hamr, motioning with his eyes toward Bolthor, who was in conversation with his steward. The skald would no doubt love to compose a saga on those outrageous subjects. Double-pronged men and vain Vikings.

"How about you, John?" Ingrith dabbed at her mouth with a linen cloth that she placed on the table, having finished eating. Then she turned in her seat to give him her full attention. "Why have you not wed? You are about the same age as I am, I believe."

"I do not intend ever to wed," he said.

Her eyes . . . beautiful, extraordinarily shaded blue eyes, by the by . . . widened with surprise. "All men of your station must needs wed for heirs, if naught else."

"Not me. I want no children of my blood. Hawk's Lair will pass to my stepsister Larise and her second husband, Sir Garreth of Sussex."

"And Gravely?"

John bristled, annoyed at her prodding into his personal affairs, but then he berated himself for having started this line of questioning. "I await a male heir. One of my stepsisters is bound to have a boy someday. In the meantime, another of my brothers-by-marriage, Andrew, acts as my castellan."

"Ah, that must be why you are so averse to having the orphans here. You mislike children."

"That is ridiculous. I like children as much as the next person, as long as they are quiet and reasonably well behaved."

Ingrith tilted her head to the side, studying him. "Is it because you are not interested in women . . . nay, that cannot be so. I have met your mistress."

At first, John was outraged that Ingrith would question his manhood. "I am not a sodomite."

"I realized that when I recalled your mistress. Sorry I am if I offended you."

"Hah! You have offended me right and left since you arrived. What mistress?"

"You have more than one?"

"What mistress?" he repeated. *I should have followed my original instinct, gone to my chamber, and buried my head under the bed furs until this pestsome woman left my home.*

Hamr was laughing, silently.

Bolthor's ears had perked up, and any minute now would be gleaning the gist of this absurd conversation.

"Joanna," Ingrith replied and nodded her thanks at one of the serving girls, who was removing dirty trenchers and placing sweet flummeries in front of them. A whipped cream concoction that appeared to have sliced peaches swirled in.

He could feel his face heat with color. "What do you know of Joanna?"

"I met her at her Coppergate stall in Jorvik. She is beautiful, John. Very beautiful."

It takes a beauty to recognize a beauty. "Joanna is not my mistress."

She made a scoffing sound of disbelief.

"A mistress implies a man providing for a woman in exchange for sexual favors. A long-term arrangement involving a house, gifts, an allowance. I give none of those to Joanna."

"You mean she does it all for free?"

Yea, she does, but not for lack of my offering. "'Tis improper for you to be discussing such a subject with me, Ingrith."

"Pfff! Those rules only apply to young, impressionable girlings. Why do you not wed her?"

John had just taken a sip of mead and began to choke.

"Yea, John, why do you not wed the fair Joanna?" Hamr inquired.

He cast a glower at Hamr and put up a halting hand to Ingrith. "No more! I will not discuss Joanna or any other woman with you."

She opened her mouth, about to speak, then clicked her teeth shut on a whooshy exhale.

He dipped his spoon into the flummery. The blend of peaches and cream and, yea, honey again, burst onto his tongue with exquisite flavor. "You really are a good cook," he admitted to Ingrith.

"I told you so." She laughed with delight.

Just then he glanced to his other side, then quickly glanced again. Bolthor was rising from his chair, and he had that dreamy expression on his face that portended a saga about to be told.

"Nay!" He jumped so quickly, he knocked his chair over, then tipped against Bolthor, who fell backward and hit the dais heavily, with John atop him. They would probably have to replace some floorboards on the morrow.

"M'lord?" Bolthor inquired, squinting up at him with his one good eye.

"Sorry," he murmured and stood, extending a helping hand to the skald to rise, too. "I tripped."

"And horses can fly." Hamr chortled behind him.

"Is he demented?" he heard Ingrith ask Hamr.

He was fairly certain she was inquiring about him, not Bolthor.

"Absolutely," Hamr replied.

"No harm done," Bolthor said. "I was just about to recite a new poem. Is that all right with you, m'lord?"

What could he say after nigh knocking the man dead?

"Oh, please do," Hamr encouraged.

"Yea, I would love to hear one of your fine poems," Ingrith said.

Dost think so, you interfering wench? It will serve you right to hear what Bolthor has to say. So be it!

After straightening his chair, John sat down and put his face in his hands.

"This is the story of John of Hawk's Lair." Bolthor cleared his throat and began:

In the land of the Saxons,
a noble knight did reign.
Then came a Viking lass
who had a heart-shaped ass . . .

Ingrith's screech of horror was probably heard all the way to Jorvik.

CHAPTER SIX

❦

Beware of rogues with angel faces . . .

Ingrith was a Viking princess raised in a keep with five hundred men, some of whom were borderline berserk, by a father who had once had a hole drilled in his head, by choice. She and her four princess sisters once killed a Saxon earl, by choice. She was on the run with the green-haired, illegitimate son of the king of all Britain.

But this . . . this situation she found herself in here at Hawk's Lair was beyond the realm of barmy. A Viking poet talking about her bottom before a room full of mostly men.

But Ingrith plopped back down to her seat when John yanked on her arm and whispered, "'Tis best to let him go. You will only call attention to yourself and prompt even worse poems. Believe me, I know."

Because he had been interrupted mid-thought, Bolthor started over.

In the land of the Saxons,
a noble knight did reign.
Then came a Viking lass
who had a heart-shaped ass.
She liked cooking.
He liked beehiving.
Both were smitten with honey
But what they did not see
Was the best honey to thrive
Was not found in a hive.

"Very good," Hamr said, applauding a beaming Bolthor.

"I do not understand," she whispered to John.

"You do not want to understand," he assured her, barely stifling a grin.

She noticed that Hamr and many of the men in the hall were grinning as well. Or smirking.

Frowning with confusion, an idea came unbidden to her. "Surely, Bolthor did not mean . . ."

John nodded. "He did."

Of a sudden, the prospect of her and John as a couple held an odd appeal. He was even better looking than she remembered. Black hair cut short in the Norman style. A body suited to his erstwhile warrior duties. And a face that the One-God's angels would envy. But then that should be no surprise. His mother, Lady Eadyth, was once referred to as the Silver Jewel of Northumbria because of her beauty.

Still, Bolthor telling one and all that she and

John were potential lovers? " 'Tis an outrage."

"That it is, but Bolthor does not mean to give offense. He truly believes no subject is forbidden. Why do you think he is here and not at home with his family?"

"Why?" she asked hesitantly, not sure she wanted to know.

"Because he wrote an ode to his wife's breasts."

She slapped a hand over her mouth, but her giggle escaped nonetheless.

"You are comely, even in boy's garb, but when you smile, Ingrith, you are beyond beautiful."

"I am not!"

"I can see why Loncaster pursues you."

"*Pursue* is the key word. I have ne'er encouraged him."

"Why? As I recall, he is a man women call handsome. Oh, he has a reputation for cruelty, but no worse than many soldiers. And he is high placed enough in his association with the king."

"He is cruel, as you say, but not just in soldiering. His aggression repulses me."

"What has he done? Surely, he has not assaulted you. If so, I will take your case to the king."

She shook her head sharply. "Everything but assault, and that is all I will say on the subject."

"You think he will come here."

"Unfortunately, he will. And stop looking at me like that . . . as if you wonder at my hidden assets to draw such a man."

"I already know your hidden assets," he pointed out, then glanced down, noticing her hands fisted on the table. "You want to hit me, don't you?"

"If it would not create a scene, I would."

"Let us make a deal, Ingrith. I can act as point guard in deflecting Loncaster's suit, but you must let me handle it my way, without your interference."

"But, you do not know . . ."

" 'Tis that, or you are on your way."

This would be the time for her to tell John that lust was not Loncaster's only reason for coming here. She should inform him of Henry's identity. And how they'd managed to rescue the girls from the brothel. And Kavil's story, too.

But she kept her silence, praying that they would be gone before John would need to know. That night she wrote a missive to her sister Tyra, asking that she find a longship to take them to the Norselands.

She would have to put up with her father's machinations for the sake of the orphans.

Finger lickin' good . . .

The next morning, Ingrith decided that she had to do something about Henry's green hair. 'Twas true, it was no longer buttercup yellow, but green would call attention to him just the same.

She came up with an idea. She would shave Henry's head. But wait, Henry's bald head would then stand out from all the others. Therefore, Ingrith decided that she would shave all the young boys' heads.

Should I ask for John's permission?

Nay, I would then have to explain why.

Besides, bald boyling heads may become the new fashion.

She was deboning pigeons early that afternoon when John came storming into the kitchen, pushing a half dozen bald boylings before him. "What is the meaning of this?" he demanded.

"Head lice?" she offered.

"We have an epidemic of head lice at Hawk's Lair?"

"Not an epidemic. More like a large amount in small children."

"Heaven help me! You are not going to shave the girlings' heads, too, are you?"

"Nay. Only the young boys are infected."

He narrowed his eyes at her. "Why do you have that nervous tic in your one eye? My sister Emma always tic'd when she told a lie."

"'Tis just from peeling onions." She could feel herself tic-ing some more.

He glanced around pointedly. Not an onion in sight.

"How are the bee studies going today, m'lord? Can I help?"

"You cannot help. The best way to help is keep the children away from the honey shed. And, by the by, Emma also m'lorded me when she had something to hide." On those words, he exited the kitchen. Thank the gods! She would like to m'lord him a good one . . . with her soup ladle.

The rest of the day was calmer than the day before as they all settled in. She figured it would be at least a few days before Loncaster would figure she was gone and begin searching. Maybe she would hear from Tyra in the meantime.

Ubbi had been charged with taking some of the older children berry picking, much to his chagrin. "Guardsmen do not act as child minders," he complained. But Ingrith needed Ubbi out of the way for a bit since he kept insult-pricking at John to get a reaction.

It was late afternoon when Breaca approached her and said she couldn't find Henry. Ingrith washed the flour off her hands and began hunting. Everywhere. It was only when she looked in John's honey shed, as a last resort, that she stopped dead in her tracks.

Henry, looking adorable rather than foolish with his shaved head, was perched on John's knee. John, sitting on a high stool before a table arrayed with various pots of honey, was explaining something about honey to the little boy. At the other end of the room, Kavil—also with a bald head, which suited him, oddly—was examining a series of honeycombs cross-sectioned to show the various stages of production. Later, she would examine it closer for her own edification.

"What are these?" Kavil asked, having moved closer to a long, rectangular box with little partitioned cubicles containing dozens of dead bees of all sizes and colors.

"Those are species of bees from all over the world," John said. "There are hundreds, mayhap thousands, of species, all different. The biggest ones are queen bees. The others are drones and worker bees."

"What is a thousan'?" Henry wanted to know.

John laughed. "Well, let's say, if you were covered from head to toe with bees, every speck of your skin, that would probably be a thousand."

Henry shivered with disgust.

"Every day the queen bee lays two to three thousand eggs to form new bees." He let that information seep in to both Henry and Kavil, who was listening intently, despite his distance. They were probably picturing three of Henry covered with bees. "Even more amazing, in just one beehive, there can be more than fifty thousand bees."

"Fifty?" Henry said with amazement. Ingrith knew that the boy understood because she had been practicing his numbers with him up to one hundred. Again, he and Kavil were probably picturing fifty bee-covered Henrys.

Ingrith was impressed with both John's patience and his ability to teach the boys a lesson at their level of understanding.

"I don't like bees," Kavil declared suddenly, stepping back from the display of bees he'd been studying. "They sting."

"Actually, bees only attack when threatened. If you don't move abruptly, they'll probably avoid you."

Kavil didn't look convinced, and actually, Ingrith was surprised that the boy even stayed in a room with a strange man. Because of his past abuse, he usually avoided contact with adult men. Ubbi was the exception.

"You should know, Kavil, that bees are very clean. They never relieve themselves inside the hive. In fact, in the winter, when you see little squirts of yellow in the snow, it is probably bee piss. Or sometimes you'll see it on light colored laundry laid out to dry in the summer."

"You jest!" Kavil said, gracing John with one of his rare smiles.

John smiled back, then turned to Henry. "Hold out your hand, Samuel," John said, at the same time motioning Kavil to come closer. Samuel was the fake name they'd given Henry.

Henry held out both hands, palm side up. John shook a flower over both of them, and a fine yellow powder settled on the skin.

"That is pollen. It doesn't always look the same, but all flowers have it. When you see a bee sitting on a flower, it is gathering pollen to take back to the hive."

Henry scrooched his nose up with confusion.

"The funny thing is, Samuel . . . the bee eats the pollen and then he vomits it up back at the hive. Eventually that's what turns into honey."

" 'Tis not!" The rascal poked John in the arm with a fist. "Yer jestin' me."

John put a hand over his heart. "I swear."

Henry shifted off of his lap and ran for the door. No doubt to inform all the other children that they had been eating bee vomit and wearing sherts with bee spew on them. Kavil followed reluctantly behind him. He'd probably have stayed behind, but would not do so alone.

John looked over and noticed her then.

"You are amazing," she said.

"I know," he replied, and winked at her.

She did not want to think what that mere wink did to her.

"Did you want something, Ingrith, that you invade my honey domain?"

Not sure if he was teasing or not, she walked closer. "I'm sorry if they were bothering you. I didn't realize they were gone."

"I was ready for a break."

"You enjoy sharing your knowledge about bees, don't you?"

He shrugged. "Sometimes. For example, bees are a lot like men and women when it comes to mating, did you know that?"

The twinkle in his blue eyes told her that he

was about to impart some inappropriate message. "First off, only the most healthy, virile drone bees can mate with the queen bee, midair, high above the ground."

"Just like men, virility being prized, I suppose?"

"Exactly. The thing is, once the mating is complete, the drone dies. Is that not just like a woman? Lets a man prick her, than stabs him through the heart first chance she gets."

"You know the wrong kind of women, methinks."

"Leastways, when you see bees swarming high above the ground, they are probably virile male drones just looking for a passing female to tup."

"You do have a way with words. I do not think I have e'er heard of tupping bees afore."

"Here's another interesting fact, m'lady." If eyes could dance, his were now. And it was a delightful sight. "There is a language that bees have amongst themselves. 'Tis called the wag-tail dance. By the way a bee wags its rump . . . the number of times, the direction, and so on . . . it is indicating to the other bees such information as the distance from the hive to a food source."

She waited, arms folded over her chest, for his zinger. It was not long in coming.

"Just like a woman. She jiggles her rump and sways her hips to send men certain messages."

"I have ne'er jiggled my body parts."

"Oh, you jiggle, all right," he asserted with a grin.

With face flaming, she wandered closer to a second long table where many pottery jars and a few glass containers were arranged in an orderly fashion. "The honey colors are so different. How can you tell them apart?"

She was surprised when he didn't just tell her to begone. Instead, he swung around on his high stool, and replied, "Long years of study. First, at my mother's knee. You know she is an avid bee-keeper. Then, studies of my own. When I went to Frankland years ago to fight for my king, I noticed the honey was different there. As it is in the Arab lands, or Cordoba, or even the Norselands."

"But the colors! None of them are the same."

"Honey can be clear as water or dark as amber. It all depends on the flowers. Unless the bees are segregated by particular plants, they gather pollen from many different flowers, producing what we call *millefiori* honey. As you can imagine, that way there is no consistency of taste or color from one harvest to the next or from one hive to the next. That is the type of honey most folks are familiar with." He glanced at her, then grimaced. "My tongue runs away with itself when it comes to bees and honey."

"I know that you study the healing properties of honey, but I wonder if different honeys would be particularly suitable for certain dishes."

"For a certainty. Blueberry honey, for example, is rich and dense. If you let it rest in your mouth afore swallowing, you can actually taste the berries. Here, try it." He put a small amount of a dark amber honey on a small wooden spoon and pressed it to her mouth.

She let it sit on her tongue, as directed, but the only thing she could think of was, *I wish he could have given it to me on his finger so that I could lick it. Like he did my fingers yestereve. What an incredible sensation that was!*

Oh, my gods and goddesses, I am becoming lustsome over a man, and not just any man. A man who has a beautiful mistress. She began to choke, and John smacked her on the back.

"You did not like it?"

"I loved it," she said, feeling foolish for her wandering thoughts. "Were these pottery jars made by your mistress?"

He wagged a finger at her. "I told you that Joanna is not my mistress. And, yea, she made most of these." He went to the end of the table and dipped a spoon into a medium-amber-colored honey. Each jar had its own spoon. "My favorite is this rare honey. It comes from the sorrel or sourwood tree that a friend brought me from a land beyond Iceland. The tree has flowers that grow in pendant-like clusters, much like lily of the valley." He handed the small spoon to her to taste.

She raised her eyes in surprise. "It tastes a bit like anise. Definitely tart, but not unpleasant."

"Like you."

"Me? Ah, you mean tart. That I am . . . when provoked."

He smiled, pleased that she agreed with his assessment, she supposed.

After replacing the spoon, he turned back to her. "You have honey on your lip. Right there." He dabbed at the corner of her mouth with a forefinger.

Ingrith forgot to breathe. How could the mere touch of a finger cause her to be so . . . so unsettled? It was like last night when he had licked her fingertips. Unsettling.

Then she did something so out of character that it shocked her even more than it did him. When he was about to withdraw his forefinger, she grabbed his wrist and held him in place while she drew the appendage into her mouth. And sucked.

For the love of Frigg! She was sucking on a man's fingertip, and it had naught to do with honey.

Her throat went dry and strange emotions swirled through her body as she glanced upward and saw the raw lust in the rogue's slumberous blue eyes.

"Ingrith," he whispered.

At the same time, she whispered, "John."

All thought fled when his hand snaked out and he yanked her forward to stand between his outspread thighs as he still sat on the high stool. He fingered the edges of her hair, then gripped her face with both hands before settling his lips over hers. "This is such a bad idea," he said thickly.

"Definitely a bad idea," she agreed . . . and wrapped her arms about his shoulders.

Oh, the pure bliss! Who knew . . . *who knew* a kiss could be so . . . mind melting? And he was equally affected. She could tell because there was a part of his body pressing against her that was anything but melting.

"Breathe, Ingrith," he urged, smiling against her mouth.

She hadn't realized she was holding her breath. With a choked laugh, she exhaled into his mouth, which was devouring her with hungry kisses. This gave him the opportunity to slip his tongue into her mouth and begin a sensual in-and-out assault that caused her breasts to ache and dampness to pool in her intimate parts.

Now, Loncaster had stuck his tongue nigh down her throat, too, and it had been repulsive. What John was doing was just the opposite. Exciting, that's what it was.

So engaged was she in returning John's kiss that it was only belatedly that she realized that he'd stood and reversed their positions so that she sat on the stool with her thighs spread under her *gunna*, and he stood pressed against the female heart of her. The hardness of the ridge in his *braies* was caressing some extra-sensitive part of her nether region.

She whimpered. And slid her rump closer to the edge of the stool.

Even through the layers of his and her clothing, it felt as if his instrument was coaxing a response from her. A chord of sublime ecstasy was rippling from that spot outward and vibrating, like the strings on a harp.

When the kissing and pressing of his hips was accompanied by his fingers stroking her breasts under her apron, she arched her neck back and her breasts forward and let out a wail of keening, "Aaaaaahhhhh!" Her body was overtaken by the most overwhelming spasms of a pleasure so intense it bordered on pain.

After several long moments, shaking still with wave after wave of fading sensation, she reeled. With her face nestled in the crook of his neck, she sighed and tasted his salty skin.

Only then did sanity return.

What have I done?

"What did you do to me?" she demanded, shoving him away and jumping off the stool. Her hair had half fallen out of its braid. Her apron had been shoved aside and her *gunna* rucked up above her knees.

"What did *I* do?" While she attempted to

straighten herself out, he laughed and pointed to a damp spot on the crotch of his *braies*.

"I did that?" she asked, horrified.

"Nay, you caused me to do that. I have not peaked in my breeches since I was an untried boyling."

It took a moment for her to understand. When she did, she put her hot face in her hands. "I am so embarrassed. Ne'er have I done such before. Was there something in the honey you fed me?"

"I wish! If there were, I could sell it for gold in any market in the world."

"You did, you rat, you put something in that honey to seduce me," she accused.

"Are you seduced?" The lazy smile he cast her way was almost her undoing. Again.

"Nay, my breasts ache and my nether region weeps all the time," she said with as much sarcasm as she could garner. "Lackwit!"

His eyes widened. "Your coarseness knows no bounds, m'lady. I love it!"

"You are laughing at me."

"I am laughing at *us*."

"What would your mistress think?"

"Joanna again! Did I mention spanking afore?"

"Do not think I will be jumping in your bed furs now."

She could tell that possibility hadn't occurred to him. Until now. "I cannot recall the last time any woman *jumped* in my bed furs."

She threw her arms out in disgust. "It is hope-less trying to talk to you." When she exited the honey shed, she almost ran over Ubbi.

"M'lady, did the troll release his bees on you?"

"Huh? Nay. Why do you ask?"

"Because your lips are bee stung."

She put her fingertips to her kiss-swollen lips. 'Twas true . . . her lips did burn in the aftermath of his torrid possession.

What next?

Next was that something else caught Ubbi's attention. He was staring over her shoulder. She turned to see John leaning against the open door-way.

"Looks like the troll got bee stung, too," Ubbi remarked.

"Oh, In-griiith," John called out to her when she was halfway back to the keep, "best you cau-tion Bolthor, or you may find yourself the subject of his nightly poem."

"He would not!" she exclaimed, peering back at him over her shoulder.

John just shrugged, but he had an evil grin on his too-handsome face.

CHAPTER SEVEN

⬥

They were certainly lippy today . . .

Gossip traveled in any castle like dust on the wind.

Leastways, that's the excuse he gave Ingrith for all the whispered remarks as they passed by on the way to yet another feast that evening. There was no way he could tell her that she looked like a wanton who had just crawled out of a libertine's bed, him being the libertine.

"I swear, Ingrith, half the fish in the lake must be lying in repose on these tables tonight." He shook his head with mock dismay. "The other half are racing to the open seas to escape your culinary passions."

And, yea, he was wondering if Ingrith's passions would extend to love play. After seeing her naked—and then having her suck on his finger, for the love of God—he was entertaining some interesting private fantasies.

Instead of being insulted, she joked back. "I

hear the pigs have bolted as well. And there is not a red deer to be found within many miles of Hawk's Lair."

"What is that green slop?" he asked, pointing to a bowl of liquidy mush. "It resembles what is often deposited in a baby's nappies."

She smacked his arm. " 'Tis Green Soup. Spinach with leeks, eggs, cream, and various spices."

"I hate spinach."

"I thought you hated cabbage."

"Spinach and cabbage."

She shook her head at him as if he were a hopeless case. "Tomorrow I am going to make you nettle soup."

"Oh, that is just wonderful! Why not just feed me nails?"

"You will love it."

"I doubt that."

"Shhh! Have an open mind. The nettles are not prickly once cooked, and they are quite delicious when combined with all my other ingredients. What do you think of boar testicles?"

He choked on the sip of mead he'd just taken. Clearing his throat, he said, "I think they are hairy buggers. Why?"

"I could use a few."

He arched his brows.

"For cooking. Fried in onion butter, they are delicious. Better yet, in a beer batter."

John's mouth dropped open, but he was saved

from having to comment because Bolthor stood and bowed toward them. John didn't even try to subdue the skald tonight. Ingrith seemed to have given up the fight, as well.

Honey is a lot like a woman.
A pain in the arse to obtain.
Sweetness it does bring,
but is it worth the sting?
Mayhap 'tis just a rite of spring
When there are other kinds of stings,
The ones that love play brings.
The bite of a kiss
Can surely bring bliss.
The pleasurable bite
Of foresport the long night.
Next time you see a swollen lip.
Do not blame the poor bees' nip.
More like it is a lover's prick.

Everyone in the hall turned to stare at him and Ingrith.

He just winked and bowed in acknowledgement.

Ingrith elbowed him in the side.

Hamr stood and applauded vigorously.

Ingrith elbowed Hamr, too.

"When is he leaving?" she muttered to John.

"Bolthor or Hamr?"

"Both of them."

He shrugged. "No doubt about the same time you depart."

She licked her lips with nervousness.

Which of course reminded him of other licking.

Good Lord! He had been in a half cockstand all day just thinking about the witch. It amazed him that, when he'd met Ingrith on previous occasions, he had not noticed her allure. He must have been blind.

"Are you a virgin?" he asked suddenly.

She turned, very slowly, to stare at him directly.

He assumed by the iciness of her regard that she was still a maiden.

"That question was inappropriate."

"I don't mean offense. Truly I do not."

"Is it because of my age? Is that why you ask?"

He shook his head. "I am perplexed that you are not married because you are so very sensual."

She gasped. "A wanton! You think I am a wanton just because—"

"Shhh! Sensual is a good thing. In fact, every man wishes that his lady wife would have a hidden wantonness."

"But I am not married."

"Exactly."

She bared her teeth at him, which only called his attention to her lips.

"Your lips *are* kiss swollen. Do they hurt?"

"Nay. Do yours?" she snapped back, no doubt hoping to embarrass him.

Not a chance of that! "Just a little, but it is a good pain, if you get my meaning." He waggled his eyebrows at her.

"What is wrong with you, John? You are supposed to be all serious and brooding, interested only in your honey studies."

"You happened."

"Oh, that is just perfect. Blame it on me. Mayhap you need to go visit your mistress."

"I swear if you mention my mistress one more time, I am going to put you over my knee and paddle your heart-shaped arse."

That turned her speechless, but only for a moment.

But wait. There had been a momentary lapse in conversation, and it appeared that everyone had heard John's words.

He turned to Ingrith, who was glowering at him.

"You want to hit me, don't you?"

"I want to do more than that," she said. "Did I ever tell you how my sisters and I killed a man?"

She was probably jesting.

* * *

I can't believe he said THAT . . .

Two things happened the next day that added to the chaos at Hawk's Lair.

    1. Bolthor's family arrived. His wife, Katherine, and five children, ranging in

ages from four to fifteen. John was going to
have a falling-over fit.

2. Accompanying Katherine and her
entourage was a messenger with ominous
missives from Lady Eadyth. John was going
to be livid.

While his men were doing military exercises in
the outer bailey, John had taken to his bee fields.
To study and harvest some of the combs, he'd
said. She suspected he just wanted to escape the
keep . . . and her.

But escape was not in the cards for him, because
Henry and some of the other children had begged
to go with him, and he'd grudgingly agreed.

"Kin I get my very own honeycomb?" Henry
wanted to know.

"I wanna see the bees rutting up in the air,"
Kavil added, recalling John's previous words.

"Kin I pick some flowers?" Breaca asked, already dragging a large basket with her.

"How do you set up a new beehive?" Godwyn
asked. "Me father once tol' me, afore he died, that
ya have ta smoke 'em out."

John listened to each of the requests and
nodded, albeit reluctantly. You had to love a man
whose heart softened to children. Not that she
loved John. And besides, he was most often a
grumpy bones about the children. This was just
an exception, in her opinion.

But then, he'd even allowed Ubbi to tag along, despite Ubbi having said, "I will keep an eye on the troll for you, m'lady."

John had gotten the last word in when he'd cautioned the little man, "Keep on bothering me, gnome, and I will plop your tiny arse on top of a hive. You'll not be able to sit for a sennight."

Even Bolthor and Hamr accompanied John, to his chagrin. "This is turning into a bloody party," John had complained.

"Oh, good!" Hamr had said. "Mayhap Ingrith can prepare a basket of food for us. Bread, cheese, fruit, leftover boar, oatcakes. Just a few things."

Ingrith had given him a not-amused glare.

"And several jars of mead," Bolthor had added.

Thus, Ingrith was alone when Katherine's group arrived in two wagons with several lone riders.

"I am Katherine of Wickshire Manor," the grim-faced woman said, introducing herself, motioning for her children to gather behind her. Ingrith could see that they were anxious to be let loose.

Katherine had seen at least forty winters, if a day. She had ample flesh about her middle and silver threads amongst her black hair, but she was still an attractive woman.

"Lady Katherine," Ingrith acknowledged, and was about to introduce herself when Lady Katherine blurted out, "Are you the lady of Hawk's Lair? I did not realize that Hawk had married."

"Oh, good Asgard, nay! I am Ingrith of Stone-heim, in the Norselands. I am just . . . visiting."

"I met your father, King Thorvald, one time in Sussex. That means . . . you are a princess?"

Ingrith nodded.

"Well, Princess Ingrith, where is the lout?" a grim-faced Katherine asked.

"Which lout?"

"You know of many hereabouts?"

"Several."

"I refer to my husband, Bolthor. Didst know that the lackwit wrote a poem about my bosoms?"

"Hey, he wrote one about my behind."

Katherine's eyes went wide, and then she burst out laughing. "I like you."

"Your husband is a very nice man. My father said that he was a fierce warrior at one time, a soldier he would welcome at his back any day."

"Yea, he is a good man," Katherine agreed. "I berated him for writing that bloody poem, but I ne'er intended for him to go away. And certainly not for two sennights. The man is twelve years older than I, but I swear betimes he acts like a boyling."

"Well, he is out in the bee fields with Lord Hawk at the moment, but I think they will be back soon. I know that he and Hamr intended to ride to Jorvik this afternoon."

"Hah! He'll be going nowhere when I get a hold on him," Katherine said, entering the great hall beside Ingrith. Then she softened her words with a wink.

It was then that Ingrith noticed the messenger in Ravenshire livery. He carried letters for both her and John. After Katherine went off with the steward to settle in two sleep bowers, Ingrith took her missive outside to the herb garden where there was a bench on which to sit.

My dearest Ingrith,

I hope all is well with you at Hawk's Lair.

Commander Loncaster was here today, looking for the boy. And you. From here, he was going to your sister's home at Hawkshire.

If you are able to get to Jorvik without detection, Eirik will provide a longship to take you and your charges to your father's home in the Norselands.

Otherwise, I would suggest that you pretend an attachment to my son as a discouragement to Loncaster's suit.

And, above all, hide Henry as best you can.

God be with you.

Eadyth of Ravenshire

An attachment to John? Holy Thor! John would fall over laughing. He had already made it more than clear he would never wed . . . or have children. Besides, compared to his other women . . . if the beautiful Joanna was an indication . . . Ingrith was not even in the competition.

Even worse, she suspected that Lady Eadyth

had suggested the same to John in the missive addressed to him. She was tempted to destroy it, but only for a moment. Her perfidy did not stretch that far.

Oh, nay! There is something even worse, she realized. John would have to be told about Henry.

Should she wait until he came back? Or go find him now?

While she still had the courage, she decided she'd best unburden herself of the true reason for her visit. Knowing John, she might very well be the one plopped onto a swarming beehive.

She started to walk in the direction John and the others had headed. After a short while, she met up with the entire group, except for John, riding in the wagons.

"He told me and Bolthor to go back to the keep and help train his troops," Hamr said.

"He said bad words when Breaca chased Signe into the flower beds," Godwyn disclosed. "Didst know that flowers have beds? Ha, ha, ha!"

"He glared at Kavil when he swatted at a swarm of bees," Ubbi told her. "What did the troll expect?"

"There is a cold repast awaiting you all if you are still hungry." She'd noticed that the food basket was empty. "Oh, and I forgot. Bolthor, your wife and children have arrived."

At first, the skald looked happy. Then worry furrowed his brow. "Is she still angry?"

"I think, if you give her a sincere apology, she is ready to forgive you," Ingrith said with a smile.

It took more time than she'd expected to find John where he was tending one of his hives. He wore a loose-woven, almost transparent cloth, covering him from head to toe, except for the openings at his eyes, nose, and mouth. Not to mention slits where his hands could emerge, when needed.

Thus covered, his reaction to her coming for him was hidden. "What now?" he griped.

Not so hidden! "I need to talk with you. There is news."

"Do not come closer without protection," he warned.

She stepped back a few paces.

"You could not wait until I returned?"

"Don't be such a grump."

He chuckled.

"What are you doing?"

"I separated one hive from another, which had become overcrowded, and brought it here. I'm checking to see if they thrive."

"That is what Kavil requested that you do, is it not?"

He nodded. "But it needed to be done."

"You have to know that Kavil has had a very tragic past." She explained to him how the boy had been sexually abused and how he usually was frightened around men.

John swore under his breath, something about bloody sodomites and cutting off private parts.

That was too serious a subject. She needed to soften him a bit before she gave him her news. "And those fields of flowers . . . it appears as if they're all the same flower."

"They are. I try to situate the hives as far apart as possible so that I'm cultivating a consistent honey. This one is heather."

She frowned. "And the bees don't just go where they want to?"

He shook his head. "Bees usually don't like to go far from the hive . . . no more than the equivalent of a hundred and twenty-five or so paces."

"You really are an expert on all things regarding bees. But you must need help to maintain all these fields."

"I have four gardeners."

She moved farther away from him to wait, sitting on the ground, then leaning back on her elbows. He kept glancing at her every few seconds, probably checking to see that she wasn't tampering with his precious flowers or bees. Or mayhap he was nervous. She knew that she was.

Finally, he took the beekeeping outfit off and folded it neatly, setting it to the side on a tree stump that also held a leather-bound journal, a quill, and a small pot of ink.

Looking down at her, he said, "You look pretty, lying there."

"A compliment? I sense a 'but' coming on."

He smiled. "But you should not be here alone with me."

"Why? Do you plan on attacking me?"

"I might." And by the serious expression on his face, he might actually do so; however, she suspected the attack might be of an irresistible nature.

He sat down next to her, also leaning back on his elbows. Then he sighed with satisfaction as he surveyed his beekeeping domain. It was a lovely, well-maintained area.

"So give me the news.

"The first news is that Bolthor's wife has arrived."

"Uh-oh!"

"With her children."

"How many?"

"Five."

He stared at her as if stunned. "Five on top of the eight you brought. I am being invaded." Then he said a foul word.

"I did not bring eight children. Two of the girls are really young women, at fourteen."

"And speaking of those two *girls* . . . why are girls that age in an orphanage?"

"Uh." *To save them from a brothel? Nay, I cannot tell him that. Not yet.*

"Hamr remarked that they seem very . . . experienced."

"They are only fourteen!"

"Your point, m'lady?"

"There is no point," she huffed. *Lies, I am wallowing in lies.*

"But you said 'first.' Please, God, let the other news be better than this."

"I wish!" She sat up and reached into the side flap of her *gunna*, taking out two folded parchment sheets. He sat up, too, and she handed him the one still sealed with his name on it.

The expression on his face got stonier. He appeared to read it through twice before she handed him the second parchment. "This one was addressed to me. I assume it is similar to yours."

When he was done reading both, he said, "I cannot marry you, Ingrith."

She gasped. "I ne'er asked you to. I merely wanted to let you know the status of Loncaster's search. And do not pretend that you cannot marry me. Let us at least be honest with each other. You *will not* is more accurate, because you do not want to."

"Not true. If it were not for certain conditions, you would be the perfect wife for me."

"Hah!" Then she could not resist asking, "Perfect in what way?"

"You can cook, and you have a streak of lust in you as wide as a Viking fjord."

"Oh, you!" She swatted him on the arm.

He frowned with confusion then. "Who is

Henry? I do not recall any of the orphans being called Henry. Or is he a lover?"

"Do not be ridiculous. Henry is Samuel."

"The green-haired boy?"

"Exactly."

She explained about Henry being the king's illegitimate child, and how the mother wanted him raised in the orphanage. She told him that she was hiding the boy because she feared the king wanted him for nefarious purposes.

"Nefarious? How?"

"I suspect he will be killed to remove yet another heir to the throne, as far removed as Henry would be."

"Oh, my God! That is why you shaved the boys' heads."

She nodded.

He inhaled sharply. "And you speak of honesty! Pfff!" he said, the iciness thick in his voice. "Continue your confession, and try to stick to the truth for once."

When she was done, John considered all she'd said and did not respond for a long time. When he did, she could tell he was furious. "You brought a horde of orphans into my keep. You told me that it was to escape Loncaster's lascivious intents."

"It is. That part is true."

He snorted his opinion.

She stood and walked a short distance away, trying to blink away the tears welling in her eyes.

He stood, too, and followed her. "Tears will gain you naught, you devious creature. You dared to hide a child of the king in my home, knowing I would be judged equally culpable when he is found. How could you?"

"I had no other choice."

"You had many choices. And damn your lying tongue for involving my mother in this scheme, too." He combed his fingers through his hair with frustration. Then his eyes sliced her as another thought occurred to him. "You attempted to seduce me as further part of your plot."

"Are you demented? I wouldn't know how to seduce a man if I could. I have not the equipment." She waved a hand to indicate her face and body.

"Oh, you have the equipment, all right. You probably suck on the fingers of all your men."

"All my men?" she sputtered. Then she stiffened. "I will go now and gather the children together. Mayhap if we travel by night we can reach Jorvik undetected, and find your stepfather's ship."

"You are not going anywhere."

She put her hands on her hips. "And how are you going to stop me?"

"Mayhap I will tie you to my bed. Naked. That way, when Loncaster arrives, as he surely will, he will at least believe that part of your story."

"You are a loathsome lout. What a crude thing to suggest!"

A smile twitched at his lips. "Tempting though, isn't it?" He chucked her under her gaping chin and walked away.

Leaving her stunned. And tempted.

"I am still not going to marry you," he called back over his shoulder.

She made a rude gesture she'd once seen her father's chief *hirdsman* make to a passing Saxon.

CHAPTER EIGHT

❧

lueless men will believe anything when it comes to sex!

John explained the situation to Hamr, Bolthor, and Ordulf, his chief *hersir*, that afternoon when they went to the bathing house following several vigorous sessions of swordplay on the exercise fields. They were all dripping wet, and not just from the muscle-straining practice in weaponry. Steam filled the room and invigorated the body.

"This is to be kept betwixt us," John warned. "No one must know that the king's son is here."

The three men nodded.

"Should I send to Gravely for more troops?" Ordulf asked, fingering his impressive mustache that matched his well-trimmed beard. He was as tall and big a man as Bolthor, but a good twenty years younger.

"Nay. Not yet. Too many fighting men on hand might make Loncaster suspicious." John did not want everyone looking guilty. That was another reason for keeping the boy's identity secret.

"It might all be a ruse to trap you," Hamr suggested to John.

"Trap me how?"

"Into matrimony."

"Pfff! Nay, Lady Ingrith's story speaks true. We all know that King Edgar will tup anything with breasts. His by-blows must be innumerable."

"Yea, 'tis true. And I recall how Eric Bloodaxe killed a dozen of his brothers to pave the way for his rise to the kingship once held by his father, Harald Fairhair," Bolthor related. "In fact, John, didst know that your stepfather's father, Thork, another of Harald's sons, escaped Eric's terror only because he renounced any claims?"

"Men in power do extreme things," John agreed.

"Ah, that is why the boylings were shaved," Bolthor said.

John nodded, and they all chuckled at Ingrith's ingenuity in coming up with the idea to hide Samuel's, rather Henry's, unique hair color.

"I think I will shave my head," Hamr said.

"Whaaat?" the rest of them exclaimed.

"It would help reinforce the head-lice tale Lady Ingrith spouts." Hamr looked at each of them, seeing they needed further convincing. "Besides, I have heard that women like bald men. It has something to do with bedplay."

They were all silent then, wondering exactly what that bedplay might involve.

"Ordulf, you would look particularly good with a bald head but keeping your mustache and beard." When Hamr got an idea, he beat it to death.

"Dost think so?"

"Women would certainly give you a second look," Hamr contended. "Especially your wife."

"Now that I think on it," Ordulf was tapping his chin thoughtfully, "Balki the Bald, that Danish berserker, claimed he could make a woman peak five times in just one bout of bedsport."

"He also claimed he could lop off three enemy heads with one swing of his battle-axe," John scoffed.

"I do not understand." Bolthor's brow furrowed with confusion. "How would a bald head help with bedplay?"

"Has something to do with a woman riding a bald horse, methinks," Hamr said, just before sliding down into the water where he stayed for a long moment. When he came back up with a splash, swinging his long hair over his shoulder, he found them all laughing.

And when they left the bathing house a long time later, they were all bald.

It was a hairy situation . . .

Ingrith was in the kitchen teaching Ardith, the

woman she was training to take over as cook, how to prepare a leek-and-dill brine for freshwater fish when Katherine rushed into the kitchen and said, "Come. Quickly. You must see this."

Ingrith wiped her hands on a cloth and followed Katherine to the back door. Coming from the bathing house, their strides wide and confident, were four big men. All of them bald as a baby's behind.

And one of them was John.

"Are they not the most handsome sight you have e'er seen?" Katherine sighed. "Methinks I will be forgiving my husband tonight."

Ingrith's eyes were filling with tears, and she held a hand over her heart. She knew why they'd done it, and it touched her to the core. And, yea, they did look handsome as sin.

"What? You are crying?" John said when he got closer. "Do I look that bad?"

"Nay, you look that good." And it was the truth. His hairless, fine-shaped head only called attention to the sculpted features of his face and his compelling blue eyes.

John shook his head at her. "Ingrith, Ingrith, Ingrith! You should not tell me that."

"Why?" She was swiping her wet cheeks with the edge of her apron.

"Because I like it too much."

"See," Hamr said, elbowing John.

Bolthor and Katherine were in close conversation. Very close. And one of John's soldiers, Ordulf by name, was surrounded by several young maidens, all wanting to touch his head, but his wife came up and dragged him away by the ear, which he allowed, whispering something in her ear. Something naughty, if his wife's blush was any indication.

Drawing John to the side, Ingrith said, "You didn't have to do this."

"I know."

"But I am forever grateful that you did."

"How grateful?"

"Tsk-tsk-tsk! You give me so many mixed signals, John. You tempt me, then repel me."

"I am mixed up inside, that is why." He gave her a look so hot her insides felt as if they were melting. "But I still cannot marry you."

She slapped him on the chest for making that objectionable statement. Again. "I have been so afraid. I felt as if a heavy burden was weighing me down."

"You are too independent by half. Mayhap you need to step back and ask for help betimes."

"I am the only one I can truly depend on."

"Not true. You have a family. Friends." He paused. "Me."

She stared at him, still weepy-eyed, then launched herself at him, hugging him tightly with arms wrapped tight around his shoulders, her body pressed against his, chest to knees. So startled was he that he enfolded her into an embrace, to keep from falling over, no doubt, but he was soon hugging her back, whether intentional or not. And it felt good.

Against the shadowy hollow of his neck, she breathed deeply of the clean, musky skin and whispered, "Thank you."

He chuckled and swept his hands from her back to her buttocks and up again, settling at her waist.

Tingles of warm sensation followed in their wake.

"My pleasure, m'lady. Definitely my pleasure."

When her emotions over this latest turn of events calmed down, Ingrith realized something startling . . . and not altogether unwelcome. John wanted her. As a man wanted a woman. She could tell by the ridge of his arousal pressing against her belly and by the fast beating of his heart still pressed against her chest.

Still maintaining her hold on his shoulders, she leaned back to study him. He did not look happy.

"This cannot happen betwixt us, Ingrith."

"Why?" Holy Thor! She could not believe she had asked that question.

"Because I cannot offer you an honorable end result."

"Marriage again! Why do you keep harping on that subject? I ne'er asked to wed with you."

"Ah, but you and I both know something is sizzling betwixt us. If we do not stop it in the bud, we will end up in the bed furs, sure as salt. For a fortnight, I suspect, if we were not interrupted."

What would we do for a fortnight? The prospect boggles the mind . . . and other body parts. She smiled, a wicked, wanton smile she did not even know she was capable of.

"Ingrith!" he moaned and pulled her tight again, kissing her neck, then murmuring against her ear. "I want you. So much!"

"I want you, too." For the first time in her life, she knew what her sisters meant when they said that women could turn lustsome, too.

To her disappointment, however, he put her away from him with his hands on her upper arms. "Enough!"

"Coward!"

"Bloody damn right I am. Your father would have my head on a platter."

"Not if he did not know." By the gods, she was begging the man. How pitiful was that?

"This is not going to happen." He walked away from her without waiting for her response. If he had waited, he would have heard her say, "Wouldst like to bet a Saxon coin on that, m'lord Hawk?"

Once Ingrith got an idea in her head, she followed through to the bitter end. Except the end she had in mind now would not be bitter at all.

*   *   *

Men weren't the only ones who were clueless . . .

John stared with dismay at the sight before him.

Hamr had left a short time ago for Jorvik with a half dozen *housecarls* to see what he could learn about Loncaster and to check on the sea readiness of the Ravenshire longship. In his wake, after spouting his baldheaded sex tales, Hamr had left at least twenty-five other males with shaven heads, and some of them very bad jobs, with bloody nicks and hairy patches in back. Even Ubbi had shaved his little head and now truly resembled a gnome. The few Norsemen in his ranks . . . everyone knew that Norsemen were known for their vanity . . . made an art form of the shaving. Some with bald pates except for war braids, some with only the back and sides shaved, some with just a narrow strip of hair left from forehead to nape.

They were creating a new fashion for men's hair here at Hawk's Lair, news of which was sure to spread far and wide. Just what he wanted. More attention directed on his home!

"Is it not nice that so many men care about protecting the boy?" Ingrith whispered to him from her seat beside him at the high table.

"Huh? No one knows about Henry, except you, me, Bolthor, Hamr, and Ordulf. The rest have been led to believe that a bald head equates with better sex."

"Oh," she said, as if she understood, which she could not have.

While on the subject of fashion, he thought, *did Ingrith have to make herself look so good?* Instead of her Norse *gunna* and apron, she wore a jade green gown in the Saxon style, its brightness contrasting with the blue of her eyes. The gown was high necked and long sleeved but formfitting enough that he was picturing what was underneath in vivid detail. Her hair, which was usually braided into a coronet atop her head, was loose tonight, long blonde waves hanging down to her waist in back but held off her face and behind her ears with a thin silver diadem.

If she only knew how much he wanted to taste the tiny lobe that was exposed, trace the whorls with the tip of his tongue, breathe into the channel.

But then he was staring with dismay at the other sight just being presented before him. A sea bass the size of a small whale sat on what had to be a specially built trencher. How she had obtained such a saltwater fish this far inland was beyond him. It was stuffed with God-only-knew-what, swimming in a sauce that resembled curdled milk, with a large apple in its mouth. The dish probably tasted delicious, but what in hell was happening in his life that he would have such a repast on a common everyday table?

"What do you think?" Ingrith asked.

"Amazing," was the best he could come up with.

"Thank you."

He had not meant it as a compliment. "Ingrith, my men will get fat if you keep feeding us like this."

"They seem to like my food." She bristled.

Did she know that when she stiffened like that it caused her breasts to thrust outward? But what was that she said? Something about his men liking her food. "Of course they do. What is not to like about such wonderful fare?" He tried but failed to keep the sarcasm from his voice.

"You are in an ill-temper again. You oaf! Your grumpiness is not about food, is it? You want me to be gone."

"You know that is not true." *And that is the problem. I want you to stay too much. In fact, I want you, period.*

"What I know is that you are hiding your emotions behind some wall." She tossed her head so that a swath on her shoulder swung to her back. The torchlight caught in the golden shades and he caught the scent of something . . . mead?

Blather, blather, blather. Now she is going to analyze my feelings. How like a woman! I wonder what she would do if I leaned over and smelled her hair. "Do not accuse me of cowardice again, I warn you."

"What I know is that you deprive yourself of what you want out of some misplaced nobility."

"Nobility is the last thing I cherish." *Definitely mead.*

"What I know is that I am sick of your seesawing gestures toward me."

"You know nothing, Ingrith. Nothing at all," he spat out, then gave in to his inclinations and put his face to her hair, sniffing deeply. "Why do I smell mead? Did you bathe in the brew?"

"I rinse my hair in beer . . . or ale . . . or mead. It makes it softer."

He touched her hair. Definitely soft. "I swear, woman, you are going to deplete my stock of honey as well as mead." *And turn all my good intentions to mush.*

"Do you begrudge me a cup of mead?"

"Only if it is wasted on hair. Unless . . . did you drink it afterward?"

"What an idiot!"

"Methinks I might need to investigate further. Perchance you need to remove your gown later, in my bedchamber, so I can see if you are mead-scented elsewhere," he teased.

But she did not seem to appreciate his lack-witted attempt at humor. "Lecherous idiot!" She shrugged away from him, giving him a look of such disgust that he flinched. *What an overreaction! I was not that lecherous . . . or idiotic. Was I?* She would have stalked out of the hall if Bolthor had not stood just then and coughed for attention.

John put a hand on her knee to force her to continue sitting.

She slapped his hand away.

"This is an ode to clueless men," Bolthor announced.

"That is just bloody wonderful," John muttered.

"Clueless men? Amen to that!" Ingrith said, glancing over to Katherine, who was grinning like a cat that had swallowed all the cream in the keep. She and Bolthor had taken to their sleep bower this afternoon and did not come out until just afore dinner. They gave proof to the fact that sex did not wane even in those of middle age seeing as how Katherine was in her early forties, and Bolthor had certainly seen more than fifty winters.

Men are a clueless lot,
Whether Viking or Saxon or Scot.
We woo our ladies
Like randy bees.
Pretty words, a lusty embrace,
Priceless jewels, a shaven face.
We coax and cajole, we take to a keg.
We even are known to get down and beg.
But who knew in the woman's mind
A mystery all men eventually find
That all it takes is a bald head
To get a woman into bed.

Everyone applauded, including John, thankful that he was not the brunt of Bolthor's jestsome sagas this time. Also thankful that Ingrith's attention was removed from himself.

"I want a favor from you," Ingrith said.

Not so far removed, he decided, moaning inwardly. He could tell by the expression on her face that it was going to be a big favor. He shook his head vigorously.

"How can you say me nay afore you even hear what I want?"

"Whatever it is, I will not do it."

"I want you to make love to me."

His jaw dropped, and he almost fell off his seat. Her words tickled his ballocks and thus caused his cock to salute the high heavens. "Have you lost your mind?"

"Nay. Nor have I lost my maidenhead, but I want to."

"Ingrith!" His favorite body part was nigh doing a jig. *Down, cock, down!*

"I have been told that women look different after they have been swived. Would that not be further evidence to Loncaster that we have an attachment?"

Concentrate, John. Do not think of bedplay, or how she looked naked, or how much you would enjoy granting her favor. You must be chivalrous. "I thought the head lice and bald heads theory was going to convince him."

"That, too."

"Your father and two hundred warriors would be here in a trice, all wanting my head."

"He will never find out."

Oh, I doubt that. Fathers have a way of detecting these things. "You said that women look different. Your father would know."

"Do not try to confuse the issue."

Confuse? I am not the one who is confused. Well, I am not the only one confused.

"You just do not want me."

If I wanted you any more, we would be entertaining my troops on top of yon table.

"If I looked like Joanna, you would agree just like that." She snapped her fingers. "She is older than I; so, it must be my lack of allure."

This subject is beginning to annoy me. I need to go off and . . . do something. "Ingrith. You have allure aplenty. This has naught to do with Joanna or how you look."

"I am almost thirty-one years old. There is little chance that I will wed. Methinks I deserve to experience lovemaking at least once."

"You think that if we make love, I would be able to stop at once?"

"Well, twice."

"How about twenty . . . or fifty?" *And about a hundred different positions and places.*

"You jest."

He just stared at her.

But the wily witch had more in store for him. Placing a hand over her navel, she told him, "You make my belly bud sweat."

He counted to ten silently.

"What does Joanna have that I do not? Are you in love with her?"

He reached up to tug at his own hair before he

realized that he had none. At least her annoying persistence had lessened his cockstand. Halfway. "Joanna is a convenience to me, and I to her. She has something that I need. Plus, the older children of her first husband have harassed her about the Coppergate stall, and I helped her establish freehold rights. I am a companion to her . . . a sexual companion on occasion, when it is convenient for both of us. That is all."

Her brow furrowed with concentration. "Something is missing here."

A whole lot is missing here, but I am not about to reveal all my secrets to you, you curious cat. He inhaled and exhaled several times. "I will not marry you, and I will not make love with you. Is that clear?"

"As water." But then she tapped her fingertips on the table, thinking away. God only knew what was going through her head now.

"So, you accept what I have said?" he finally inquired.

"Of course not. I am thinking of ways to change your mind."

That's what he was afraid of. And chivalry be damned!

CHAPTER NINE

You could say she was going a-Viking . . .

Ingrith was pretty sure she was under a spell.

In all her almost thirty-one years, she had never felt aroused just by looking at a man. In fact, she wasn't sure she had ever been aroused at all.

He looked at her, and she melted.

He licked his lips, and she melted.

He brushed against her in passing, and she melted.

He blinked his sinfully long lashes, and she melted.

He stared at her when he thought she was not aware, and she melted.

She was even aroused by his stupid bald head.

"How do you undo a love spell?" she asked Katherine, who sat next to her in the kitchen where they were pitting sour cherries for a sweet tart. Ardith, the new cook-in-training, was at the other end of the long table preparing a dozen stuffed capons to be roasted for the evening meal, under Ingrith's subtly watchful supervision.

Katherine cast Ingrith a speaking glance. "The Hawk has you under his spell?"

"Well, not *his* spell precisely. If he had his way, I would be long gone. I, on the other hand, have developed this odd attraction to the lout."

"Odd in what way?"

"When he looks at me, I feel the embers of a fire spark to life within me."

Katherine nodded her head. "Does the heat start in your oven?"

"My oven?" Ingrith squeaked, then giggled. "You could say that."

"I married and buried three husbands afore I met Bolthor, all of them swine. I swore I would not wed again, despite the efforts of King Edgar, my cousin many times removed, and certainly not a Viking. I grew up in Saxon lands, fearing and hating the Norse invaders. But when I first met Bolthor, I was lost. And, yea, betimes all it takes is a smoldering gaze."

"I am almost thirty-one years old. I grew up in a royal household surrounded by fighting men, many of them too virile for their own good. More than a score of men have offered for me, several score, truth to tell, and not all of them were unacceptable. Not once was I tempted as I am by Lord Hawk."

Katherine shrugged. "Wise men through the ages have attempted to understand this concept of male/female attraction. Methinks God, or the gods, designed us to be a puddle of desire for our men so that we would agree to procreate. Otherwise, we might just send the clueless dolts on their way."

"But see, that is the problem. John keeps telling me that he will not marry, ever. And he does not want children, ever."

"Hmmmm. Now that is strange. Still, if you really want him, there is no way he could resist."

"Hah! That is just what he is doing. Resisting me. I must confess, I asked him to make love with me . . . without the benefit of marriage . . . and he refused."

Katherine's eyes went wide with surprise. She set down her small knife and shoved the bowl of cherries aside. "You need a plan."

"A plan?"

"A temptation plan."

"Oh, my gods!"

"Are you interested?"

"Oh, my gods!" She braced herself. "Absolutely."

"You must think of yourself as a spider, and Lord John as the hapless fly. What you must do is lure the man into your web."

She moaned at the prospect. A web of deceit, she feared.

"Here is what you should do," Katherine advised, "Number One . . ." She began to detail a series of ploys that Ingrith could try to lure John to her bed furs.

By the time Katherine got to Number Twelve, Ingrith's jaw was nigh touching her chest.

"Dost think you have the nerve?" Katherine inquired. "Do you dare?"

Ingrith had her answer then. "My father always said, 'Never dare a Viking.' And I am Viking to the core."

"Lord Hawk does not stand a chance," Katherine declared with a hoot of laughter.

Ingrith could only hope.

Oh, honey!

It was late the next afternoon before Ingrith was able to put her plan into action.

There had been several crises to handle before that. Henry was becoming increasingly distraught as he realized he was in some danger. He was too small, at five, to understand kings and power plays, but someone must have told him that bad men wanted to kill him. As a result, he was behaving in a clinging manner that would only call attention to himself when Loncaster finally arrived.

And Hamr had already sent word that the Saxon commander would be there within days. Loncaster was currently harassing the folks at

Larkspur in the far north, where Ingrith's sister Breanne resided with her husband, Caedmon.

After much soothing and patient explanation, Henry settled down. He and the other children were made to understand how important it was that they keep their secrets, and that included the two girls from the brothel, who had been calling attention to themselves with some of the men.

Then there was Ubbi. Really, the little man was becoming more than protective of not just the children but also of Ingrith herself.

"I see ye eyein' Lord Hawk like a sweetmeat. Doan be thinkin' the troll is fer you," Ubbi advised, hitching his child-size pants with self-importance.

"What is it that you have against Lord Hawk?" she'd asked, which had been a mistake. It only gave Ubbi the reason to launch into a tirade.

"The troll is full of himself. All this nonsense about bees and such is jist a cover fer his licentious nature."

Not so licentious if he will not accept my offer. "Really, Ubbi! How would you know that?"

"Us men have ways," he assured her. "In any case, didst know he has some of his people engaging in perverted sex acts, all fer the sake of preventin' babies from bein' born?"

"*What?* I have never heard of anything so outrageous."

" 'Tis true." Ubbi was nodding his head with

conviction. "He has these couples tuppin' like rabbits, with honey coatin' the men's cocks."

"Ubbi!"

"Fergive the coarse words, m'lady, but 'tis a fact. Lord Hawk calls 'em ex-parry-mens to prevent a man's seed from takin' root in his bed partner, but I say it is jist bloody damn wicked."

Ubbi expected her to be outraged, but Ingrith wondered if there must be a connection between these experiments and his assertion that he cannot, or would not, have any children. In fact, she saw Ubbi's charges as just another piece of the puzzle that was John of Hawk's Lair. The only question was why.

Finally, she was free to pursue the rogue. She knew from observation that John usually worked on the exercise fields with his men in the morning . . . sword practice, archery, lance throwing. In the afternoons, he worked in his honey shed, researching the properties of honey and treating some of his cotters with honey treatments for various ailments.

As the first part of her temptation plan, Ingrith altered a gown she'd owned for years. It was crimson, in a wool so soft it appeared to have a nap, like a kitten. It was modest in style, with a rounded neck, long sleeves and hem, but because of the material, it clung to her body's curves. No apron today, that was for sure.

When she got to the honey shed, she stepped

inside, but then stood near the open door against the wall. At the far side, there were several people lined up for their master's help.

The first was a young girl who had her *gunna* raised to her knees. She seemed to have an angry rash on her lower legs that had become irritated. The skin was red and raw in places.

"This is a mixture of honey and vinegar and several other ingredients that forms a paste," John was explaining as he applied the ointment to her legs. "It should relieve the pain and begin the healing process, but you must not scratch. If you do, it makes the rash worse and it will spread, as well."

The girl sighed with relief when John finished, patting her on the head as he handed her an oiled parchment cone filled with the cream.

"Me mother said ta tell you she'll send some turnips from our garden in payment."

"Good. I can never have enough turnips," John replied, barely hiding a grimace. Ingrith suspected that he had no taste for the *neeps*, in any form. That and cabbage and spinach.

Next up was a woman holding a coughing infant. "Ah, little one, what is the matter?" John took the baby into the cradle of one elbow, while using his free hand to peel back the blanket and swaddling clothes.

"Herbert has been coughin' like this fer days," said his mother, with tears in her exhausted eyes.

"You should have come sooner, Mary. Now, Herbie, let us see what the problem is." Using a fingertip dipped in honey, to make his intrusion more palatable, he examined the child's mouth and throat. Soon, he was handing the mother a honey-and-cherry-bark syrup to alleviate the cough. " 'Twould not hurt to put a little mead on your nipple when you nurse the mite, as well. The child will sleep more restfully."

Mary gifted him a handwoven wool horse blanket.

Three more people were served by John and his "healing" arts while Ingrith waited. His payment for these services was a jug of Frankish wine, several ells of the transparent cloth he used in his beekeeping, and a kiss on the cheek by a nubile dairy maid with promise of more if he was interested, which he did not seem to be.

Ingrith could not help but be impressed with his knowledge and compassion. If she was not already half in love with the man, she would be now.

Finally, he was done and exhaling with relief. That was when he noticed her standing there.

"Oh, nay! Not you! Again!"

Not very encouraging to her plan.

"Are you stalking me?"

"Can a lady not seek out a man to talk?"

"Nay, nay, nay! No more of your kind of talking. The last time you 'talked' to me, you asked

me . . . well, suffice it to say it took me a long time
to recover."

Good! I must affect him, after all. With a smile, she
stepped closer. *Come here, fly. Let me show you my
spiderweb.*

His gaze swept her body, taking in the clingy
material. She could feel her nipples peak at his pe-
rusal and wondered if he could tell.

His survey snagged when passing over her chest.

Yea, he noticed.

Still, he resisted. "You will not bend me to your
will, Ingrith. Do not even try."

"I would not know how." She could already see
the tendrils of her web reaching out to him.

"Hah! That gown alone speaks for your intent."

She did not try to deny his accusation, but instead shrugged. Her heart hammered against her
ribs as she proceeded with her seduction, ill prepared as she was for such an activity.

"Do not step any closer, Ingrith."

"Why are you staring at my lips?"

The edge of his mouth quirked, but then his
face went bleak as he repeated what was now a
familiar refrain, "I will not marry you."

She was mystified and entranced by this silent
sadness that came and went over his face. What
was it that troubled him so?

At the same time, with their bodies almost
touching, she could feel his heat and arousal, like
an erotic cloud reaching out to her. His cheek-

bones, heightened in color, were like red flags of surrender. To her, leastways.

"You are attracted to me," she insisted.

"Of course I am. I am a red-blooded male. But you are perilous to all I hold dear."

"You treat your people for all their ailments. Why not me?"

That brought a full-fledged smile to his lips.

If he only knew what his smiles did to her!

"And what is your particular ailment, m'lady?" he inquired with a lazy drawl.

"I ache."

He arched his brows.

"Here," she said and put a hand to her lower belly.

"God help me," he said on a moan, then opened his arms to her.

Sometimes spiders do not catch the fly . . .

John closed his eyes and shuddered as he held Ingrith in a tight embrace. How could something so wrong feel so right?

So aroused that he felt disoriented, he trembled with his efforts to maintain control. Ingrith's eagerness excited him, without a doubt heightened by his long period of self-denial. But he must put a stop to this temptation.

"Ingrith. Sweetling." He tried to set her away from him, but her arms were wrapped so tightly about his neck, like manacles, and . . . Good Lord!

She was rubbing her breasts back and forth across his chest and making little mewling, catlike sounds of satisfaction. She had to be aware of his raging enthusiasm pressing into her abdomen.

"Stop!" he said firmly, prying her fingers off his neck and forcing her to stand an arm's length away. With his hands on her shoulders, arms braced, he made her stand still. "This cannot happen."

"Why?" she whimpered.

With a deep sigh of surrender, he told her, "I will tell you why. God help me, but I will tell you why." He lowered his hands to her waist and lifted her to sit on his high stool.

He walked away a short distance, unable to speak at the look of passion, and disappointment, on her face.

"You know that I am the illegitimate son of the Earl of Gravely."

She nodded. "What has that to do—"

He halted her further words with a raised hand. "My birth is the result of Steven of Gravely raping my mother."

She gasped. "I did not know."

"Not many people do. Steven was an evil man, Ingrith. Insane, if you must know. And I carry the same blood."

"Oh, John, I carry the same blood as my father, who is arrogant beyond belief. And cruel in battle, I am told. And lustsome?" She rolled her eyes. "Needless to say . . . five wives speak for itself."

John smiled sadly. "That is different. The despicable things my father did in his short life are evidence of a madness I have difficulty describing, and it wasn't just in battle. Rape is the least of his sins. Murder, even of children and innocent women. Torture. Sodomy. God only knows what else. 'Tis said that his brother Elwinus entered a cloistered order of monks as a young boy due to the things he saw at the Gravely estate. Mayhap he experienced the insanity himself."

"What is it that you are trying to tell me?"

"I am telling you that insanity runs in my blood, and I refuse . . . I absolutely refuse . . . to bring a child into this world with that prospect hanging over its head."

Tears welled in her eyes. Pity, no doubt. Pity he could do without. He stiffened and raised his chin defiantly. "That is why I meet with Joanna on occasion. She is barren."

"Why have you not married her? Leastways, you could ease your body on her without repercussions whenever your sap rises to overflowing."

"My . . . my sap?"

"Is it because she is of a lower class?"

"I am still stuck on the rising sap."

"Do not pretend that you do not understand. 'Tis when a man's dangly part gets so filled with sap it must find relief or burst."

She can't be that gullible. Can she? "I have ne'er

heard that theory afore, especially in reference to dangly part."

She narrowed her eyes, trying to determine if he was mocking her.

He maintained a straight face, though he was in fact laughing inside.

"You did not answer my question. Why not marry Joanna?"

"I have asked Joanna to wed, and she declined."

She flinched and closed her eyes for a moment, as if he had hit her.

"Joanna prefers her independent life in Jorvik. And she refuses to give up the trade her husband established to his greedy children."

"I'm sorry . . . for you."

"Do not be sorry for me," he snapped. "I have told you, ours is merely a convenient affair."

"No heart pangs involved?"

He smiled. "None at all." The sadness on her face pulled at him. "I do not want to hurt you, Ingrith. 'Twould seem that bluntness is the only way I can make you understand."

"I still do not understand, you fool." She swiped at her eyes and slid off the stool. "Have you ever struck a child? Have you ever raped a woman? Do you feel an urge to do perverted things?"

"Only with you," he said, then immediately regretted his levity.

"I cannot accept that you have bad blood. I just cannot."

"Ask your sister Tyra's husband. Adam the Healer. His stepfather Selik suffered sorely at my father's hand. Not only did my father rape Selik's first wife, but he also carried his infant son's head about on a pike."

Disgust finally seeped into Ingrith's thick head, and she almost swooned on her feet. He put his hands on her upper arms to help her keep her balance.

"Now you see why I cannot be with you. I cannot risk pregnancy. You must not develop an attachment to me."

"I fear it is already too late," she said, gathering the skirt of her *gunna* in one hand. As she turned to leave, she told him, "I think I have fallen in love with you."

CHAPTER TEN

❧

In the battle of the sexes, men rarely win . . .

It was two days before John was within talking, or touching, distance of Ingrith. He was avoiding the too-tempting wench like a bad rash.

But she was determined, if nothing else. In fact, he was beginning to refer to her in his mind as "the Burr," meaning that she stuck fast to someone or something until she got what she wanted. Why else had he ended up harboring a herd of orphans, including the king's illegitimate son? The Burr, for sure.

Bolthor could probably create a great saga with that title, he thought with a silent grimace.

But she found him finally . . . well, trapped him . . . in the hall outside his bedchamber as he was about to go down for the evening meal, to be followed by an evening session in his bee shed. Work was his salvation.

He almost jumped out of his skin. "Ingrith! Why are you sneaking about, pouncing on me?"

"I did not pounce. I merely waited in the shadows until you came out." She must have just come from the bath house, because her braid was damp with wet tendrils framing her flushed face. She was wringing her hands nervously.

He didn't want to ponder why her face was flushed or why the usually unshakeable woman was now nervous. It no doubt boded ill for him.

"If I were pouncing, I would have barged into your bedchamber."

Now there is a thought! "Could you not wait 'til I came down?"

"Nay. You are avoiding me."

"And that does not tell you something?" *Like . . . stay away!* "Where is your chaperon?"

"Chaperon?"

"The gnome. He usually shadows you, to protect you from my lascivious intents. Little does the pestsome gnat know, I am the one needing protection."

Her wringing hands were now fisted.

Holy saints! It was fun riling the woman.

"You are being mean to me."

Mean to be kind. "Is it working?"

"Nay. I need to tell you something important . . . something I just learned, which you may not be aware of. For a certainty, I did not—"

His head shot up. "Is Loncaster here?"

"Of course not. Your guards would have sounded the horn. Besides, Ordulf would have been the one—"

"Not another secret that you neglected to share with me! Nay, that cannot be it. Your eye is not twitching." He sighed deeply. "What is wrong now?"

"How can I tell you if you keep interrupting me? This is personal."

"Uh-oh!"

"We should go into your bedchamber to discuss this."

"We definitely should not go into my bedchamber." *Now would be the time for me to run. Fast.*

"Why? Are you afraid of me?"

"Terrified." *Run, Hawk, run!*

"Enough jesting!"

"Who is jesting?" *If she licks her lips one more time, I just might . . .*

She skirted around him to open his bedchamber door. Then she turned to glare at him in the middle of the corridor. "Well? Are you coming in?"

"Do I have to?"

She reached for his arm and dragged him in, then closed the door after them.

Under normal circumstances, he would be amused, but Ingrith was going too far. Being unbiddable was one thing, forcing her attention on him was quite another. He leaned back against the closed door, arms folded over his chest. "Get to it, Ingrith. I am hungry and would go down to eat. What feast are we having tonight, by the by?"

She ignored his sarcasm as she paced the small room, seeming to be struggling for the right words. "I was speaking to Katherine, and she told me there are ways to prevent conception."

"What?" he shouted. He barely restrained himself from going over to shake the troublesome woman. "You dared discuss my problem with Bolthor's wife. Bloody hell! The skald will be composing an ode to celibate men."

"Of course I didn't tell Katherine. We were speaking in general of women who bear too many children, to the point of death, and how convenient it would be if they could prevent a man's seed from meeting fertile ground, at least on occasion." She released a whooshy exhale after that long stretch of blather.

"I have ne'er in all my life had this kind of conversation with a woman." He put his face in his hands and counted to ten, then confronted her. "I am aware of those herbal remedies. They may or may not work, usually not. I would not take the risk."

Her face fell with disappointment.

"This is my problem, not yours." He attempted to be gentle in his words when he would really like to throttle the wench for her interference.

"It is my problem when it prevents you from making love to me."

Oh, good God, we are back to that forbidden subject.

"And if you say that you are not going to marry me again, I think I might just scream."

He almost smiled . . . until she came out with another of her outrageous suggestions.

"Sometimes at the orphanage we rescue girls from brothels. They have told us . . . things."

"What kinds of things?"

"Sex acts that do not involve . . . um, penetration," she said quickly, as if she might not have the nerve if she hesitated.

Every single part of John's body went on alert. Sex alert.

The kind that thickened the blood and hardened essential parts. He could swear he heard a buzzing in his ears . . . a buzzing that presaged surrender. This woman made him so damn angry . . . and aroused. A man could take only so much.

"So be it!" he said. "You want to make love, without intercourse? We will, but only under my conditions."

"What conditions?" she asked, hesitantly.

But her hesitation had come too late. He was the one determined now. "You will do everything I order. Everything. Without question."

"But—"

"And once you agree, there will be no going back."

"But—"

"Everything. No matter if it is coarse, rude, wet, noisy, brazen, or wanton. Sex play . . . good sex play . . . is not for the faint of heart."

"Whaaat? John, you know that I am a woman in control above all things. It would be nigh impossible for me to do such things without question."

He shrugged. "That is precisely what I would ask you to hand over. Control. In the bedplay only. You may rule the kitchen roost as you will. Cock-a-doodle-do all you want, but in my bedchamber the rules are mine."

Her chin rose haughtily. There was no way that this prideful woman would give him such power.

"Agreed."

"What?" he choked out. "Ingrith, I offer you one last chance for escape. You are nobly born. Women of your class do not engage in such activities."

"Noblewomen do not engage in illicit liaisons?"

First dangly parts and rising sap. Now liaisons. Where does she get this information? "Not when they are virgins!" He stared at her for a long moment. "I know I asked before, but you are a virgin, aren't you?"

"Yea, I am. A thirty-one-year-old virgin! And I am damn tired of it! Like an albatross, my maidenhead is."

He would have burst out laughing, but this situation was becoming nigh ridiculous, and not in a humorous way. Enough! Time to scare the wench. Force her to stop this nonsense.

He steepled his fingers and pinioned her with a deliberately lecherous gaze.

She did not waver. The willful witch!

"Despite all caution, your virtue would be forfeit."

"Oh, please! Get on with it!"

The irksome woman was driving him barmy! If she thought to take the reins in this ride, she was in for a jolt.

"Very well. Take off your clothes. All of them. Slowly."

He bit his bottom lip to keep from smiling and wondered how quickly she would run away, calling him every foul name in her vast vocabulary.

Instead, she surprised the spit out of him.

Slowly, very slowly, she took off every bit of clothing, including her shoes and hose. She stood before him in all her naked glory with a full-body blush and squared soldiers. A sex siren off to war.

She was tall . . . long-waisted and long-legged, with many intriguing curves to soften the bones. Little hills and valleys that begged exploration. Her breasts were high and that unusual pale rose flesh color. Her buttocks were still firm . . . no sag at all, which was surprising for a woman her age. But then she had not borne any children which usually caused the belly to go soft and the bottom to expand. In his experience, and it defied his understanding, happily married men loved those marks on their women.

"Unbraid your hair and finger comb it out."

She did as he asked, the pose causing her

breasts to lift in the most enticing manner. When she was done, Ingrith stared at him, nervously awaiting his response.

How could he tell her now that it was all a jest? A tactic meant to prove how unsuitable she was for this kind of wicked bedsport.

Instead, the joke was on him.

He fought a silent battle to be chivalrous . . . and lost. He was powerless to resist the intense attraction that blossomed between them, as it had from the first she entered his keep.

"Well? Are you going to stand there like a turnip?" she demanded, hands on hips. "Do you yield?"

Heat ignited, then unfurled to all the extremities of his long cold body. He never knew that surrender could be such a sweet burn.

She was a fast learner . . .

For the first time in her life, Princess Ingrith of Stoneheim, a woman of sensible . . . some might say priggish . . . nature, stood before a man, naked.

And she liked it.

She liked the way his nostrils flared as he pretended he was unaffected.

She liked those wicked things he'd said about sex play being wanton and not for the faint of heart.

She liked the fact that finally . . . *finally* . . . she would understand what her sisters meant about peaking and bliss, even if it wouldn't involve penetration.

And, gods help her, she liked John.

Without looking down, she knew that her nipples were pearled into hard points, and her nether folds wept with the dew of her arousal. A new, strange inner excitement made her restless and anxious to begin the game.

Oh, she knew that John's order that she disrobe was a blatant attempt to humiliate her into withdrawing from his reluctant agreement. But she could not care.

He grinned wolfishly and flicked his fingers, a gesture designed to annoy her. "Turn."

She arched a brow.

"So that I may examine the goods."

She would like to give him the goods . . . with a smack upside the head. "Just so you know . . . I will be examining your goods later, too."

The laughter that burst from his lips had a sharp edge to it. "I cannot wait."

He flicked his fingers again.

She gritted her teeth and turned slowly, full circle, hoping he wouldn't note that her bum was a bit jiggly or that she had big feet.

"Again," he said in a choked whisper.

With a foul word muttered under her breath, she twirled again, this time faster. "Do I meet with your approval?"

"You will do."

Her upper lip curled. "So, I am lacking when compared to Joanna?"

"Why do you keep bringing up Joanna? She has naught to do with us." He inhaled and exhaled as if to give him time for his next words. "You are who you are, Ingrith. Beautiful."

Her heart lightened. Oh, she knew she wasn't beautiful, but at least he found her somewhat pleasing.

But then he added, " 'Tis a blessing that you do not have dimples in your buttocks as women your age are wont to do."

Her eyes shot up to spear him. Was he teasing? Or really viewing her as a woman of advanced age?

His deliberately blank face told her naught as he walked over to a hardback chair and sat down. "Come here, Ingrith."

When she got closer, he tugged her to stand between his outspread thighs.

Under his steady scrutiny, she could scarce think. "This doesn't feel right," she said, "with me naked and you clothed."

"Do you protest our arrangement already?"

"You would like that, wouldn't you?"

"Actually, Ingrith, I would not. You beguile me."

"I do?"

The expression on his face *was* hungry and lustful.

She was oddly pleased that she could tempt such a man.

He lifted her breasts from underneath and strummed the already erect nipples with his thumbs.

"Eek!" He could have warned her that he was going to do *that*. Her breasts ached and she could swear there was a pulse, like a heartbeat, betwixt her legs.

"Do you like that, sweetling?"

Lackwit! "Nay. My knees fold on me all the time."

"Never fear. I will catch you."

"Must we talk?" *Let us get on to the good stuff.*

"Have you ne'er pleasured your own breasts?"

Huh? "Of course not." *I did not know I could.*

He spent an excessive amount of time playing with her breasts then. Cupping them. Massaging. Tweaking and strumming the nipples. On and on he continued the blissful torture, until she was mewling for satisfaction. Only then did he take a nipple in his mouth and draw her in deeply.

"Aaaaaaahhhhh!" she keened. Was there ever such a comparable pleasure in this world? With each suckle of one breast and fondling of the other, every hair on her body stood on end, even on her scalp, which prickled with sensation. The pulse between her legs was now a series of spasms.

"You taste wonderful," he murmured, open-mouthed, against her breast. "Do you like my touching your breasts?"

"Do frogs spit?" *Talk, talk, talk. The man is becoming a chatterer.*

He choked out a laugh, then resumed his delicious torture. From one breast to the other, he alternated his attentions

And then he stopped.

His blue eyes were glazed and at half-mast. His lips were parted with a soft panting. "We need to slow down."

Is the man mad? "Nay. We need to hurry up," she insisted, drawing his hands up to her breasts again.

"I am captaining this ship, Ingrith," he said, and withdrew her hands, but almost immediately he lifted her by the waist up high, so that he could arrange his legs together and her astride his thighs.

Oh. My. Gods! "This is scandalous," she protested, trying to draw her knees together to cover her exposed nether parts.

"Yea, it is," he agreed. "Isn't it wonderful?"

She gurgled out a further protest, but he spread his thighs, and hers, wider. She was shocked into speechlessness.

But then he put a hand to her nape to pull her closer to his lips, his hand massaging the tense tendons on the back of her neck. At the same time his other hand was moving over her back and bottom in wide sweeping caresses. His lips moved over hers from side to side, as if adjusting to the perfect fit. And then he was kissing her fervently.

Besieged by sensations from so many directions, she wanted to pause the kiss, or swat one hand or the other away from their distracting, albeit wonderful, forays so that she could concentrate on one thing at a time. It was too much. And not enough. How was she to know what she liked if everything was happening at once?

And then he stopped once again.

Puzzled, and highly aroused, she gaped at him.

His eyes were closed and his head thrown back. She could see the wild pulse beat in his neck. When he was seemingly back under control, he looked at her lazily through half-closed eyes.

"Methinks 'tis time to go down to dinner," he said.

"You jest!"

"Nay, 'tis always best in bedplay to stretch out the anticipation."

"Best for whom?"

"Both parties."

She smacked him on the chest and attempted to wiggle off his lap. She had felt only a twinge of humiliation standing naked before him. But now she felt full-blown humiliation as she sat spread before him like a ripe peach ready for the plucking, whilst he remained cool and casual as to whether they continued the game or not.

Well, the game was over for her.

"Let me go," she demanded, fighting his grasp on her upper arms. "This arrangement is over. Ne'er did I bargain for one-way bedplay. Dost get satisfaction turning me breathless and wanting as you remain an indifferent observer?"

"Ingrith! Is that what you think?" He laughed.

She hit him again.

He took one of her hands and placed it over the large bulge in his *braies*. "That is how indifferent I am to you, sweetling."

"Then why did you stop?"

"Because Katherine is knocking on the door."

"What?" she squealed. "How long has she been knocking?"

He smirked.

"Lackwit!" This time he let her wiggle off his lap. Grabbing a *gunna*, she held it up in front of her and opened the door a crack. "Katherine, sorry I did not hear you sooner. Is something amiss?"

"Nothing is amiss lest you consider a scorched fig pudding a problem." Katherine was grinning in a knowing fashion.

"I'll be right there," she said. "In the meantime, take it off the heat and pour it into several bowls. Be careful not to scrape the burnt bottom."

When she closed the door and was about to turn back, she noticed John staring with interest at her bare arse. *Men!*

"I must hurry. Dinner will be ruined."

He slouched in the chair, grinning. "I thought you were training a new cook."

"I am, but she is slow to learn. Oh, where is my undertunic? There. Under the bed."

"Let me help you dress."

She raised a brow at that.

To her amazement . . . though she soon understood why . . . John preferred that she don the red *gunna* she'd worn to the honey shed a few days past, the one that clung to her body like a second skin. His helping her dress was foresport in itself, with all his presumably inadvertent touches. And he insisted she wear naught beneath.

"Why?" she wanted to know. "Why no undergarments?"

"Anticipation. Remember what I told you. Betimes anticipation can be as intense a pleasure as the end result."

"I have ne'er heard a man favor waiting. For anything."

"See? I am teaching you new things," he said, and whisked the backs of his fingers over both breasts so that the nipples stood out, even under the fabric. "See?" he told her with an arresting smile of overblown male arrogance. "Another new thing. Now, when you walk and your *gunna* rubs against your turgid nipples, you will think of what is to come."

"Yea, I see," she told him, mimicking his arresting smile of overblown arrogance. And she whisked the back of the fingers of one hand over the front of his *braies*.

If his groan was any indication, they were going to be equal combatants in the bed battle.

"I have changed my mind," John said suddenly. "Take your garments back off." Already he'd removed his belt and was raising his tunic over his head.

"What are you doing?"

Instead of answering, he tossed his tunic over his shoulder and sat down on the side of the bed. "Help me remove my boots."

It was a sign of her melting brain that she knelt to do his bidding. "You said anticipation is to be highly valued."

He shrugged. "The best warrior knows to change tactics as the battle progresses."

"Is this war?"

"Most definitely."

"I have always thought I would make a good soldier."

He shook his head at her persistence for equality, even in the bedsport.

"We really should go down to dinner," she said.

"We really should not."

"I thought you were hungry."

"I am. Ravenous, in fact." Glancing up at her through smoldering eyes, he told her in a passion-raw voice, "But not for food."

CHAPTER ELEVEN

Sometimes the best meals involve no food . . .

John let Ingrith study his naked body with its rampant erection for a long moment. He hoped she wasn't too shocked.

"I have seen many a naked man," she began.

Mayhap not so shocked.

"But none of them waving a flagpole at me." She grinned.

The impudent wench! Does she have a shy bone in her body? "So, a connoisseur of male flesh, are you?"

"Tsk-tsk-tsk! My father had hundreds of warriors in residence. They had no qualms about exposing private parts to women, even five Viking princesses. Betimes they even practiced battle exercises in the nude, like berserkers."

"And how do I compare?" *I cannot believe I asked such a pitiful question.*

She tapped her chin and pretended to study his body once again. Well, no pretense, she *did* look him over in detail. "Truth to tell, John, you are a finely made man, all over, even with your shaved head."

"Thank you very much, m'lady." He bowed at her, which probably looked ridiculous with his "flagpole" waving. "I will show you later what I can do with that shaved head . . . and flagpole."

Her head shot up . . . she had been giving his "flagpole" extra attention, turning her head this way and that. No doubt she would have got on the floor to examine the underside if he hadn't spoken.

John knew his way around the bed furs. And he knew what to do now, for damn sure. He had taken a deliberately long time putting Ingrith's gown back on, but it took him only the blink of an eye to remove it now. With both of them naked, he tossed her, shrieking, up and onto the middle of the bed. Then, with a triumphant war cry, he came up over her. He could only imagine what those below stairs were thinking about the noise.

"I am going to eat you like one of your delicious honey cakes," he promised.

She smiled, uneasily. "I am not nearly as tasty."

"I beg to differ, sweetling. Let me see. First, I will lick you. All over. Like I do all sides of your juice-seeping pastry." He demonstrated by giving her ear a wet lap of his tongue. Then he blew it dry. After that, he licked her lips. The inner skin of her elbow. Her breastbone.

She shivered. With pleasure, he hoped. "Are you saying that I seep juice?"

"Only if I am lucky."

"What next?" the impatient wench prodded. "With honey cakes, I mean."

"I enjoy nibbling along the edges." He gently bit the edge of her stubborn chin, the curve of her shoulder, and the aureola of one breast. "Yum!" he said.

"Am I permitted to participate in this meal?" she inquired with mock docility.

This woman had never been docile. She no doubt came screaming from her mother's womb, trying to organize the birthing room. In truth, her eagerness excited and frightened him at the same time since he was unsure whether he could really resist her in the end. "Definitely. Later." He moved down her body so that he straddled her knees and put his face to her woman-fleece. "I especially want to eat you here." He dipped a finger inside, which came out wet. "Didst know they call this woman-honey?"

Her feet shot up and her arms flailed out. She almost knocked him off the bed. "Get away from there, you perverted oaf."

He was laughing so hard he could scarce speak as he moved up to lie on his side, with one leg pinioning her to the bed. Best not to give her an opportunity to bolt. "I thought you were going to let me do anything I wanted."

"You stipulated wanton things, not perversions."

Stipulated? Where does she get this stuff? "A sex kiss is not a perversion."

"It isn't?"

Mayhap a little. He shook his head. "But mayhap it is too soon in our arrangement. I will give you time."

"You are too generous."

"Uh, uh, uh!" he chided. "Sarcasm has no place in bedsport."

"Methinks you make these bedsport rules up as you go."

"Open your legs, Ingrith."

"Not so you can put your mouth there again." She turned slightly away from him, as far as she could go with his leg thrown over hers.

He smacked her lightly on the rump. "Do as you are told."

Amazingly, she lay back again and spread her thighs a bit.

"More."

With a muttered curse, she widened the space so that he could settle himself over her with his overenthusiastic cock nestling where it most wanted to be.

When she felt him there, her shock rippled out through all parts of her violently shivering body. "Oh, my!" was all she of the usually blathering mouth said. "I thought men looked more like worms there, but yours is surely a snake."

First, I am a flagpole, now a snake. What next? "You tremble, Ingrith. Are you fearful? Of my snake?"

She shook her head. "I tremble with . . . anticipation," she said, throwing his own word back at him.

"I am going to have such fun playing with you," he murmured against her parted lips.

"Good!" she murmured back at *his* parted lips. "I have not played since I was a youthling."

" 'Tis not youthling play I have in mind." Then he proceeded to kiss her to silence. She surprised and pleased him at every turn. When he thrust his tongue in and out of her mouth in the rhythm of the type of sex he would not be able to enjoy with her, and explained it to her, she was soon mimicking his actions. The first time she inserted her tongue inside his mouth, way far in, by the by, and began to stroke him, he almost peaked, way too soon.

He flipped her over on her stomach, and kissed and caressed, examined and stroked, every bit of skin from nape to feet, even her buttocks. "Your big feet are ticklish," he told her.

"My big feet suit me well and good," she told him with a hint of chagrin.

He had been teasing. She did have long feet, but he liked them. Including the slim toes, high arch, and shiny, neatly trimmed toenails.

"If you do not stop looking at my feet, I am going to sleep," she pronounced.

He licked her arch.

She would have jerked upright if he had not placed a palm on her back. "Not asleep now, are you, dearling?"

"Lout!" she muttered.

"A lout mayhap, but your lover-lout," he corrected, rolling her over again. More endless kisses. Soft and hard. Gentle and hungry. Coaxing and demanding. Submitting and dominating.

"You taste like cherries," he said.

"Katherine and I made cherry tarts. Dost like cherry tarts?"

Oh, God! Now we are going to talk about food. "I like your tart tongue."

She smacked his shoulder. "Are we supposed to talk when doing . . . this?"

"If we want to." *But only about sex.* "There are no set rules, Ingrith. Like your recipes. Surely, there are dozens of ways to make a tart." *Now I am the one bringing food into our bed talk!*

"This is fun," she said, brushing her breasts back and forth across his chest hairs.

He saw stars behind his eyelids. "And to think we have scarce begun."

"By the runes! My insides are already melting out from betwixt my legs. Soon we will have a flood."

He burst out laughing and could not stop, to her chagrin. "Truly, you are priceless," he told her when he finally settled down. Then he moved down her body to her breasts and said, "Let us see what else we have at this feast. Ah, aspic cream cups topped with tiny strawberries."

"What?"

"Hey, if we're going to discuss food, it might as well be my way. Now, where shall I start?"

"Aspic? Holy Frigg!" She gripped his shaven head and pulled him down so that his mouth landed over one breast . . . nipple, aureola, and half her breast in his open mouth. "That is where you should start," she told him.

Never let it be said that Ingrith was a timid pupil.

He lifted his head, despite her attempts to hold him down. "Ingrith! Let me lead, for once."

She meekly—*Hah! She wouldn't know meekness if it hit her in her pert nose*—rested her arms at her sides and let him examine her breasts in detail. He was fascinated with the hardness and softness. The silkiness of her skin. The perfect little nipples. Most of all he loved her reaction to all his different touches.

"Your breasts are very sensitive, aren't they?"

"How would I know?" she snapped. "If you mean that even the lightest of your touches makes my woman-fleece weep, then, yea, I am. If you mean that I crave your suckling, then, yea, I am. If you mean that your breath alone on my breasts can make me swoon, then, yea, I am."

"One answer would have been sufficient," he griped, even though he was highly pleased.

"When do we get to the peaking business?"

"Jesus, Mary, and Joseph! Will you stop trying to guide this ship?"

"As you wish!" Her pretense of compliance did not fool him, not one bit.

He got his control back quickly when he suckled one breast deeply and moved a hand down to part her nether folds, stroking the slickness.

Almost immediately, she arched her hips up for more, moaning and rocking her head from side to side with rising passion. "Please, please, please," she kept pleading, for relief, though she was probably not sure what form that would take.

He knew! And he played her now with all the expertise he had perfected over the years. He licked and sucked on her nipples at the same time that he touched and then vibrated a finger at the pearl of her passion, which stood out from the slick folds as testament to her—*What did she call it?*—rising sap. She was close to her peak; he could tell by the stiffening of her legs and fisting of her hands. With a middle finger inserted inside her body and a thumb pressing against her pearl, he could feel the spasms that began inside her and then spiraled outward. He did not need her scream . . . and, yea, she did scream . . . to know that she was peaking.

His ability to please her brought inordinate pride to John. He'd seen this female phenomenon more times than he could count. After all, he'd swived his first maid sixteen years ago, when he was fifteen. But it felt like the first time here with Ingrith.

She stared up at him, stunned.

"Can I take my relief on you now, Ingrith?"

She nodded. "How?"

"Do not worry, sweetling. There will be no penetration." He went over to get a drying cloth from the washstand and came back to arrange the cloth under her buttocks.

"I was not . . . eek! Do you actually fit that thing inside a woman? It's huge."

He chuckled, and, yea, man that he was, he was *hugely* complimented. He arranged himself over her with his cock riding her outside female channel and her knees raised to cradle his hips. With arms braced on either side of her head, he began the strokes that would lead to his satisfaction. Not inside, which he would of course prefer, but still a remedy that sufficed.

He lost focus then and had no idea how she reacted to his thrusts, except that he must have been hitting her bliss spot on the return stroke because she began to moan with rising passion, *again*.

Then she splintered. He could see and feel the ripples passing over her belly.

At the same time, he peaked, too. His head

was thrown back with ecstasy, and his cock was pressed tight along her slickness, but he spilled onto the cloth beneath her. Not the best way to end sex play, but satisfactory nonetheless. More than satisfactory, truth be told.

For a moment, he lay heavily upon her, harsh, uneven breaths searing his lungs. She was strangely silent beneath him. When he was finally able to raise himself, he saw that tears were streaming from her eyes.

"Ingrith!" he said with concern, swiping the wetness beneath her eyes with his thumbs. "Did I hurt you?"

She shook her head. "Nay, it is just that it was so wonderful. Was it wonderful for you, too?"

"It was," he said, kissing her forehead.

"But it would be better if you . . . you know . . . came inside me?"

"Definitely."

"I don't see how it could be? Firstly, you would not fit."

"I would fit, Ingrith, never doubt that."

She frowned, trying to figure out how.

"If I were inside you, my cock would grow even larger, and your inner muscles would shift to accommodate my size. I would feel your heat, and you would feel mine. Like satin and steel. The way God made our bodies to fit. You have experienced peaking now, but when inside you, it would be a different kind of peaking."

She listened carefully to his explanation. "Better peaking?"

"Different."

She shrugged. "Can we do it again?"

He laughed. "If you give me a little time to raise my enthusiasm again."

She reached between their bodies and took his cock between her fingers.

Immediately, the traitorous part began to swell, which prompted her to squeeze. "Aaarrgh!" he gritted out. He had to pry her fingers off of him, very carefully.

"Are you enthusiastic now?"

"I am getting there."

"This time can I do all the tortuous touching?"

His heart lurched, then seemed to expand, taking his breath away. It took a few moments for him to reply. "If you insist."

It was a new role for her . . . and not a food roll, either . . .

Ingrith was no fool. She knew she was only getting half a meal with this kind of sex play, like eating a piecrust without the filling. Or soup without the salt.

Still, she had enjoyed the shocking things John had done to her. She wanted more. If she had to be satisfied with half a pie, that would have to suffice, because she did understand his concern about passing a deformity of mind onto a helpless child. They'd had a boy at the orphanage one time who was always in a foaming rage, maiming animals, hitting other children. Nothing seemed to help his inner torment. When he was twelve, he went after the wrong older youthling and was killed in the process. A shame, really!

John removed the damp cloth from the bed and went over to the pitcher and bowl, where he proceeded to wash his phallus. All very sensible. But not so sensible when he came back to the bed with another wet cloth and attempted to cleanse her nether parts. She swatted at his hands. "I can do that myself."

"Let me," he insisted.

And she did, besotted fool that she was becoming.

And was that really her, lying here bare-arsed naked, waiting for whatever he would do next? When had she become so biddable?

When he lay back down, splatted on his back, he almost bumped her off the bed. With his arms extended outward in a pose of surrender, he grinned at her, and she knew that she was more than besotted. She was falling a little bit in love with the man. An impossible situation that could only lead to her being hurt. But who could stop this avalanche of emotion?

"Well? I'm waiting," he teased.

"For what?"

"For you to have your way with me."

"You are a rogue," she said, turning on her side so that she could begin her own game. A tantalizing prospect.

"Is that a compliment?"

"Definitely," she said, rubbing a palm over his head. "You are getting bristles already. Will you shave again?"

He nodded. "Until after Loncaster comes and goes. Besides, I have an idea how to please you with those head whiskers."

She tried but could not figure out his meaning. "How?"

He chucked her under the chin playfully. " 'Twill be a surprise."

"Mayhap I will have some surprises for you, too."

"I am counting on it."

She leaned over to kiss him, and he put his arms around her waist to embrace her. She shoved his hands aside and said, "Nay. I need to concentrate on one thing at a time. You confuse me when you kiss and touch and press and prod and tickle all at once."

He chuckled. Her mouth was almost over his when he inquired, his hot breath like a caress in itself, "May I kiss you in return?"

She pondered a moment. "Yea, as long as you follow my lead. I am the one making bold with you . . . this time."

He chuckled again, and she could feel laughter

rumble in his chest, under her breasts. That, too, was like a caress.

"Kissing is a new experience for me," she told him.

"Truly?"

"Not that I haven't been kissed in the past. Of course I have. After all, I am almost thirty-one years old."

"Ancient, really."

She smacked his shoulder. "But the men were the aggressors in all those instances. Now I get to do whatever I want, and it is a heady prospect."

His smoldering eyes told her that he was pleased.

She licked her lips first, and then his. Lapping like a kitten with fresh cream. He muttered something under his breath that sounded like, "Help me, Jesus!"

Once she had wetted him, she shaped his lips with hers 'til she got the perfect fit. Then she opened her mouth and his, almost gobbling him with her lips. She angled her head from side to side, giving the hungry kisses different nuances. And then she plunged her tongue inside, beginning the dance he had taught her. She did not need to look down to see that he was aroused. She could feel his excitement in the way he kissed her back, by the rapid increase in his heartbeat, by his soft groans. In truth, she was exciting herself.

She was not nearly satisfied that she'd had enough kisses, but she had more territory to cover, and she was not sure how long he would allow her free rein. Sliding lower, she touched his flat male nipples with the tips of her fingers. "Does it feel good when I touch you here?"

"Very good."

She put her mouth to his nipples and suckled. Not as much to grasp onto, but by his sharp inhale, she figured she was doing things right.

Traveling lower, she examined his phallus in detail, mesmerized by the way the skin was loose and pliant on the outside and hard as a marble rod inside. The mushroom-shaped head was already seeping his seed, which was apparently encased in a milky fluid. "Does it hurt?" she asked.

"What? Your touching me? Nay, it feels wonderful, but be gentle with me, sweetling. I am tender there."

She nodded. "I meant, does it hurt when your dangly part gets hard?"

He choked out a laugh. "Only in a pleasurable way."

Her brow furrowed with confusion, wondering how pain could be pleasurable, but her mind was already moving on to new activities. Rising up on her knees and leaning forward with her hands on his shoulders, she straddled him and arranged his staff along her female channel with the bulbous tip against the newly discovered bud of pleasure. "Am I doing this right?"

He made a gurgling sound through kiss-wet lips, and his eyes were misty blue with passion.

She tried to ride his staff to give them both the most pleasure, and seeing how awkward she was, he put his hands on her hips and showed her a rhythm and position that worked for both of them. This time, they peaked at the same time. Ingrith could not imagine how much more intense sexual penetration would be, when this particular activity gave so much satisfaction.

While she lay in his arms afterward, he murmured sweet compliments and answered her questions.

"Do you want to go down to the kitchen with me and find some food?"

"Nay, I would not want to run into anyone who would surely question where we have been and what we were doing. Tomorrow is soon enough for that."

"No one will question you," he assured her. "They will just think it."

"Oh, that makes me feel better." But she could not regret what she had done. Yawning, sleepy with satiety, she fell asleep. But that was not to be the end of their bedsport.

In the middle of the night—she assumed it was the middle of the night, since the candles had burned out—she awakened to find the brute with his face at her nether parts and her legs over his shoulders. "Have you lost your— aaaahhhhh!" He was using his tongue and teeth in the most extraordinary way. "This has got to be wicked."

"Wicked good," he agreed. After inserting his tongue inside her body, he used a middle finger to strum the erect bud—*What he had done to get it that way, she could only imagine*—and a palm over her stomach to hold her down. Over and over and over, he brought her almost to peaking. Then stopped. And resumed. And stopped. And resumed. Her mounting urgency was so intense that when her shattering finally came, it was with fierce convulsions rolling over her in waves that almost made her faint.

"I ne'er knew," she said when her pounding heart slowed down to a mere racing.

"Ne'er did I," he said, kissing her ravenously.

How could the man be ravenous when she was so sated? Ah, he had not peaked himself, she realized.

He rolled over on his back and coaxed, "My turn?"

"How?"

And he showed her the age-old ways of pleasuring a man with her mouth. Blessed gods and goddesses, he did show her!

The next morning, Ingrith took special care braiding her hair, donning a sedate gown, and attempting to cover the whisker burns on her neck. To no good end.

When she stood at the entrance to the kitchen, alone, Ubbi took one look at her and said, "I'll kill the troll."

And Katherine yelled out toward the open courtyard door, "Bolthor, heartling, you must come and see this."

Good thing Hamr had not yet returned from Jorvik. He would no doubt give a hearty Viking cheer of approval.

"It is not what you think," she lied. "I had trouble sleeping last night and rolled off the bed into the straw."

Ubbi snorted, and Katherine giggled.

None of which was helped when John came up behind her and kissed the back of her neck, walking the fingers of one hand down her back, from shoulder to buttock in a teasing, lover fashion. But then he glanced ahead and saw their audience.

"Uh-oh!" he said.

She just moaned. What else could she do?

CHAPTER TWELVE

The shortest distance between two people is a smile . . .

John moved about his ordinary duties that day as lord of Hawk's Lair. Exercising hard on the practice field with his men. Checking his beehives and flower patches. Discussing the honey birthing-control project with its participants. Making a list with his steward of items needed to purchase from market.

But there was nothing ordinary about the way John felt. He could not stop smiling.

When he missed his target three times on the archery field, and grinned, Ordulf remarked, "Methinks your bald head is causing your brain to melt.

"Pfff!" he said.

But Bolthor disagreed. " 'Tis another part of his body that is melting. His heart."

"Pfff!" he said again.

"Fergit the meltin'. 'Tis what's been gettin' hard

that bothers me." Another person had entered the conversation. John glanced down to see that Ubbi had come up to stand at his side, and he was not a happy gnome.

"Go away!" John told him, whisking his hand as if Ubbi were a bothersome bug, which he was.

Ubbi hitched his little breeches and straightened his age-humped back. "I'll not be goin' away on yer say-so. I'm here ta warn ya, troll. Besmirch my mistress's reputation, and I'll have five hundred Vikings here, led by her father. Lopping off yer randy manroot will be the least of yer woes then." On those words, he stomped off, back to the keep.

John, Bolthor, and Ordulf exchanged glances of amazement. He'd just been insulted by a dwarf.

"How about *my* reputation?" he yelled to Ubbi's back.

Ubbi kept walking but he made a rude gesture over his shoulder, one understood equally by Vikings and Saxons alike.

That incident didn't hamper John's good mood at all.

When answering a missive to his mother, who was concerned about the welfare of the children and "that sweet unmarried Viking princess," he did not even tell her in no uncertain words to mind her own business. Instead, he was gentle in telling her to mind her own business, and he smiled as he did so. He did not even curse when the thick encaustum ink splotched on the parchment, looking like a gummy teardrop when he blotted it off.

Next his mother would be rushing here to rescue her weeping, melancholy, unmarried son. Worse yet, Bolthor would be writing a poem about it. "Tears of a Knight," or some such nonsense.

Still, he smiled.

He resisted until noon his overpowering desire to track down the source of all his smiles, the woman who had more than pleased him through the night. He felt feral and predatory chasing after her, but he could not help himself. He found her in an underground storage room. Not surprisingly, she was organizing the goods on all the shelves.

She glanced up to where he stood on the steps, and smiled.

He smiled back at her, like the idiot he was becoming.

She was wearing traditional Viking attire today. With her hair braided into a coronet atop her head. And a long, lavender, open-sided apron over an ankle-length purple gown. She even smelled like lavender, from her soap no doubt. Gold brooches in writhing dragon patterns secured the straps of the apron over her shoulders. Her lips still looked bee stung from his kisses, as his probably did, too. He took inordinate pride in the bite mark on her neck. He had one on his belly.

"Do you know what I would like to see you wear?" he asked as he came closer and took the spice jar from her hands and placed it on the shelf. Cloves, he thought irrelevantly.

"What? A samite silk gown embroidered with silver thread? A crown of precious jewels? An ivory-linked belt?" She was staring at his lips. Was she imagining the things those lips had done to her?

"I would like to see you wearing that apron . . . and nothing else."

"Is that so?" Her blue eyes flashed impishly. "Dost know what I would like to see you wear?"

"Nothing?" he guessed hopefully.

"That, too," she said. "Nay, I was thinking of you in that beekeeping veil . . . and nothing else."

"Mayhap we can arrange both our desires," he murmured against her neck, having tugged her into his embrace, which she did not fight, thank the saints! Cupping her face in his hands, he studied her face. "You are beautiful."

" 'Tis lust speaking," she replied, linking her arms around his neck. "But thank you just the same."

It was unclear where her insecurity about her appearance came from, but she was wrong if she thought herself less than comely. "Thank *you* for one of the most memorable nights of my life."

"Truly?" She kissed the side of his mouth gently and was about to pull back when he yanked her back for a more thorough kiss. God, he loved kissing her. Each time he discovered a facet he hadn't expected. A surprise, that's what she was. A sexual surprise.

"Truly," he finally answered.

"Even without . . . ?"

"Intercourse?"

She nodded.

"I will not deny that it could be so much more, but you gave me immense pleasure. I wish I could give you more."

"I cannot imagine more," she said. "Was I too . . . wanton?"

He chuckled. "A woman's ardor is a man's delight," he assured her.

The whole time they were talking, he was unpinning her apron, which puddled at her feet, and lifting the hem of her *gunna*.

Cupping her bare buttocks, he whispered, "Wrap your legs around my hips." Then, even as he kissed her hungrily, he walked to a far wall, where he braced her in place. With loosened breeches about his knees, he arranged his now exposed cock along her cleft.

"You are wet," he said, raising his head with surprise.

"I have been thinking about you all morning," she confessed. Scarlet stains colored both her cheeks. After all they had done, she could still blush. Amazing!

"Ah, Ingrith!" he sighed, beginning to thrust between her slick folds. At the same time, with one hand holding her around the waist and the other massaging a breast through her wool gown, he kissed her deeply and thoroughly, as if he could sink into her, make them one.

Then he stopped and took his cock in hand, using the knob to stroke the raised bud at the top of her channel.

She began to beg, "Please, please, please . . ."

He resumed his thrusts then, matching his tongue thrusts to the same rhythm, and they both peaked together. To his embarrassment, he had not pulled away quickly enough, and he'd soiled the back of her gown.

"I am sorry," he said.

She put a fingertip to his mouth. "Shhh. I will arrange my apron over it before going to my room and changing. Truly, 'tis no problem."

He blinked at the sudden burning in his eyes. "I have felt like a cripple, Ingrith. You make me feel whole."

She had been straightening her clothing, as he had been, but she stopped and cradled his face in one hand. "I am the one who has been crippled, without realizing what I had been missing. For the first time in my life, I feel like a woman."

They stared at each other for a long time as something frightening sizzled between them.

"I wish I could give you more."

She shrugged. "I wish you could, too."

"I still will not marry you," he said, and could have bitten his tongue.

She flinched, and walked away.

Even if it was true, the words did not need to be said aloud. Not at this time. He felt lower than dragon piss.

What could he do to make it up to her?

Skinheads aren't all bad . . .

Ingrith was in her bedchamber, changing her *gunna*, when she heard a rustling sound under the bed. At first, she thought it might be mice among the rushes, but soon discovered in was Henry.

His tear-tracked face was woeful when she dragged him out.

"What are you doing under there?" she asked as she wiped his wet cheeks with the edge of her apron and took him onto her lap.

"I doan want my head lopped off."

"What?"

"I heard Lord Hawk and Ordulf talkin'. They say my father wants ta kill me."

"That is not true, Henry. He wants to meet you, but the men who surround him might do you harm. That is why we are hiding for the moment. We will protect you, though. Do not doubt that."

"But what if . . ."

She shook her head. "I promise, you are safe, as long as you do as you are told. You must pretend to be Samuel, and we must keep your hair shaved. But only for a little while, until matters are resolved. Do you understand?"

He nodded, but she could tell he was still scared. Therefore, she did not chastise him when he nipped at her heels for the rest of the day. And, truth to tell, she needed a diversion to keep her mind from dwelling on John's hateful words at their last parting.

Oh, she knew he would not . . . in his mind, *could* not . . . marry her, but his timing had been cruel. Could he not at least pretend affection for her?

She would like to think that she would avoid him now. That she could stop the sex play. But she knew herself too well. Now that she knew what lovemaking entailed, she wanted to experience everything. Even if it was only for a short while.

So, that evening at dinner, when she sat down next to John and he tried to apologize, she raised a halting hand and said, "Nay. No regrets. I knew coming into this that it was not to be permanent. If you think that you are using me, do not. I am using you."

"*What?*"

"By the time I leave Hawk's Lair, I expect to be well-versed in the love arts. Mayhap I will be more receptive to men's attentions now that I know what I was missing. Mayhap even one of the suitors my father has presented will do. Or else I will become a courtesan of sorts. A Viking courtesan. I like the sound of that."

"You cannot do that!"

She frowned at him. "Why not?"

"Because . . . because it would not be right."

"How do you figure that?"

"What I am teaching you is for us alone."

If it were any other man than John, she would swear that he was jealous. Was that possible? Hmmm. She decided to test the waters. "The only man who can make such a demand on me is my husband, and you will ne'er be that, by your own proclamation." She patted his hand, which rested on the table. "Not to fear. I will be in your bedchamber tonight. I have much to learn yet."

His face flushed. Even his shaved head had heightened in color. He *is* jealous, Ingrith concluded, and smiled to herself. She would decide later how to best use that information.

"Think I am funny, do you?" John prepared to stand and no doubt stalk away, but Bolthor put a hand on his shoulder and shoved him back down.

"Wait. You must hear my latest endeavor," Bolthor insisted.

Katherine, leaning forward so that Ingrith could see around both Bolthor and John, pointed to her husband, then to John, and winked.

Oh, good gods! What would the skald say now?

"This saga will be called 'Ode to Shaven Heads.'"

Ah, that wasn't so bad. John was to take the brunt of Bolthor's warped humor. She was to be spared.

Or so she thought.

Men are vain creatures
So aware of their features,
Like smoldering eyes,
Or muscled thighs,
A manroot of immense size,
Charming tongue to romantize,
All to gain the woman prize.
But what if they lose their hair?
From bedsport will bald heads scare?
Or will those bare-skinned heads
Lure more women to their beds?
Mayhap a bare-skinned roof
Will permit a sex play that is foolproof
One which lets a woman peak,
And peak, and peak, and peak.
Tell us true, Ingrith and Katherine,
Did bald heads worship at your shrine?
And did it feel like a porcupine?

"This is all your fault," she said to John, and stood.

"Me? I am as much a victim here as you are."

"You have honey enough for your experiments. I have decided that I do not want to be one of your subjects."

"Subject?"

"Bedplay experiment."

"Ingrith! Where do you get these ideas? You know I . . . oh, what the bloody hell! Go if you must! I do not need you."

Her heart cracked a bit at those word-arrows. "You have made that abundantly clear from the start."

As she lay in her lonely bed that night, she wondered if this was what they meant by cutting off your nose to spite your face. Except that it wasn't her face that was suffering, lest it referred to her pride. Yea, losing face had become too important to her.

She buried her head under her pillow and tried to sleep. Forget about counting sheep. She counted bees.

Would you like to see my . . . garden?

John resisted his base inclinations until the following afternoon.

After a sleepless night, which ended in a most unsatisfactory self-pleasuring; after a morning in which his men snickered behind his back; after an hour in his honey shed, where he was unable to concentrate, he stomped into the kitchen, surprising Ingrith, Katherine, and a half dozen maids, including the woman Ingrith was presumably training as her replacement cook. Oh, that there could be a replacement lover! But, woe to him, there could never be another Ingrith, he was fast discovering.

"What are you doing?" Ingrith asked as she paused in the midst of stuffing some bird . . . a pigeon or sea bird or small chicken, he could not tell. No matter! She wiped her hands on a damp cloth and followed in his wake through the kitchen and into the pantry.

He was tossing various items into a leather saddlebag. A wedge of hard cheese. A circle of manchet bread. A hunk of smoked ham. Two apples. A flagon of wine.

"John, I asked you what you are doing."

He turned to confront her. "Do you care?"

"Care what? That you are messing up all my shelves?"

Her shelves? He grinned and proceeded to make an almighty big mess, tossing fruit, jars, spices, and various other foods onto a table in the middle of the room. "We are going for a ride."

"We?"

"You and I."

"Why?"

"I have something to show you."

"Methinks I have already seen it."

"Not that, sweetling."

"Do not call me sweetling."

"Why . . . sweetling?"

She bared her teeth at him and growled.

"You are getting quite good at that."

She blew out a breath of frustration. "What am I getting quite good at?"

"Snarling at me." *And other things.* He put an arm over her shoulders. "Will you come with me for an hour or two? I would like to show you a special section of Hawk's Lair. It will give us privacy to talk."

She hesitated, then nodded. "As long as talk is all you have in mind."

"Of course." *Ha, ha, ha!*

With Ingrith perched on the horse in front of him, John had the opportunity to tease her at will. A forearm brushing against a breast. A hand inadvertently touching the delta of her thighs. His raging enthusiasm pressing against the crease of her buttocks.

He had been taking it as a sign of her receptivity when she didn't protest . . . until she raised her rump and sat down hard on his bulging enthusiasm, which was instantly no longer bulging. "Oops," was all she said. It was enough.

They finally arrived at their destination, and he helped her dismount.

"Oh, my! The scent is fantasic here. What is it?" She visibly sniffed the air. "I know. Roses."

He smiled at her correct guess. Tethering the horse and grabbing his saddlebag and blanket, he said, "Come." With their fingers laced, he led her up to the top of a rise.

She gasped at the sight below.

Rows and rows of roses of all colors from white to darkest red provided a spectacular picture over more than a *sulung* of land. Six beehives were arranged in the midst.

Turning to him, she said, "It is like a painting. Almost too beautiful to believe."

"I bring back rose cuttings from wherever I travel, even when fighting for my king in other lands. My family members do the same. Not all roses thrive in this climate, but many do."

He walked to one of the nearest bushes and used his knife to cut the stem and clip off the thorns.

When he handed the bloodred rose to her, she seemed overcome with emotion. "Thank you for sharing this place with me."

"Am I forgiven?"

She pretended to be unsure, but then she squeezed his hand. "Of course. I was at fault as well for losing my temper."

He spread the blanket and emptied the food out of the saddlebag, handing her the flagon of wine to pour into two small cups. Once he'd arranged himself in a reclining position where he could view the flower fields and he'd taken a sip of the red wine, he glanced over at her, in a similar position.

"I missed you last night," he told her.

She turned on her side so she could see him better. "I missed you, too."

"I had every intention of seducing you here today, but I have changed my mind. I will not be making love to you."

"Oh, please! You are not going to start the 'I will not marry you' nonsense again!"

He smiled and tapped her playfully on the chin. "That is not what I was going to say. I am proving to you that you are more than sex to me. Not an experiment, as you said."

"And by doing so, who are you punishing? Me or you?"

He chuckled. "Not a punishment, you willful wench. If I had set about a seduction, you would have protested that, too."

And so they ate the food and drank the wine and talked about inconsequential things. His goals for the honey experiments. Her plans for the orphanage. Funny stories of his being a Saxon growing up in a Viking keep. Funny stories of five Viking sisters being on the run after killing a villainous earl.

There was not even one kiss or caress. Even so, John knew that he treaded dangerous territory. He was falling in love with a Viking princess.

When he yawned widely, and she followed suit, he lay down on his back and pulled her to his side with her cheek on his chest and his arm around her shoulders. Under the warm, summer sun, the previous night took its toll, and they fell asleep.

In his dream, John was making love to Ingrith. Really making love. And it was wonderful. Except . . .

Cough, cough, cough!

He was about to thrust inside her dream body.

Cough, cough, cough!

Only gradually did he realize that it was not Ingrith coughing, or him. He slowly opened his eyes to see an amused Hamr standing over them.

Immediately, he set a drowsy Ingrith aside and stood up. "You are back."

"Obviously."

"And?"

"Loncaster was at my back. I expect he will be here by nightfall."

"Whaaaat?" Ingrith shrieked, jumping to stand at his side. Addressing Hamr, she scolded, "You stand there like a fig tree taking all the time in the world. Do you not recognize the danger?"

"All is well back at the keep. Bolthor and Ordulf have the children in hand. They'll pretend everything is normal. And you two . . . well, there will be no doubt in Loncaster's mind that his affections for Lady Ingrith are not being returned." He stared meaningfully at the mark on her neck and their rumpled clothing.

When they got back to the keep, everything was surprisingly calm. They dismounted in the stables, and Ingrith was about to rush off when John grabbed her forearm, pulling her into a hug.

Against her ear, he whispered, "Loncaster will not prevail. This I promise you."

She leaned back to gaze up at him. With tears in her eyes, she stunned him with those most unwelcome words: "I love you." Once a woman uttered that declaration, it was the beginning of the end for him . . . although he hadn't had much of a beginning yet with Ingrith.

"Ingrith," he chastised. "We agreed."

She waved a hand dismissively. "Oh, do not get your *braies* in a twist. Besides, I told you . . . um, *that* before."

"Nay, you did not say *that*. What you said was, 'I *think* I have fallen in love with you.' There is a vast difference."

"Have you lost your mind?"

Probably.

"The words just slipped out. Forget I said them."

Hah! *Not bloody likely.* "Those are words that cannot be unsaid."

"Let me modify them then. I want you."

"I want you, too." *More than you know.* "Does that mean you will do that one thing I told you they do in the Arab lands? The one with the marble wand."

"You are being unnecessarily loutish. Let me modify my words even more. I do not want you. In fact, I wish I had never come here. Go away. I have better things to do than prattle with you." She threw the rose he had given her at his chest.

I could have handled that better.

Before he could respond, not that he had anything to say, she was off to organize the world, or leastways his keep. You had to love a woman like that.

He only wished he could.

CHAPTER THIRTEEN

*T*he *terrible trouble arrived . . .*
   I am pitiful.

Ingrith came to that conclusion immediately upon having blurted out those three words that she knew shocked John into speechlessness. He had made it more than clear from the beginning that her softer affections would be unwelcome; so, he must view her declaration as a betrayal of sorts.

In her defense, she'd been unable to help herself, so overcome had she been at the realization that for the first time in her life she was in love. Who wouldn't be, after that visit to the rose garden? But, if she'd thought even for a second, she would have kept her big mouth shut.

He doesn't want me, and I have to accept that, she told herself over and over as she bustled about the keep instructing the children on their behavior once Loncaster arrived, mostly to say nothing. She gave several of them, including Henry, a last-minute head shave. By her count, there were fifteen boylings and twenty-two men with bald heads. Henry would stick by Ordulf's wife, Anne, alongside their daughter Beth; Anne would be holding a baby, the implication of course that Henry was Ordulf and Anne's son. Luckily, Anne had blue eyes, like Henry's.

Maybe I could seduce John into changing his mind, she argued with herself, watching him from across the hall as he donned a *brynja* under a black surcoat. What a different picture from the man who only wanted to work with bees! A sword was sheathed on one side of his waist and a long knife on the other. His men were stationed throughout the keep and courtyard with deliberate displays of arms. Loncaster would know he was coming into a hostile environment.

But, nay, even if I had the seduction skills, John's reluctance is not about good lovemaking. John has good reason not to marry. To him marriage entails children. When he glanced her way, and their eyes held, she knew that he was unhappy about her declaration of love. Maybe he was having the same troubling thoughts she was.

Walking up to her, he asked, "Are you ready?"

She nodded. *Mayhap if I agreed to never have children . . . Nay, that wouldn't work. We'd never last a month, let alone a lifetime, sharing a bed without consummation. Eventually, he would find a woman with whom he could complete the sex act. A woman unable to conceive.*

"Why do you look so doleful?"

Could he really be that thickheaded? "I'm afraid Loncaster will get me alone."

"I'll stick close to you, if I can. Otherwise, Hamr will be nearby."

She nodded again. *I need to face facts. Someone like Joanna is more suitable.* "John, about what I said earlier. I didn't mean it. It was a jest." *Believe that, and I have a desert to sell you in Iceland.*

"Nay, nay, nay! Those are words that cannot be taken back."

What? Is he saying he welcomes the words? Or is he pricking me at the idiocy of my sentiments? "Well, don't worry that I will be doing anything about it."

"Like what? I have an idea." He grinned. Then he winked at her.

And with just that twitch of his lips and wicked wink, she was hopeful. Maybe they had a chance after all.

"You could come to my bed furs tonight. I'll show you the marble wand."

Not so hopeful after all. It still came down to loveplay. Half-baked loveplay, in her opinion, if all it encompassed was sex. *Why can't I be content with just that?*

There was no opportunity to pursue the subject further, because the sound of horses' hooves on the wooden drawbridge echoed through the open double doors of the hall.

John squeezed her hand and was off to join

a contingent of his men who waited outside. A greeting party, so to speak.

She stepped up to the doorway and watched as Loncaster and a dozen armed men dismounted. Immediately John approached Loncaster, and they began arguing. Both John's *housecarls* and Loncaster's troops had their hands on the hilts of their swords. A tense moment, to say the least.

Loncaster noticed her standing in the doorway. With his face turning nigh red with anger, he was about to stomp up the many steps to confront her when John put a hand on his shoulder and stopped him. They exchanged more angry words. Soon, though, both men began the ascent while Ordulf and Hamr led Loncaster's men toward the stables.

"Lady Ingrith! You defied my order by leaving Rainstead," Loncaster said right off, pointing a finger sharply in her direction. "Methinks you are either daft or unaware that my orders carry the weight of the king."

"You did not order me to stay at Rainstead. You merely said you would be coming to visit sometime." She backed up a bit, and John moved quickly to her side. Looping an arm around her shoulders, he pulled her against him into a pose that bespoke a close relationship.

"What is going on here?" Loncaster's piercing eyes took in the position of John's arm as well as the mark on Ingrith's neck, which she'd made sure to expose by arranging her braided hair atop her head.

"Watch the way you address my betrothed," John warned.

Ingrith had to bite her bottom lip to stop herself from saying, "Whaaaaat?"

"Since when?" Loncaster demanded.

John motioned for a serving maid to bring ale, and he led her and Loncaster to a nearby table. She noticed Bolthor standing nearby with a battle-axe in his hands along with several of John's *house-carls*. Some of Loncaster's *hird* had entered the keep, as well, and awaited orders.

After they'd sat down, she and John on one side and Loncaster on the other, John replied, "Ingrith and I have known each other for years. I would have wed her long ago, except she resisted my proposals. Didn't you, heartling?" John gave her a besotted look that would have looked silly on anyone else.

"Why did you lead me on?" Loncaster demanded of Ingrith.

"I did not lead you on," she said huffily. "Besides, I was not betrothed last time we met."

"You do not fool me with this ploy, Hawk, and you will not get away with such deceit. King Edgar promised the wench to me, and I *will* have her."

Ingrith groaned inwardly. Oh, this was bad. Very bad. How dare the king make a decision about her life? The answer: Because he could. *I should have stayed in the Norselands. At least the only danger there was a wart-nosed suitor.*

"The 'wench' is a lady," John reminded Loncaster. "Speak to her with respect, or you will not address her at all."

For once, Ingrith was satisfied to let someone do the talking for her.

Loncaster let his rude gaze survey her silent form. "Suddenly she has become biddable?"

John chuckled and squeezed her shoulder. "Not at all. It is one of the things I love about her."

Did he say love? He probably didn't mean it. But, oh, gods, how good it sounds!

"And what is going on with all the shaved heads?" Loncaster eyed John's and Bolthor's bald pates with distaste.

"Head lice," John said with disgust. "We had a large head-lice problem here at Hawk's Lair. The buggers get in the ear and nose hair, too. Be careful where you lay, lest there be some still about."

"Enough games! Where is the boy?"

"What boy?" Ingrith asked.

Loncaster growled. He actually growled. If John hadn't been sitting beside her, he would probably have throttled her. "The king's whelp. Henry. I have instructions to return with the child to Winchester." He slapped a folded parchment with the royal seal on the table between them. While she and John read, Loncaster lifted his cup and drained it of ale to the bottom in one long swallow. Immediately, a maid scurried up to give him a refill, to which he didn't even give a nod of thanks. Instead, he continued to scowl at them.

John shoved the letter back to Loncaster, and Ingrith said, "The boy is not here."

"You lie, m'lady. Have a caution. If I do not believe you, that means the king does not believe you." Loncaster's dark eyes accused Ingrith. He might be a bully, but he was an intelligent one. "That bloody orphanage outside Jorvik emptied quicker than a bladder of piss when you knew I was coming for the boy. An orphanage which is, by the by, now burned to the ground."

Ingrith gasped with horror, and she could feel John tense beside her.

"Wouldst care to explain the reason for the hasty exit?"

"It is always good to get out of the city during the summer months. The heat and flies and such."

"Pfff!" he scoffed. "Either you have Henry, or you know who does."

"Why is the boy so important?" John inserted.

Loncaster shrugged. "Every single succession to the throne in the past century has been contested. While Edgar has two legitimate children, Edward and Ethelred, they are young. If something happened to the king, there would be a flurry of rats like you could not imagine to influence who accedes to the throne and who will be the guardian. Archbishop Dunstan, who has the king's ear, for one. Then, there is Edgar's second wife, Elfrida. Have you met her?"

John nodded. "A great beauty."

"Hah! You would not think so if you were around her for long. The woman seeps ambition for her son Ethelred like venom. Any who dare dispute her claims gets snakebit, for sure."

"What has Henry to do with this?" Ingrith asked. "There are two legitimate heirs . . . and Edgar is young yet . . . only twenty-seven, I believe. He may have other children."

"M'lady, you do not understand court politics. In order to secure the throne, all contenders . . . and I mean *all*, must be eliminated. Edgar is a good king, in many ways, but he has the sexual appetite of a satyr. God only knows how many illegitimate children around the countryside carry his blood. Like Henry. All are considered threats. Even the daughter being raised in a Wilton convent by that abbess he raped."

"You can see then why we . . . I mean, people . . . would want to protect Henry," Ingrith said. "His life is in danger."

"Not if the king, or even Dunstan, takes him under their sheilds."

"What if Henry renounces any claim to the throne? My stepfather's father, Thork, a son of King Haraldsson, did so. Wouldn't that be enough?" John asked.

Loncaster shook his head. "Mayhap if he were

older. But the word of a child of five would be discounted. In any case, release the child to me, and I will take him back to the king."

"With the assurance that naught will happen to him?" Ingrith returned Loncaster's grim look, stare for stare.

"Whilst under my protection, he is safe," Loncaster promised.

"And when Edgar, or Dunstan, takes him in hand, I assume the boy would be fostered out to some friend of the court," John said.

"No doubt," Loncaster agreed. "But that is not my problem."

But it is mine, Ingrith thought, and repeated her lie, "The boy is not here. You may search, if you do not believe me."

"Oh, you can be sure we will search. And do not think that the business betwixt you and me is over, m'lady. I will return with the king's order forthwith. There'd better not be a marriage in the meantime."

Unfortunately, there would not be.

For the next several hours, Loncaster and his men examined every nook and cranny of the keep, the stables and other outbuildings, even the privies and garderobes. Riders rode in four directions to see if the boy might be hidden somewhere on the outer extremities of the estate.

Ingrith forced herself to stay in the kitchen preparing a cold meal for Loncaster and his men to eat . . . before departing, she hoped. John, Ordulf, Hamr, Bolthor, and even Ubbi stayed in strategic places, watching the men search. It was only through a surreptitious whisper from Katherine that Ingrith learned how Henry had fared. Very well, mainly by not saying a word, and hugging the legs of his "mother."

She had just gone into the laundry room, which was located in a separate building attached by a covered walkway, when Loncaster trapped her, alone. Yanking her inside, he slammed her against the wooden wall and held her there in a painful grip on her upper arms.

"Where is the boy?" he spat out.

"I don't know," she stammered through chattering teeth.

"You lying bitch!" With the pincer-hold on her arms, he shook her so hard that her braided coronet started to unravel. "Where is the boy?"

It took all her nerve to raise her chin. "I don't know."

His attention riveted on the love mark on her neck then. "Another thing . . . I would have married you afore, but now that you have given your favors freely to another, I will make you my whore. Do not doubt my words. Edgar owes me too much not to grant me the boon of your body."

"Never! You will ne'er have me, you brute."

"Defy me, and you will find yourself living in

hell. I will kill any who stand in my path. Your lover, first of all."

"You would kill John?" she asked tremulously. "Mayhap you are not aware that he has friends in high places. Including his stepfather, who is on the king's Witan."

Loncaster shrugged. "A stab in the back in a dark corridor. An arrow to the heart when he is out beekeeping. A fall down a cliff. Who could tell who the culprit was?"

"What has he done to harm you?"

"He took you and shielded the king's bastard. The king will thank me."

Just then, the door flew open, and John stormed in, yanking Loncaster away from Ingrith. "You bloody whoreson! I told you not to touch my lady."

"I did her no harm. Did I, *m'lady*?" He glanced pointedly at John so she would get his meaning. Tell John what he had done and said, and John would be dead. If not now, some time in the future when he least expected it.

She shook her head to indicate she was unharmed. It was only later when Loncaster and his men were gone that John went to lead her to the hall for dinner, and she flinched with pain.

"What?" he asked.

" 'Tis naught. A draft of cold air."

"There is no cold air. What happened?"

"Do not make a fuss over nothing."

Refusing to accept her words, he took her hand

and led her into a solar, where he undid her apron brooches and released the laces at the neckline of her *gunna*, tugging it down to the elbows. There were two black and blue rings on her upper arms, which would soon turn yellow, as well. Loncaster had almost broken her bones, so hard had he gripped her.

"I will kill the man," John seethed after he'd taken her down to his honey shed and put warm honey poultice on both bruises. He kissed one, then the other arm.

Not if he kills you first, she thought. Even if John wanted her now for more than a quick romp, she couldn't stay and jeopardize his life. Henry and Loncaster were her problems, not his.

Fortunately, or unfortunately, he didn't try to make love to her now. Or make lust, she corrected herself. Either way, he had more important things to do back inside the keep. Even if he had taken her in his arms now, it wouldn't have made any difference.

First thing on the morrow, she was leaving Hawk's Lair.

She was worth the risk, after all . . .

At least a dozen of his men complained about the meal that night. Not that it was bad, but prepared by the new cook, it was just regular fare.

Where was Ingrith?

That's when he discovered the horrible truth. She was planning to leave Hawk's Lair.

The orphan children were weeping, the cook was complaining that the job was too hard, Bolthor and Katherine were giving him dirty looks. And Hamr just grinned as if he knew something John did not.

He would have gone for her immediately, but Bolthor insisted he stay for his latest creation: "The Lesson of Danger."

Danger ever lurks when man is near.
Cruelty abounds to make all fear.
Even children are not exempt
When greed does the powerful tempt.
But one good thing about a death threat
It reminds good men to ne'er forget:
Cherish what is most important in life.
Good health, a roof over one's head,
A longship sturdy, a body well fed,
Strong ale, family, and good friends,
But most of all, when life ends,
The thing most missed is a woman's love.
Truly it is the gods' gift from above.
The wise man grabs it when he can.
This I tell you is the best plan.
Love overcomes danger any day.

As far as Bolthor's poems went, this one was not so bad, and John told him so. To which Bolthor replied, "Then heed the message, fool, afore your love is gone."

"What love?"

Bolthor just shook his head at him.

It was only later, as one person after another turned away when he got near, that he finally found out the reason for the shunning. The reason the new cook had prepared the meal . . . the reason why Ingrith was missing from the dinner table . . . wasn't due to her head megrim, which she'd claimed to have earlier. She was packing up to leave in the morning.

"Where is she?" he demanded of Ubbi after finding both his and her bedchambers empty.

The little man, who was eating in the kitchen, did not even look up.

"I asked you, gnome, where is your mistress?" he gritted out.

"Go away. My mistress has no need fer a troll."

What if I need her? He picked Ubbi up by the scruff of the neck and shook him. "Tell me where she is or you will be turning on yon spit, and all in my keep will dine on roast gnome come morning."

Ubbi spat out a series of foul words, but the new cook, Ardith, interceded for him. "She is in the stable packing the wagons. She plans to sleep there tonight to be ready for a dawn departure."

"Oh, she does, does she?" He stomped toward the back door and turned at the last moment to point a finger at Ubbi, who was rubbing the back of his neck. "Stay here if you value your life."

Wearing the tunic and *braies* she had arrived

in—*Was it only a sennight ago?*—she was indeed up on the wagon, arranging various leather bags and blankets, along with stacks of bread and various other foodstuffs to carry on the road to wherever she planned to go. The wagon bed was covered with straw, no doubt to make beds for children on which to sleep along the way.

By the light of two wall torches, he could see her every action in the dark barn. He paused, relishing the sight. Right now, she was bending over, exposing to him one of her best body parts as the fabric of her *braies* stretched over her rump. She was wrapping a sword in protective cloth. God only knew how she planned to use the weapon.

"Going somewhere, Ingrith?" he inquired as calmly as he could when fury boiled his blood.

"Uh." Guilt bloomed like fire on her cheeks.

He reached up and lifted her to the ground.

She was too surprised by his arrival to protest.

"You were leaving without my permission?" He stepped closer to her . . . in a menacing manner, he had to admit.

She bristled and moved back from his close proximity.

As if he would let her escape!

"I do not need your permission. You are not my husband."

"Let me rephrase that. You were leaving without even saying good-bye." He moved closer again.

She backed up more. " 'Tis better that way."

"Better for whom?" He saw an empty stall behind her with fresh straw and a blanket. Her bed for the night, he supposed. It would be a bed all right, but not for sleeping.

This time when she backed up, she realized where she was and panic filled her blue eyes.

Why the panic? "You need not fear me, Ingrith, lest you consider being naked and being stroked to screaming ecstasy a danger to fear. I intend to punish you for this transgression, but in a way you will ultimately enjoy." That had not been his original intent when seeking her out. Leastways, not that he'd been aware.

"I don't want this."

"Liar!"

Tears filled her eyes. "I want this too much, then."

I do not need tears now. Tears dampen enthusiasm. "And that is why you leave?"

She nodded, watching intently as he removed his long surcoat, tunic, and belt, hanging them over the stall gate, which he had closed behind them. As he toed off one boot, then another, she began to speak. "I can't stay here, John. It's too dangerous."

I'll tell you what is dangerous, m'lady. Trying to talk down a raging enthusiasm. "And you think traveling on an open road with only a gnome to guard you is not dangerous?" He inhaled sharply for patience. "Where were you going, by the by?"

"Jorvik. To find your stepfather's longship and go to Stoneheim."

"Jorvik!" He cursed under his breath. "And Loncaster? Didst not imagine he is watching the road from here to Jorvik?"

"I planned to camp in the woods a few hours from here, and then travel by night."

"God above!" He shrugged out of his *braies* and yanked off his hose.

"God above!" she exclaimed, but she was not remarking on the idiocy of her plans, as he had. She was staring at the cockstand that pointed at her like an accusing finger. A giant accusing finger, if he did say so himself.

It was only when he began to remove her apron and loosen the neck ties of her tunic that Ingrith struggled, then put her hands on his shoulders to stop him. "Wait," she said. "I really must go. Opening my thighs to you will only make things hard when I go."

"Things are already hard, if you must know," he muttered, and he didn't mean difficult. Aloud, he said, "Your mention of opening your thighs doesn't help your cause."

"Tsk-tsk-tsk!" Apparently she knew good and well what he'd meant. "Loncaster will kill you if I stay. He told me so."

He paused in his attempts to undress her squirming body and tilted his head to the side. "He cannot kill me when I have an army behind me, and, believe me, the combined forces of Hawk's Lair and Gravely are an army."

She shook her head in dispute and ducked under his arm, which had been raised to loosen the braid arranged atop her head and to finger comb it over her shoulders. He grabbed her by the neck of her tunic when she attempted to open the gate. The tunic ripped right down the center of her back, as much to his surprise as hers.

Turning, she blinked at him in dismay and leaned against the stall to hold the back of her tunic in place. Useless effort, that. He merely yanked on the sleeves and had the garment off and lying in the straw before she could speak. And speak she did. The woman did like to talk. Which would be fine under other circumstances, but right now he had other plans for her mouth.

"Loncaster would not use obvious means to wield his evil. He would find a way to stab you in the back when you least expect it."

For a moment, he did not understand, his brain having gone blank at the sight of her perfectly round breasts with their palest rose nipples. He wanted to taste them and touch them and bring her to ecstasy when he finally suckled. But wait. What had she said about Loncaster? John rubbed a hand across his mouth, studying her. It was true concern he saw in her eyes. Concern and, yea, mayhap even love, which he did not want. Did he? Not unless it meant she would give him her body freely and without inhibition.

"You were going to risk your life for me?" His heart was beating so fast he could scarce breathe.

"Yea, but not just you. Loncaster would go after others I lo . . . care about, too. Like Ubbi. Or the orphans. Look what he did to the orphanage for spite. A man like that would stop at nothing."

The woman risked all for me. Does not matter what she says. To protect me, she was going to expose herself and the children to Loncaster's threat. "How could you think I would want to hide behind a woman's shield? What honor is that? Methinks death would be better than a loss of manhood."

"That is lackwit talk. Dead is dead. Pride need not be your downfall."

"You are my downfall, Ingrith, but not because of some miscreant military commander." He touched the tips of her breasts with his fingertips only, but they bloomed into hard points of arousal.

"What . . . what do you mean?"

"You and I have unfinished business."

As he removed the rest of her clothing, she gave up on shoving his hands away with a groan of surrender. "Why are you doing this, John? You know it's best for all of us if I'm gone. You've said as much more than once."

"Can a man not change his mind? Can a man

not say lackwit things without being reminded of
them forever and ever?"

"Huh?"

He smiled at her and saw the way her lips
parted on a sigh. She'd told him more than once
that his smile melted her. He could only pray that
it did so now. With that in mind, he smiled some
more, besotted lackwit that he was.

"We're going to make love, Ingrith."

"Really make love?"

He could tell she was skeptical. "We are."

"Do you mean . . . oh, my! But why now? What is
different now than it was . . . let's say, yesterday?"

*Blather, blather, blather. If I am not careful, we are
going to talk our arousals to death.* "It was inevitable,
but Bolthor brought home to me tonight how fleeting life can be. Danger lurks everywhere. Best we
cherish each day as it comes." *That was good! I did
not realize I could be so poetic.*

"You are taking advice from Bolthor now?"

He grinned. "Amazing, isn't it?"

He was lowering his mouth to hers when she
stopped him again. "Will you be doing that honey
thing?"

"Honey thing?" *I wonder if my eyes are crossed
with frustration.*

"The things you make the people do in your
birthing-control experiments?"

That stopped him short. *She knows about that.*

Truly, my people cannot keep a secret worth a damn.
"Nay. One of the females in the experiment is breeding, which means the honey paste is not foolproof. Plus, methinks breeching a maidenhead would be more than hardened honey could withstand." He flicked her woman-fleece with his fingertips and chuckled. "After having touched you here, I know how hot you are. Your woman-heat would melt a stone, let alone a honey cap."

She blushed and attempted to cover her breasts with one arm and her nether parts with the other, but he took both hands and placed them on either side of her on the stall's rail, a position that made her breasts present themselves in the most tempting manner.

"And afore you get offended, woman-heat is a good thing."

He kissed her bare shoulder and licked first one nipple, then the other, pleased at the moan it produced. "I will withdraw afore spilling my seed. There is still a risk, but not as great."

"Is that a risk you really want to take? We can do . . . you know . . . what we did before. Oh, my gods! Do *that* again."

He had just rubbed his chest hairs back and forth across her breasts.

"Happy to oblige." And he did. But to answer her question: "Heartling"—it was the first time he'd seriously used that most precious endearment to her, and she knew it, he could tell by the softening of her expression—"you were willing to risk your life for me. How can I do anything less?"

"I don't want payment. Can't you see—"

"Shhhh!" He was exploring the inner whorls of her ear now with the tip of his tongue, an activity she seemed to enjoy immensely. He did, too. "Our making love was going to happen eventually. We both know that. This way, I can at least take a modicum of caution."

And thus began a sexual journey the likes of which he had never experienced, not since he'd learned the full extent of his father's insanity by age fourteen. He only hoped it would not end in tragedy.

CHAPTER FOURTEEN

You could say it was a sexual healing . . .

Ingrith still intended to leave Hawk's Lair
in the morning, as planned, but when the gods
plopped a gift in your lap, you did not say them
nay. And making love with John, *really* making
love, was a gift, to be sure.

At almost thirty and one, she was a strong
woman, accustomed to the loneliness of a single
life. She would be strong again, despite the soul
wounds she was bound to carry, but not for anything would she deny herself this one night of
bliss.

For now, she was lying on her back in the straw,
watching John as he watched her. Then, levering
himself on his elbows and nudging her knees
apart, he settled himself over her. Raising her
eyes, she saw him scanning her face, intently.

"I want you." His thick voice was like a velvet
caress.

It was a heady feeling, having this particular

man want her. "You make me feel beautiful and special."

"You *are* beautiful and special."

At first his lips coaxed a reaction from her. A kiss of persuasion, that's what it was. Little did he know, she was already persuaded.

With her fingers gripping his shoulders, she opened her mouth to him, welcoming the bite of his teeth and slide of his tongue. She could smell the musk of arousal on his skin.

When his kisses moved to her neck and shoulders, she sighed. "My easy surrender should shame me."

"Never! Your ardor is my pleasure. Surely God meant for two people to share bedjoy. Why else would He have made it so exciting?"

"Methinks Adam said the same thing to Eve."

"Or Eve said to Adam, since she was the one tempting him with the forbidden apple," he corrected.

They smiled at each other, sharing the humor and the intense physical awareness that always resonated between them, more so now. Squirming a little, she enjoyed the sensation of skin on skin, male on female, rough on soft.

"Temptress," he chided, and rolled over onto his back.

At first, she felt off balance and embarrassed, but he arranged her legs so that she kneeled astraddle his belly, with his erection nestled against the crease of her buttocks. "Oh, I do not know about this," she protested.

"For me, Ingrith," he coaxed. "Do it for me."

With a sigh of surrender, she settled her rump on him. "I do not know what to do, precisely."

"I'll show you. Remember how I taught you to ride my finger? You will do the same with my . . . member."

If she had not been blushing before, she was now, in remembrance of that wicked activity.

"But that will come later," he said. "We have roads to travel afore reaching that destination."

His first stop on that road was her breasts, which seemed to fascinate him.

"They are not very big."

"They are perfect.

He palmed her breasts in a circular fashion, and she could feel the nipples prodding his skin. When he touched her nipples with a forefinger each, then began vibrating back and forth, she tried to jerk back, but he grabbed her hips and held her in place. "No trying to escape now, sweetling."

As if she could! As if she would!

He continued fluttering the tips of her breasts, making them grow bigger, and there was an echoing flutter between her legs. In fact, she could feel moistness seeping from inside her onto his belly.

With a moan of equal parts embarrassment and ecstasy, she closed her eyes.

"Nay, do not think of shutting your reactions

away from me. Open your eyes, Ingrith. I want to watch your reactions. To see what pleases you. Do you like this, for example?" He tugged her forward a bit and he leaned upward so that he could kiss each taut nipple. Then his mouth closed over a breast which he had lifted from underneath while the other hand played with the opposite breast.

"Yiiiiiiiiiiiiii!" she squealed.

He lifted his mouth from her breast and glanced upward. "Does that mean you like it?"

"Are you demented?"

"I take that as a yea." He chuckled, and even his hot breath on her aureola drew an answering ache low in her belly. "If you like that, methinks you will love this." And he began the serious business of suckling. Hard, then soft. Alternating with licks of his tongue and nips of his teeth, he soon had her keening out her agony of ecstasy. And then—*Holy Valhalla!*—he moved to the other breast. Soon she was rising to an imminent peaking, which she did not want to happen with her in this position, alone. She tried, futilely, to break away, and her thighs braced, fighting off the impending explosion of sensations too intense to bear.

"Relax, dearling," he said, lying back to watch her.

"Relax? You really are demented. Dost enjoy torturing me so?"

"Delicious torture, I hope. I know it is for me."

Laughing, he made her sit upright on him, even though she was inclined to hide her face on his chest. He did the most scandalous thing then. Cupping her buttocks, he lifted her slightly, and his expert fingers stroked her slick folds from behind.

"Let it come," he urged.

And she came, all right. Wave after wave rolled over her, making her lightheaded and flushed all over. Her breasts had swelled and ached. The slickness down below felt like hot syrup surrounding a spasming bud of pleasure. Even her inside woman channel was spasming.

When the peaking ended, she opened her eyes, not having realized that she'd closed them. The look in John's eyes was worth the embarrassment. And Holy Thor! When had he rolled them over with him molded over her?

"Are you ready?"

"M'lord, I have been ready for years."

He laughed and slapped her buttock. "That is for m'lording me." Then he turned serious. Lying between her legs, he raised her knees and spread them wider. Then he twined his fingers with hers and raised their hands above her head. Slowly, so slowly she wanted to scream, he worked the knob of his phallus just inside her woman channel. To her embarrassment, she felt herself grasp him in a welcome peaking.

"Jesus, Mary, and Joseph!" he murmured.

"Sorry," she said.

"Do not apologize for giving me more pleasure than I have had since . . . since forever." Beads of sweat stood out on his forehead as he shoved in a little bit more, then almost pulled out. She wanted to grab hold of him and yank him in to stay. Instead, he took her a bare finger span at a time. In. Out. Each time, her inner muscles clenched him in an attempt to bar his escape. The friction was unbearable and blissful at the same time.

Finally, he was filling her. All of him penetrating nigh to her womb, which was a miracle to her. No one had ever told her that a woman's channel expanded with pleasure to accommodate a man's size. Or that the fullness of a man was a joy in itself. There was a oneness to the sex act that had a celestial aspect to it. Two people made one.

"Are you all right?" he asked.

She nodded. "It only pinched for a moment."

"You feel like the tightest, warmest glove around my cock," he told her.

"You feel like hot, living steel. As if your manpart had a mind of its own."

"It does. Believe me, betimes it does."

She almost wished that he would stay unmoving inside her. To do otherwise would break the spell. She thought that until he began to move, and she entered another level of paradise. "Oh, my!" was all she said.

"I agree," he choked out.

Then began the real business of sex. Like swordplay, it was. Lunge, then retreat. Lunge, then retreat. At first long and slow strokes. Then shorter and faster.

He whispered wicked words and promises into her ear.

She writhed from side to side with incoherent pleas for relief. His impatient hands were everywhere, discovering all her hidden erotic places. Who would have ever guessed that the backs of her knees were as sensitive as her breasts? He left her no secrets.

It was all too new and unbelievable for Ingrith to take in. Physical delights beyond any she ever could have imagined assailed her from all sides. And John was equally affected. She could tell by the violent shiver that overtook his body.

Her world narrowed to the scent and feel of her lover. The only sounds were those of their heightened breathing and the erotic, wet slap of sex parts. Only occasionally did a horse made a noise in a nearby stall.

And then he threw his head back and seemed to be counting silently. But, nay, he was waiting for her to peak first, which she promptly did. With mounting tensions, all of her insides were wound tighter than a ball of yarn, and then—Oh, thank you, gods!—it unfurled, sending sparks of relief to every part of her body, especially the thrumming bud between her legs.

Only then did John release a roar of satisfaction as he withdrew and spilled his seed into the straw. She could feel his chest heaving as he lay heavily upon her, his face buried in the crook of her neck. Instinctively, she caressed his back and the dip behind his waist, one of her favorite spots on his body.

Ingrith wanted desperately to tell John that she loved him because, of course, she did. But she had learned her lesson once. Those were not the words he wanted to hear from her. She had shown him, though, through her lovemaking. If he knew, he would probably run for the hills.

When he raised his head, finally, she thought he would grin and make a teasing remark about her wanton ways. Or he would make some cutting remark about how he wasn't going to marry her.

Instead, although the familiar silent sadness that entranced her was gone from his eyes, his expression remained serious. As he lightly traced her lips with his fingertips, he said, "God help me, Ingrith, but I feel as if I have long been sick, and now I am healed."

First she churned his butter, then she milked his . . .

John couldn't believe he had revealed himself in such a pathetic way. He rolled them over onto their sides and studied her face. To his relief, there was no pity there. Just a wonderful satiety, for which he was proudly responsible.

He lifted her thigh so that it rested on his hip. After what they had just shared, there was no way he was letting her escape him now.

"I feel the same," she said.

No one can feel the way I do right now. I am a god. I am Adam before he ate the apple. I am King Solomon and King David combined. I am an idiot. "What same?"

"What you said about being healed."

You cannot possibly know what it's like to carry insanity in your blood. Always on the alert that it will finally manifest itself. "No offense, m'lady, but you are healthy as a prime horse on racing day." He deliberately teased to lighten their conversation, and besides, what need was there for conversation when he was naked, and she was naked, and . . .

"Loneliness is a sickness of sorts. Even though I am often surrounded by people. Growing up with my sisters. A royal estate overflowing with Viking warriors, cotters, and household servants. All the children at the orphanage. Still, I felt alone without realizing it. It wasn't until I experienced all this"—she motioned a hand between the two of them—"that I realized what I was missing."

"All this?" He grinned.

"You know." She attempted to smack him on the chest for his teasing.

He grabbed the hand before it could do any harm and kissed the knuckles instead. "Nay. Tell me."

"I feel fulfilled as a woman. Do you . . . I mean, since you didn't actually . . . does this satisfy you?"

Did I not shout my satisfaction there at the end? Am I not now as limp as a winter stale carrot? "Unlike you, I am perfectly aware of what is missing from our joining, but it was still good, Ingrith. Better than good." *I cannot imagine how it will be once you gain some experience. I may die of satisfaction then.*

"Did I . . . did I do things right?"

"More than right. But . . ." *Time to put an end to this blather.*

When he rolled onto his back and didn't immediately answer, she prodded, "But . . . ?"

"But I have a need." *Will she fall in with my game?* "A yearning, really." *Mayhap I should bat my eyelashes.* "I wish . . ."

She braced herself on one elbow and leaned over him. "Your wish is my command, m'lord."

Thank you, God! "Ooooh, Ingrith, do not make such statements to a man with ideas."

"Within reason," she amended.

"I want you to touch me." *Teasing aside, that is the truth. Forget want, I need her touch.*

"All over?"

"All over." *Please, please, please.*

She winked at him mischievously. "That I can do. In truth, I, too, have yearned to touch you."

Oh, Ingrith! You could not have said anything to please me more.

"In all the ways that you touched me."

All the sated parts of his body blinked to attention.

"An exploration, really, since you are the first man I have seen naked up close."

First sounded as if there would be more. For some reason that bothered him. But he couldn't be too upset. The woman had promised to touch him. Intimately.

Before she even started, his cock was rising with enthusiasm. By the time she was done, the enthusiasm had bloomed into a full-fledged, let-me-let-me-let-me cockstand. And, oh, the pleasure in between!

"On your belly, knight," she ordered with an exaggerated sternness.

He did as she asked, gladly, and laid his face onto his folded arms. That way he hid his grin of satisfaction.

"For a beekeeper, you have a well-muscled body," she remarked.

"I must needs be a warrior for my king, as well. 'Tis the law," he explained. "Do you like my body?" *How pitiful! Now I am reduced to begging for compliments.*

She chuckled. "You know I do."

I do? "Show me."

Thus began a tortuous venture starting with a wet sensation on his shoulder. Was she licking his skin? By the saints! She was. Now it felt as if she was lightly scraping the surface with her fingernails.

What followed fulfilled all his longings for her touch. Sweeping caresses from his back to his ankles. Deep massages that soothed sore muscles. Kisses at the small of his back and the backs of his knees. When she sucked on one of his toes, *and thank God I bathed tonight*, he'd had enough of her torture and turned over onto his back.

"Methinks you need new territory to explore," he husked out, "but not below the waist. I do not want to disgrace myself by being overeager."

This should be a particularly enjoyable exercise since he could not only experience the pleasure of her touch, but he could watch her doing it. Men were visual characters. They liked to watch whatever they were doing.

But back to Ingrith. Her eyes were fixed on his erect phallus. "Methinks your 'new territory' has a different idea."

Hah! Ideas like you wouldn't believe, sweetling.

Before he could stop her, she lifted his cock and peeked closely underneath at his ballocks as if they were wondrous objects.

Do. Not. Peak, he ordered himself, and he meant *peak* as in spill his seed, not the kind of peeking she was doing. *Do. Not. Peak. Do. Not. Peak.*

"They are like peaches, with that fine fuzzy hair."

Peaches! That was a new one! He tried to laugh but it came out as a gurgle. "Enough of this 'territory' for now," he told her and lifted her body up so that they were face level. He was about to kiss her when she tapped his lips with a fingertip. "Uh-uh! I am leading this expedition."

Am I in Valhalla? Is she a Valkyrie come to grant all my wishes? But wait, I am not a Viking. I am Christian. She must be an angel. A fallen angel?

She leaned over to touch the tip of her tongue to one of his flat nipples, which was nice, and not nearly as dangerous as her foray into his manparts.

"Are your nipples as sensitive as mine?" she asked.

He blinked through the haze of his arousal. " 'Twould seem so."

"Good," she said. And spent an inordinate amount of time playing with them.

Then the hair that ran from his chest in a *V* down to his crotch fascinated her, with a few dips along the way in his navel. "I hate a hairy man. You have just enough," she declared. "I saw a man once who had so much body hair he looked like a bear. My father said it kept him warm in winter. Hah! He smelled like a bear, if you ask me."

John couldn't believe a naked woman with breasts brushing his belly was discussing some Viking man's body odor. "Could you move on, Ingrith? Please."

She skipped over his most important parts, which was just as well, considering the state of his excitement, and went to his feet once again.

"No sucking of toes," he warned her.

"You're ticklish," she hooted with glee. Then, as she licked and kissed her way up one leg and thigh, she glanced up at him and inquired with her usual disarming bluntness. "Are you as aroused as I am?"

He choked out a laugh and waved a hand at his bobbing cockstand. "How can you even ask? Come here, sweetling. We are going to have to continue this touching exploration another time."

He lifted her up to lie on top of him, and what an excruciatingly delicious position that was, with her breasts nestled in his chest hairs and her curly mons touching the tip of his cock. "Top or bottom?" he asked against her parted lips.

"Both."

"You greedy wench!" He helped her to rise on all fours, then ease herself down onto his cock. When he was in to the hilt, and every drop of blood in his body had drained from his fevered brain, she rose up on her knees and cast him such a tantalizing smile that his heart lurched.

She jiggled her rump on him, even as she was impaled, to get a better fit, he supposed.

Bloody hell! He closed his eyes. He was fairly sure his eyeballs were rolling back in his head.

Before he could catch a breath, she began to move on him. He didn't know where to look. At her sliding up and down his cock. At her breasts jiggling with her energetic bouncing. Or at her glorious hair with its mass of blonde waves tumbling down her back, over her shoulders, and brushing his chest when she leaned forward.

"This is fun," she said.

Fun would be a vast understatement.

"Look, when I spread my knees and lean forward a little, I hit that little bud in my woman-folds on the downstroke. Can you see?"

"I see. I see," he husked out.

"How am I doing?"

I am in sex heaven. "Fairly well."

"Oh. I thought you wanted me to be gentle. Guess I'd better work harder."

"I was only teas . . . oh, my God! What are you doing?" Blood was pounding throughout his body, all running thickly to that part of his body Ingrith was using like her own personal butter churn. "Easy, dearling, easy."

She stopped suddenly, and her eyes went wide with wonder as he felt her inner walls grasping and ungrasping—milking, for the love of all the saints!—his cock in a seemingly never-ending peaking. "Oops!" she said, when the peaking stopped, but not to worry, she was about to resume her bouncing.

Worry? Hah! Enough of this torture! "Bottoms up," he said, putting his hands on her hips to hold himself inside her channel, then rolled over. He stared down at her as he arranged himself better, cupping her buttocks and tipping her up.

Propped on extended arms, he began to ride her hard. He couldn't help himself. To his amazement, her inner spasms resumed, and it felt as if he were plunging into a flexing fist.

It was the most incredible sexual experience of his life.

And it wasn't over yet.

Fierce tremors overtook him. Even worse, his emotions were out of control. He had never intended to let himself fall under Ingrith's spell, but all his good intentions were for naught under the onslaught of his desire for her.

What happened to the sane, logical man of yestermonth?

And who the bloody hell cared?

His head and shoulders reared back as he felt his ballocks tighten and rise, presaging an imminent peaking. He wanted desperately to stay inside Ingrith, to shoot his seed to her womb, not to breed children but for the sheer pleasure of the natural culmination of the sex act. But that was not to be.

He disengaged quickly and spilled his essence off to the side. Then he turned away from Ingrith, not wanting her to see him in this state. But sensing his distress, she curved her body into his, knee to knee, breast to back. With one arm wrapped around his waist, she kissed his shoulder. "Regrets?"

"Shouldn't that be *my* question? I'm a selfish bastard, Ingrith, taking your maidenhead."

"You took nothing, you idiot. I gave."

"To answer your question. How could I be sorry for such an experience? Thank you."

"I know you don't want to hear this, John, but I have to tell you. I love you. Nay, nay, nay," she said as he started to turn, "stay where you are."

Which was all right with him. He didn't want her to see his face when he was this defenseless.

"I don't expect you to return my sentiments. You are safe."

Dolt that he was, he said nothing, and soon he felt her even breathing against his back. He put his hand over hers, which was resting on his waist.

Only then did he whisper what he could not in good conscience say aloud. "I love you, too. God help me, but I love you, too."

CHAPTER FIFTEEN

✧

He never promised her a rose garden . . .
When Ingrith was young, she loved to climb trees. One time she even hung from a limb by her knees, her *gunna* fallen down to cover her face, and the summer breeze warm on her nether parts.

But she was a girling no more, and she couldn't recall the last time she'd climbed anything higher than a bush. Still, she was hanging, and—

Her eyes flew open, and she saw by the torchlight that John was lying between her legs. Correction. John was kneeling between her legs, and her knees were in the shameful position of hanging from his bare shoulders.

"What?" she shreiked. "This is surely perverted. Do not try to convince me it is not. Put my legs back down, you . . . you lecherous lout."

"Shhh. Do not wake the horses. I am just doing a bit of exploring myself." He blew a warm breath against her exposed cleft.

She realized then where the breeze of her dream

had come from. The lackwit was the windbag at her most intimate parts.

"See. There is this cave here that begs exploring. But first an expert explorer must brave the slick water of the channel that protects the cave opening."

She wanted to protest his actions, to get her legs down to a modest position, but she burst out laughing. *I never realized that sex could be fun.* Until, that is, said explorer's tongue did a long, lapping survey of the wet folds. *I am definitely not laughing now.* "Oooooh," she groaned.

"You like that, do you?"

She refused to answer, just wallowed in the erotic skills of his tongue and, yea, his teeth, too.

"Hark! I see danger up ahead. A little boulder."

"A what?"

He parted her folds wider with his fingers, then flicked that nubbin of pleasure she had only discovered under John's tutelage. *Oh, that boulder.* She was about to marvel to him that she was almost thirty and one and was just now discovering her body parts when he began to suck softly on that bud of pleasure and at the same time stuck a long finger inside her.

Holy Thor! Instant peaking! "Oops!" she said, mortally embarrassed at her hasty, wanton response.

"Oops indeed!" He grinned. "Now, my dear, there is something I have wanted to do ever since you forced me to shave my head."

"As if I could force you to do . . . aaarrgh! Get your head out of there."

He was rubbing his shaved head against her slick folds and the erect bud. The short bristles caused the most incredible friction. To her shock, she peaked. Again. *Is there a crack in the earth where I can fall in?*

He chuckled and rose to his knees. There was an embarrassing dampness on his fool head.

Yea, a big wide crevice where I can hide my shame for an aeon or so. "Where do you learn these things?"

"Needs must," he said. "When you cannot have children, you are forced to be inventive."

"But how—" Her question was cut off. In fact, she forgot what she wanted to ask as he cupped her buttocks and slid his erect phallus into her tight inner channel, which welcomed him in its usual way. With her muscles clutching him a heated vise. *Is there any pleasure in the world, for a woman, that matches this fullness . . . this sense of becoming one with the man you love? I cannot believe my sisters never told me. All they ever mentioned was men's dangly parts that turn from snake to pole in a matter of seconds. I will have a few words for them, to be sure.*

He made a hissing sound through gritted teeth, which she assumed meant that he was equally aroused. "You are incredible."

"I am?" She wanted to participate in this mating but was unable to do so with her legs locked wide and her knees still planted on his shoulders. It was a vulnerable position, and she did not like giving up all this control. Not one bit.

Liar! her conscience immediately chided. She was liking it too much. "Release my legs so I may participate," she demanded.

"Participate all you want, but you are not lowering your legs. Touch your breasts while I swive you, Ingrith."

Did he actually say . . . ? "What? Nay, I will no—"

Even as he was buried inside her, he took her hands and encouraged them to play with her own breasts. She had not realized that she could pleasure herself in this way.

"That's the way, sweetling."

Unbelievable! Ingrith felt as if she were floating above her own body and could not believe that wild, uninhibited creature was her.

Whilst she examined her nipples with tentative fingers, he pummeled her below with deliberately long and slow thrusts, deeper than before because of the tilt of her body, she assumed. "It is hard concentrating on two titillations at once, you brute. Halt and let me catch up."

"Titillations!" He laughed, a joyous sound coming from a man who had so little humor in his life. "Do not concentrate then. Just let it happen."

"In other words, give up control," she gasped out.

"Exactly."

As John worked his magic strokes in her, she

admired his body with her own magic. Caressing his wide shoulders. His sensitive paps. The hard ridges of his abdomen. The well defined muscles of his arms, which were braced on either side of her. His blue eyes were stormy with arousal under half-shuttered lids. His deliciously full mouth was parted as he panted with excitement.

This time, she rose to an even higher peak and surrendered to all the sensations assaulting her. A heated flush covered her from forehead to toes. Blood thickened and rushed to her female parts. Breasts swelled and ached. And then, as his lunges became shorter and harder, she arched up, mewling little cries of agony . . . a sensuous agony. She could scarce see John through the haze of her need.

And then . . . and then it came with a wild shattering. The scorching heat stemmed from the place where they were joined, but it was flaring out to all her extremities. She must have fainted, because when she came to consciousness, she was lying on her side in his arms, and he was making soothing sounds of comfort.

"Did you peak?" she asked.

He chuckled and kissed the top of her head. "Yea, I did."

"In the straw?"

"Of course."

Ingrith might not know exactly what it was like to complete the sex act, but her woman instincts knew and missed having him spill himself inside her body. How much more incomplete it must feel for him. "Oh, John!" she started to say.

At the same time, he started, "About what you said earlier . . ."

She knew that he referred to her declaration of love, a revelation she should have kept to herself with a man who shunned such emotion.

"Ahem!"

They both jarred to attention, finding Hamr leaning over the stall rail. Dawn light was coming into the stable. She quickly grabbed for the blanket, almost knocking John over in her attempt to tug it out from under him. When she was covered, she ducked her head with embarrassment. How long had the rogue been standing there? She feared she knew the answer.

John had already risen and was donning his *braies*. "How did you find me here? And what is so bloody urgent that you had to disturb me?"

"I found you because all the stable hands were sleeping in the cow byre after you ordered them out of the stable last night. And, yea, it is urgent."

"Oh, my gods! Is it Henry?"

"Nay," Hamr assured her. "But Loncaster has struck."

She and John both stiffened with dread.

"You know that rose garden you have on the south boundary of the estate?"

She and John exchanged glances.

"Yea, what of it?" John asked. He'd already pulled his tunic over his head and was fastening a braided belt around his waist.

"Burnt to a crisp."

You could say he was the Marquis de Hawk . . .

For the past three days, Ingrith had become a regular watering pot, leaking tears all over the place. All because of his ruined rose garden.

"Ingrith, it was only flowers. It can be replaced. No one was injured. We must count our blessings." He said this to her as she knelt in the burnt flower field along with two gardeners. They were pruning back the plants to see if any could be saved.

Some could.

Most could not.

Actually, this reprehensible act of Loncaster's enraged him. And there was no doubt in his mind that the Saxon commander had done the deed, or leastways his men had. *How dare he destroy my personal property? Even worse, what or whom will the spineless cur target next?* But he was a methodical man. He did not act impulsively . . . well, not usually, he thought, his one act of recklessness staring at him through beautiful blue eyes.

"But you told me yourself that it took years to gather these roses, and that some of them are very rare. You must be devastated."

Bloody hell! She's weeping for me. He shrugged.

" 'Tis not seemly for you to be digging in the dirt like a laborer."

"Pfff! You surely planted some of these yourself."

He would tell her that it was different for a man, but he'd lost that argument before. "Come back to the keep, Ingrith. A hundred of my men have arrived from Gravely, and your new cook is threatening a kitchen revolt."

"Oh," she said brightly, standing and rubbing her dirty hands on her dirty apron. If there was anything to grab her attention, it was a challenge . . . better yet, a cooking challenge.

She was a remarkable woman in so many ways. How could he have not seen that in the past? Her blonde hair hung in a single braid down her back. A few new freckles dotted her nose from being in the sun. Her skin glowed with good health. In essence, she looked comely beyond all reason to him, especially since he knew what was hidden underneath her garments.

"I brought my own horse." She pointed to a gentle mare tethered to a stake in the ground. Apparently, she'd been talking whilst he'd been only half attending.

He went over and saddled the horse for her. Before helping her mount, though, he took her into his arms and inhaled her sweet scent. Even so, he said, "You smell like dirt."

"You smell like horse."

He pinched her rump playfully. *Playfully? By thunder! When did I turn playful?*

She pinched him back . . . on his rump, independent wench that she was.

They smiled at each other.

He leaned down then, meaning only to give her a quick kiss, but her softness drew him in, and he was soon tongue kissing her with fervor. And she was returning the favor, bless her Viking soul.

It was only the awareness that they were being watched by the two gardeners that made him stop, finally. "I missed you," he said, putting her away from him. And, Lord help him, she was staring back at him with glazed passion in her blue eyes. How he enjoyed her quick arousals!

"How could you miss me? I just left your bed at dawn, and it is scarce noon now."

He put out cupped hands to help her mount her horse. She rode astride, with her *gunna* bunched between her legs. Never let it be said that Ingrith did things in the usual female way.

"I cannot get enough of you, and you know it," he replied. "Methinks you and I need a sennight or two in bed without disturbance."

"And then you will have enough of me and send me on my merry way?" He could tell she regretted blurting out that question even before she added, "Forget I asked that."

John saw the brief flash of pain on Ingrith's

face. She pretended that his resistance to marriage didn't matter, but it must. He should let her go. Let her find a man who could offer marriage, give her children. But he could not. He just could not.

On the other hand, Ingrith had said on more than one occasion that she was resigned to not having children, that at her age she no longer expected to marry. Mayhap they could come to an arrangement. Mayhap she could be content with her menagerie of orphans. Mayhap marriage was not impossible. Mayhap—

"You're looking very serious," she said, riding alongside him.

"I have a lot on my mind. Now that we have additional men here, I can feel secure in leaving."

"What will you do when you find Loncaster?"

"I'd like to kill him outright, but he is the king's man. In the best case, we would capture him and take him to the Witan for trial. If that doesn't work, we will take matters into our own hands. Either way, he will be punished."

"I am divided in my thinking about Loncaster's fate. On the one hand, being drawn and quartered seems a perfect punishment for him. On the other hand, I wish we could just let him go. I know he burnt the orphanage and your rose fields, but now that we know how dangerous he is, we can be better prepared. Defense is the best weapon betimes. Then again, a sword to his heart would not come amiss."

He noticed how often she used "we," and oddly, he didn't mind.

"And I can always go to the Norselands with the children. Henry would be safe there." She made this offer through quivering lips.

It was his cue to say that he didn't want her to leave, but once again guilt hammered at him, and his confused brain wavered.

If Ingrith thought she was divided in her thinking, she ought to look inside his muddled head.

Could a woman really accept the kind of marriage he could offer? He doubted it. Eventually it would wear thin. Or when contemplating a lifetime of lovemaking with one woman, especially one as responsive as Ingrith, there might be a time when he was so overwhelmed in the bedplay that he failed to pull out in time. Odds were not in his favor.

He was so confused, but now was not the time for that particular matter. "Henry is going to be a problem that needs resolving," he told her. "He is the king's son, and a man has a right to his own blood. Don't give me that angry look. I'm not suggesting that you turn the boy over to Loncaster, but 'kidnapping' is not an answer either, and believe you me, taking a royal child out of the country would be considered a crime." *Besides that, I do not want you to leave. Leastways, not yet.*

"What are you suggesting? I will not hand Henry over as long as there is any danger to him. I don't care what you say. I won't."

"Hold, Ingrith! I care about Henry, too. Did you know he has been helping me gather honeycombs? And he eats only half of what he harvests."

She nodded and smiled tremulously at him.

"Trust me. We will resolve this situation. And Loncaster will pay."

"When will you leave?"

"I await word from my stepfather. Hopefully within the next few days. He is attempting to set up an emergency meeting of the Witan. When I go, I'll leave Bolthor and Ordulf here for your protection."

"But—"

"You will stay," he said emphatically, sensing her resistance.

"The waiting is hard for me. My inclination was to chase after the buzzard and mow him down the instant the fire was discovered."

He knew that good and well. And she would have been leading the charge with sword and soup ladle in hand. "A wise man once told me that in the most successful battle no blood is shed."

She frowned, perplexed.

"More can be accomplished through diplomatic, lawful means," he explained. "I would like to put a sword through Loncaster's heart as much as you would, and I may still do so. But he is acting on the king's orders. Let me work this with my stepfather and the Witan. The most important thing is defense right now. Protecting Hawk's

Lair, Gravely, and all within, including Henry."
And you.

"There is honor in killing, too," Ingrith persisted. "Mayhap it is my Norse blood speaking, but some men just need killing."

"Are you questioning my honor, Ingrith?" he said sharply.

"Of course not. Just your methods." Seeing his growing anger, she quickly added, "But I do trust you, and I am willing to accede to your wishes." Unspoken but clearly apparent were the words *for now.*

"Are you sure?"

"Yea," she said hesitantly.

Foolish maid! She should never make such an open offer to a man. Especially a man with a rising enthusiasm. He could not believe that this prim lady was the wanton who had been in his arms all night. Nor could be believe the pleasure of having intercourse with her, even with the less-than-perfect endings.

Leaning forward he whispered in her ear, "My wish is that you go up to your bedchamber and take off all your clothes. Then lie on the bed with your arms raised over your head, and your one knee raised."

Her face bloomed a pretty rose color. "You cannot be serious. It is still daytime."

"I am willing to accede to your wishes," he repeated her words back to her. "So soon you renege? Ah, well, mayhap sex play is too wild for a tame lady like you."

She raised her chin defiantly. "I can be as wild as you can."

Oh, God, I hope so. "One more thing. Bring a skein of heavy yarn with you."

"Huh? Are you planning to weave?"

Only a net to lure you in. "Nay, I just had another idea involving bedsport."

"Seems to me you have an overabundance of bedsport ideas."

You have no idea. "Yea, I do. 'Tis one of my best traits."

John watched her walk away with what appeared to be an exaggerated sway to her hips. The witch! He smiled. Then he realized that Hamr, Bolthor, and Ordulf were gazing at him as if he'd grown two heads.

"What?"

"You're smiling," Hamr observed.

"So?"

"You hardly ever smile," Ordulf added.

"Methinks . . ." Bolthor started.

John walked away before Bolthor could compose a poem about a sappy, smiling knight. Still, he was smiling as he went. He was happy, he realized. His rose fields were no more. He had an irksome woman and a herd of children in his keep. Loncaster was proving to be more than a nuisance. And him? He was bloody well happy.

He was even happier when he got to Ingrith's bedchamber and saw that she'd fulfilled his wishes . . . and then some. Somehow, she'd found an ell of his beekeeping veils and she'd managed to wrap it around her body like a sarong he'd once seen on a caliph's houri, except that one had little bells on it. He wondered if . . . never mind.

"Do you like it?"

"Do dragons roar?"

She did a little dance around him as he removed his clothing. All his motions were slowed down by the spectacle she was putting on for him.

"I thought you were too shy to make love in the daytime," he said, grabbing for her, but she managed to dance away.

"I thought so, too. Surprise, surprise!"

He would give her a surprise. A big surprise. Lunging for her, he took them both to the bed. "Now, are you going to pose for me, sweetling?"

"Only if you will do the same for me later."

"Gladly."

He stood, very aware that his staff was already past the point of being enthusiastic and bordering on ecstatic. She was aware, too, if the seductive gleam in her blue eyes was any indication.

She lay back with her hair loose, spread out on the pillow and over her shoulders. With her hands holding on to the posts of the headboard, she bent her knee, as he'd requested. Staring up at him, she licked her lips. And waited.

Somehow, the transparent cloth was almost more erotic than bare skin. Almost.

He unwrapped her like a gift, taking a long time so he could savor all the good parts along the way. When he was done and lying on his side, leaning over her, her little nipples were pearled and she was breathing heavily. He would wager she was moist for him.

"Now that I have had you, really had you, I cannot get enough," he admitted in a husky voice he scarce recognized.

"I feel the same. I am going to kill my sisters when next we meet for not telling me how good sex could be."

"Uh, I don't think it's a good idea to discuss what we have been doing."

"Why? I am not ashamed. Are you?"

He *was* feeling guilty, but not enough to stop.

"There are so many things I want to do with you. Hundreds of different ways of having sex. Ones I have tried, and many I have not. We will be sex virgins together."

She laughed. "Are they perverted?"

"Some."

"Good."

He had to hug her with sheer joy at her lack of inhibitions. May she never change, he thought, but grimaced when he realized he probably would not be around to appreciate her evolution.

"Now, did you bring the yarn, like I suggested?"

She motioned over to the washstand.

He got up, and using a small knife, cut the red yarn into four arm lengths. Approaching the bed, he twirled them in one hand. "This is called the rope game," he told her.

"That is not rope. It's yarn."

"Same thing. How adventurous are you, Ingrith?"

"I ne'er said I was adventurous."

"You are adventurous, all right. The question is to what extent? And whether you truly do trust me."

"Are we back to the trust issue again?"

"We are. Do you trust me enough to play this game?"

Turns out she did.

Ingrith stared at John as he arranged her spread-eagled on the bed with the yarn tying her to the four bedposts. He had not been jesting when he said this would be perverted. As he was tying the knots, he caressed her along the way and spoke in a hushed voice of all the things he would like to do to her. She became aroused by his words alone.

"Your breasts are so pretty. The nipples like tiny pearls."

"Does your fleece weep for me?"

"Just looking at you makes me hard."

"Lick your lips, sweetling. Just so."

But he had more in store for her.

She hadn't realized that he had carried an

ornate carved chest into the room with him, much like some highborn ladies used to store jewelry.

"My Uncle Tykir gave this to me years ago, but I never had the opportunity to explore its contents."

"Frigg's foot! Exploring again?"

"Yea, but this will be a different kind of exploration."

"I imagine that is what all men say."

He swatted her playfully on the thigh as he sat on the edge of the bed next to her restrained body.

"Have you any idea how depraved it feels to be carrying on a conversation with a naked man pointing his dangly part at me?"

"Except my dangly part is no longer dangly." He waggled his eyebrows at her. "Are you not curious about what is in the chest?"

Oooh, I do not like that gleam in his eyes. "More like suspicious."

Using a tiny key, he unlocked the chest. To her amazement, inside was not jewelry, but feathers. Feathers of all kinds. Everything from stiff chicken-like feathers to swan down to peacock plumes.

She was confused.

"Torture implements," he explained. "Erotic torture."

"Oh. Good. Gods!"

"Would you like to be blindfolded, or not?"

"Oh. Good. Gods!"

"I take that as a nay. I am told it enhances the pleasure. Mayhap next time."

Ingrith might have protested all these perversions, except they did not seem perverted when John was smiling thus at her. Where was the brooding, sad man? If her "trusting" him could lighten his mood, how could she refuse? Besides, John had been right. She liked an adventure.

Thus began what seemed like hours but was probably only half an hour of "exploration" by her torturer. He started with an extra-soft feather of indeterminate origin, its strands like a thousand silky threads. He used it to "fluff" her body. All over. Even her inner thighs and the bottoms of her feet.

By the time he got to the more rigid feathers, she was a moaning, writhing mass of heightened nerves. He used the harder feather to flick at her engorged nipples and the aching bud betwixt her legs. She'd had no idea that her lips were an erotic area, but their pleasure points were surely sensitized by a tracing of the hard feather.

"Enough, John!" she demanded.

"But I am not nearly done."

She stared pointedly at the bead of his man seed peeking from the end of his marble-hard phallus. "I think you are."

He laughed and began to undo her ties. No sooner was she free than she grabbed for him, catching him off guard. He fell across her body.

"Kiss me," she demanded, cupping his face and drawing him down to her.

He choked out a laugh at her taking control of the game, but then he did indeed kiss her. And, whoa! The man did know how to kiss. She hated to think where he'd gotten all that kissing experience and with whom. But then, she was benefitting, and that was the most important thing.

Soon, she changed her demands. "Suckle me," she whispered, adding, "I find it hard to believe I have the nerve to even say the words aloud. What a wanton I have become!"

"Lucky me!" John replied as his mouth opened wide over one nipple and aureola and began to suck at her hard and rhythmically, at the same time his fingers delved into the slickness down below.

She screamed her bliss as she peaked, over and over and over in waves of almost excruciating pleasure. He watched intently, sparing him no hiding, even of her deepest emotions.

"I cannot wait," John told her and arranged himself betwixt her spread thighs. As he worked his hardened staff inside her, she peaked again, the fullness in itself an overpowering aphrodisiac. "Oh, sweetling, how good it feels. Truly, your sheath was made to hold my cock."

She tried to laugh but choked at his unromantic sentiment.

After that, she had the need neither to laugh or choke as he began pummeling her with strokes that surely crashed against her womb. Wrapping her arms around his shoulders, she leaned up to kiss him as he performed his magic down below. They peaked together this time, even with him outside her body, and the rippling aftereffects were almost as powerful as the sex act itself.

A short time later, as she lay in his arms, her face resting on his heaving chest, she glanced up at him and said, "Now is it my turn to tie you up?"

He laughed and kissed her quickly. "Ingrith, you are a treasure."

And he made her feel that way. He really did.

In fact, they treasured each other, off and on, for the rest of the day and night, never going down to eat. As they were sated and sated and sated, their lovemaking took on almost a desperation, aware that they would soon be parted.

It was a special loving time for Ingrith, one she would never forgot. Somehow she sensed that it would never be matched by another man. It was as if a glow of unspoken love surrounded them.

All things changed when they went down to the great hall, soon after dawn, ravenous finally, for food. A short missive with Loncaster's seal had arrived overnight. John read it aloud.

*   *   *

My Lord Hawk:

Please come visit me at Winchester where I
have taken my newest mistress. Joanna of Jorvik.
Bring Henry.

> *Leo of Loncaster*
> *Commander, Jorvik Garrison*
> *Liege to King Edgar*

CHAPTER SIXTEEN

※

*T*here was nothing sweet about the sorrow in this parting . . .

"What is it?" Hamr asked as he came into the hall with Bolthor and Ordulf and saw John crumpling the parchment. John's face had gone ashen with horror.

"Loncaster has Joanna." He turned away from Ingrith. "Hamr, gather the troops at once. We leave for Winchester. Ordulf, you know what to do to secure Hawk's Lair. Bolthor, you will make sure the women and children stay within the keep."

"I am so sorry," she said, but John was already in leader mode, ordering a squire to bring his armor . . . leather helmet, *brynja*, gauntlets, *chausses*, two swords, and a lance.

"I'll be leaving within the hour," he told them all. "One hundred men will accompany me. There are a hundred guarding Gravely, and the rest will stay here at Hawk's Lair."

"So, it is to Winchester we go then?" Hamr asked.

John nodded as he cursed under his breath.

Fear rippled over Ingrith. Winchester was the king's primary residence. How could John, even with a hundred men, hope to prevail in that setting?

"Wait," Ingrith said, tugging on his sleeve. "You are not thinking clearly. You need a plan."

"What I need, Ingrith, is for you to go about women's work and leave me to do what I am trained to do." He shrugged her hand away.

She flinched as if he had slapped her.

He was too preoccupied to notice her reaction. In his defense, he had too much on his mind to pay attention to her. Still, she had an opinion, and she resented his dismissing her so handily.

And, while she was as horrified as he was at this latest outrage, and while she conceded that Joanna was in danger through no fault of her own, a small, mean part of Ingrith was jealous. Why was John so quick to rush to the rescue of his mistress, or whatever he wanted to call her, whereas he had been willing to wait for the Witan just hours ago? Did Loncaster's missive spark John's true emotions to the fore? Did he love Joanna, after all?

She hated herself for these less than honorable thoughts.

"What can I do?" she asked Bolthor.

But John heard her and turned. "Stay inside the keep. The drawbridge will be up and no one permitted to enter lest they pass Bolthor's approval. Take care of Henry."

"Mayhap I could go with you—"

"Nay!" he shouted, pointing a finger at her. "Listen to me, for once. I cannot concentrate on rescuing Joanna and watching after you at the same time."

She stiffened at his tone. Where was the loving man of the previous night? "What I was going to say before you interrupted is that I got you involved in this situation, and I should be responsible for helping to correct it."

"How, pray tell?" he asked, hands on hips.

Oh, I would like to smack you. "Sarcasm ill suits you, m'lord," she shot back. "Loncaster might consider a trade. Me for Joanna."

His face, which had been ashen, was red now. Even his bald head had a glow. "Have you lost your bloody mind?" The pointing finger was in action again. "You are staying here even if I have to tie you to my bed."

"You've already done that."

He threw his hands out with frustration.

"Don't get your bowels in an uproar. If you don't want my help, so be it." She spun on her heel and was about to stomp away, not wanting him to see the tears in her eyes. Besides everything else, John was going after Loncaster, facing danger. She hated that they would part with angry words.

When she'd gone only a few steps, he grabbed her arm, almost yanking her off her feet. Framing her face with both hands, he said, "Wait for me. We have much to discuss when I return."

Before she could reply, he kissed her quickly. And left.

Ingrith very much feared that she would never see him again.

The first cut was the deepest . . .

For two days, Ingrith paced about Hawk's Lair with no word from John, Loncaster, or anyone else. She felt John's cold departure like a cold cut to her heart.

Bolthor composed a poem, presumably to lighten her mood.

> *Love hurts.*
> *Love heals.*
> *Love soothes.*
> *Love excites.*
> *Love is the honey of life.*
> *Love is the gall of life.*
> *Love turns men into blithering lackwits.*
> *Love turns women into muddleheaded wantons.*
> *The gods created love*
> *To show humans*
> *That betimes neither sword nor lance*
> *Can bring men and women to their knees,*
> *Whereas love conquers all.*

Ingrith said, "That's nice, Bolthor," but what she thought was, *Love is a pain in the arse.*

"Katherine, I need to leave Hawk's Lair," she

said later when she was in the kitchen helping to prepare the evening meal. "Can you keep a secret?"

"Oh, nay, do not be telling me things I cannot share with my husband. And did you not promise Lord Hawk to stay here until he comes back?"

"Nay, I ne'er made any promises. He told me to wait, but I did not agree."

"Methinks you are parsing words."

She shrugged. "Here's my thinking. I brought this mess to Hawk's Lair by repudiating Loncaster's suit and by hiding the king's illegitimate son. I must be the one to put an end to it."

"I fear to ask, but how?"

"First, I will travel to Jorvik with Henry and put the boy on a longship to the Norselands. My father has no fear of the Saxon king."

"And you will go with Henry?"

"Nay. After I know he is safe, I will go to Winchester and offer myself in trade for Joanna as hostage."

"Did Lord Hawk not already forbid such barter?"

"He did, but he is not my master, or even my husband. John and his stepfather can continue to work through the Witan, or they can wage a battle 'til they all lie dead, but I cannot in good conscience let another woman suffer for my 'crime.'"

Katherine sighed wearily. "What do you want of me?"

"Care for the other orphans and do not tell anyone of my departure until tomorrow."

"You will leave tonight?"

Ingrith nodded. "I will take one horse and have Henry ride with me. Ubbi will come with us for protection."

Katherine snorted her opinion.

"Believe me, I will be careful, and I do know my way back to Jorvik."

Katherine groaned and put her face in her hands.

"One more thing. John has told me repeatedly that he will never marry me. He has never said that he loves me. His swift attempt to rescue Joanna speaks of strong affection, in my opinion. In many ways, I will be making it easier for John to return without having to face me. For all I know, he will be bringing Joanna here."

The "other woman" was a deciding factor for Katherine. "I can see why you want to be gone in that circumstance. Will you send for the other orphans later?"

"That depends on what happens to me. If I am not able to send for them, someone at Rainstead will. Already it is being rebuilt."

Katherine hugged her and choked out over her tears, "You are the bravest woman I know."

Ingrith shook her head. "On the contrary, if I were braver, I would stay and fight for the man I love."

*   *   *

It was the calm before the storm . . .

Two sennights and he was still chasing his tail at the Winchester court of King Edgar. There was so much hissing and backbiting and slithering that the royal enclave truly did resemble the snake pit to which it was often likened.

John wanted to go home where people were honest, where his beekeeping research called to him, where Ingrith waited for him and he had an important question to ask her, not to mention an almighty enthusiasm to be satisfied. First he must kill someone, preferably Leo of Loncaster, but the king would do, as well.

Not that he and Loncaster hadn't come into contact with each other, so to speak. Despite ten days having passed, John still had a swollen lip and a sword slash on his abdomen that had needed stitching. Loncaster sported a broken arm in a sling, a stab wound aimed for his heart but which had ended up on his shoulder, and a limp, which unfortunately would not be permanent. One of them would have ended up dead if Archbishop Dunstan had not intervened and ordered them to keep a distance betwixt them until the Witan could meet. In the meantime, the holy man, if he could be called that, had levied huge penances on the two of them, mostly involving knees on cold chapel floors and praying. John hadn't been able to find the chapel yet in the Winchester maze. Leastways, that was his story.

The only thing he'd accomplished thus far was the release of Joanna into his custody at Dunstan's order, but he was forbidden to leave with her until a meeting of the Witan could be held . . . a meeting that had been delayed, and delayed, and delayed, until every single member could be present. His stepfather, Eirik of Ravenshire, an ealdorman on the Witan, had arrived days ago, and he was boiling mad over the delays, too. If all this wasn't bad enough, his *hird* of one hundred soldiers had been forced to camp outside the castle grounds, or else give up their weapons to accompany him inside.

Winchester was the seat of English government, a favorite home for Saxon kings. Fed up with constant invasions by the Vikings, King Alfred, almost a hundred years prior, had ordered a system of *burhs* throughout Britain, with a fortress or garrison, or in some cases a castle, located within twenty miles of every village.

Plans were in hand to expand Winchester Castle, a glorifed wood castle at this point, into a lavish stronghold made of stone, but that could take decades, even a century if the elaborate plans were any indication. Really, who ever heard of a round table hung from the ceiling? Or a great hall in the shape of a double cube? In the meantime, the hammering and chiseling of construction work added to the usual court chaos.

"Well, we finally have a date for our hearing. Tomorrow afternoon," Eirik said, coming up to join him and Joanna, where they had been seated in the great hall, well below the salt, halfway down from the high table. The fancy, many-course meal . . . not nearly as delicious as Ingrith's fare . . . had been going on for hours. By the time they were served, the food was cold.

"Will I have to speak before the king's council?" Joanna asked.

Although she would not disclose details, Joanna had been misused by Loncaster. It had been one of the reasons for his sword fight with John, and one of the reasons Dunstan, disgusted with Loncaster, had released her to John's care.

"You will have to be present, but I doubt your testimony will be required. The issue before the Witan is Henry," Eirik explained.

"I'll make sure your kiln and trading stall are repaired," John added, squeezing her hand, which rested on the table. The gesture did not escape his stepfather's attention.

"I appreciate that," Joanna said, squeezing his hand back. He had not realized he was still holding her hand.

"If I do not leave soon, Eadyth will be riding here hell-bent on avenging my honor. News often reaches Ravenshire of the queen's lascivious activities."

"She has attempted to seduce you, too?" John inquired.

"Hah! Elfrida would tup a troll if she thought

it would assure her son's ascendancy to the throne."

"She's incredibly lovely," Joanna inserted.

"On the outside," John and his stepfather said at the same time.

"Like minds," Eirik remarked.

They exchanged warm smiles.

"Do you think she is behind the attempts to bring Henry here?" Joanna asked.

John shook his head. "Nay, but only because she did not think of it. It is Edgar, with Dunstan's backing, who wants to see the boy."

"The older I get, the more I understand my father's rejection of the Norse throne," Eirik said with a shake of his head.

"Truly, the little boy would be in danger?" Joanna, like many softhearted women, found it hard to believe that a child could be killed for political gain.

"Yea, but no more so than the king's legitimate sons," Eirik told her.

"For all we know, the king may want to meet Henry for nonthreatening reasons, but who can tell? And what may be safe today could be dangerous tomorrow, as the political climate changes," John added.

"And what of this woman who brought the boy to Hawk's Lair?" Joanna asked. "Princess Ingrith, I think she is named? Loncaster told me that you are betrothed."

John noticed his stepfather sit up alertly, this being news to him.

He did not want to discuss Ingrith and their relationship, especially not until he'd had a chance to discuss an important question with her . . . one that had multiple ramifications. So, he told Joanna, "We pretended a betrothal to get Loncaster off her scent."

He saw the look of relief on Joanna's face, which confused him. "I met Princess Ingrith once. She is very beautiful."

"She said the same about you," John said.

What an insane conversation! Was he really discussing one woman with another, both of whom he had been engaged with sexually?

Just then, Joanna turned on the bench so that she could look directly at him. She licked her lips several times as if trying to garner courage. "John, you asked me several years ago to wed you, and I rejected your proposal for good reason, at the time. I wonder . . . well, I have changed my mind. I *would* like to marry you."

Whaaat? He was so shocked he could not speak.

"Unless you have changed your mind, of course." She lowered her eyes, shyly.

His instincts told him that Joanna was frightened and made her suggestion not out of love, or even lust, but because of fear for her well-being once she returned to Jorvik. He would insure her safety, and would tell her so once they were alone, but nay, he would not be marrying Joanna. He had other plans.

But those plans came to a screeching halt as a feminine voice said behind him, "A betrothal. How wonderful! Leo, call for a servant to bring wine for the toasting."

All three of them . . . himself, Joanna, and Eirik, who had been staring at him, mouth agape, the whole time Joanna proposed . . . turned on their benches to see Elfrida standing with her hand on the good arm of Loncaster, who smirked at John.

"What? Another betrothal? How convenient!" Loncaster said, and Elfrida giggled, swatting the commander playfully on the chest.

"I . . . I . . . I . . ." he stuttered.

By the malicious gleam in the queen's eyes, John sensed that she knew she was placing him in an impossible situation. Soon, he and Joanna were being toasted with crisp red wine from the Franklands by the queen, Loncaster, and everyone surrounding them. If he were not careful, Edgar would be stepping down from the dais and joining them.

So, John made as quick an exit as he could. He and Eirik escorted Joanna to her bedchamber, then made their way toward the room they would share. He had not put Joanna straight on the betrothal business, figuring there was time enough for that after the Witan meeting tomorrow.

"By the scowl on your face, I take it that congratulations are not really in order," his stepfather said, humor twitching at his lips.

" 'Tis no occasion for mirth."

"But you actually announced a betrothal to Ingrith, King Thorvald's daughter? A bloody princess?"

He could feel his face heat. "It seemed the most expedient thing at the time."

"Ex-ped-i-ent?" Eirik rolled the word on his tongue as if it were a strange substance.

"Whether I am betrothed to Ingrith or Joanna or no one at all is not an issue here. It is Henry, the outrages Loncaster has inflicted thus far, and the continuing threats to anyone associated with this case."

"Hopefully, it will be resolved tomorrow by the Witan. I must caution . . . the queen strolling about on the arm of Loncaster bodes ill . . . if the queen as well as the king is supporting Loncaster . . ." He shrugged.

"But I have you at my back."

"That you do," Eirik said, looping an arm over John's shoulders as they arrived at their designated bedchamber, then moved the bed against the locked door once inside. They were taking no chances of a surprise visit during the night.

As John fought sleeplessness later that night, he wondered what Ingrith was doing. Was she experimenting with new foods in his kitchen? Was she playing with the children within the keep, as he had ordered? Was she digging up dead rosebushes, against his orders? Was she missing him as he was missing her?

He would have sent her a letter apprising her of the progress here, except there was no progress of note.

Once this whole mess was over, John planned to spend a considerable amount of time with Ingrith. God willing, mayhap a lifetime.

CHAPTER SEVENTEEN

Even a thousand years ago, men were clueless . . .

"Bloody damn women! Gods spare me! Stupid, bloody scheme! Ought to stay home in the bloody kitchen making bloody lutefisk."

"Stop cursing," Ingrith told Rafn, her brother-by-marriage, as they walked through one of many corridors at the Winchester Palace, heading toward the council room. They were surrounded by four of the king's *housecarls*. "I don't know how Vana puts up with you."

"I have talents," he said, waggling his eyebrows at her.

Rafn was a very attractive man, Viking to the core. In fact, he was once called Rafn the Ruthless before her sister tamed him . . . or tamed him as much as any dark Norseman could be tamed.

"If yer so talented, how come we're here in the king's palace without a sword or knife betwixt us?" Ubbi snorted with disgust. "I coulda pretended I needed me lance fer walkin'."

Rafn, who was uncommonly tall, even for a Viking man, glowered down at Ubbi, whose head scarce met his chest. "As if anyone would have bought that story!" Rafn scoffed. "You should have planted your little arse back with the troops."

"Me little arse has been carin' fer Lady Ingrith jist fine."

"That is why the two of you were strolling around the Jorvik docks, big as you please, looking for any longship headed to the Norselands. Could you have been any more visible?"

Almost immediately after arriving in Jorvik with Ubbi and Henry, Ingrith had been fortunate to run into Rafn, who was unloading one of her father's merchant ships. After she explained the dire situation, Rafn put the little boy on his longship. He had wanted Ingrith and Ubbi to get on the same ship forthwith and make haste for her father's stronghold, but she'd refused. She couldn't let John or the others continue to suffer because of events she'd set in motion.

"Your father will have a heart fit when he hears about this," Rafn had argued.

"'Tis the honorable thing to do. Me offering myself as hostage in Joanna's place."

"Honor be damned when you're dead as a squashed bug."

"I am going to Winchester," she'd insisted. "Just get on your damn ship and take Henry to Stoneheim."

Rafn had sighed deeply. "Well, then, I'll have to accompany you."

"But Henry . . . ?"

"Henry will be safe with Bjorn. The oarsman has five children of his own. The boy will be comfortable with him until we return."

So it was that Ingrith found herself with a giant and a dwarf for her protectors in Winchester Castle, where they'd been told on arrival that the Witan was about to convene. She realized that while her mind had been drifting, Rafn had been continuing his tirade about her and Ubbi traveling alone from Hawk's Lair to Jorvik. "Between the two of you, there's not enough brain to fill a pigeon's head."

"I resent that."

"Resent all you want! This plan of yours is insanity, and you know it. Lord Gravely had the right of it, telling you to stay at Hawk's Lair."

"He threatened to tie her to his bed," Ubbi told Rafn, "but Lady Ingrith said he'd already done that."

Rafn stopped, and she and Ubbi did, too, along with their four frowning guards. Rafn turned, very slowly, to stare at her. One of his eyebrows was raised in question. Only one. It was a particular skill of his.

"Ubbi, you talk too much," Ingrith said huffily and resumed walking, leaving the two dolts behind with the confused guards, who were not sure whether to stay with them or follow her. "How far is this council room, anyway?"

A passing maid thought she was talking to her and said, "Just around the next bend, m'lady."

Ingrith nodded her thanks.

Rafn and Ubbi caught up with her.

"So, have you been sharing the Saxon's bed furs?" Rafn inquired with the subtlety of a battering ram.

"That is none of your bus—".

"Yea, she has," Ubbi offered.

She glared at the little man.

"What? 'Twas no secret, was it?"

Of course, it was a secret. Does he really think I wanted one and all to know of my wanton ways?

"Ingrith! For shame!"

"Oh, do not give me that 'for shame' nonsense, Rafn. You and Vana were not celibate afore your wedding, that I know."

"Ah, but we were betrothed. There is a difference."

"Lady Ingrith is betrothed," Ubbi said.

"Could you manage to halt your blathering tongue?" she chided Ubbi.

"I was only bein' helpful." Ubbi's wrinkled face stiffened with affront.

"A betrothal? I had no idea, Ingrith. Wait 'til your father hears about this. He has been trying to get rid . . . I mean, get you married for many a year."

"How nice of you to mention my shortcomings!"

"Truly, he was running out of prospective husbands for you. Last I heard he was sending to the land of the Danes for new blood. In fact—"

"That will be enough, Rafn," she said, glancing his way to see a grin twitching at his lips. He had been teasing, of course.

Finally, they arrived at the council room. After Ingrith and her party identified themselves, one of the two guards in royal livery opened one of the massive double doors to let them enter, leaving the four *housecarls* behind. There was already a discussion taking place at the front of the room, where twelve men, along with King Edgar and Archbishop Dunstan, sat on chairs on the curved dais. Benches were arranged below the dais, all filled by at least three dozen people, men and women both.

John's stepfather, Eirik of Ravenshire, was one of the Witan members up on the dais. The Witan, or *Witenagemot*, was the king's advisory council, a powerful political body that had the power to select new kings. The members were appointed for life; so, the king needed to be diplomatic in how he crossed them.

In the front row, with their backs to Ingrith, sat John and Joanna. John had an arm wrapped around Joanna's shoulders, holding her close.

Joanna wore a lovely lilac-colored gown of samite silk, with inverted pleats of violet lace, matching the lace edging on her sleeves and bodice. Her black hair was piled loosely on her head, held in place by amethyst-studded combs.

Attired more sumptuously than Ingrith had ever seen him, John wore a fur-lined mantle, attached at his shoulder with an intricate gold circular brooch. It covered a tunic and *braies*, all of the finest soft wool in a dark blue shade. A gold-linked belt held in the tunic at his waist.

Ingrith's heart felt as if it were being squeezed inside her chest. It was probably nothing. Joanna had to be distraught. He was just comforting her.

A nobly dressed woman was standing next to her, and Ingrith whispered, "What's happened so far?"

"Not much. They're about to listen to Lord Gravely present his case. That's the handsome man in the front," she pointed to John. "The one with his arm around his betrothed."

"His betrothed?" Ingrith choked out.

"Yea. Their betrothal was announced yester-eve. Queen Elfrida led the wine toasts."

"Are you sure it was John . . . I mean Lord Gravely?"

"Yea. Do you know him?"

"I thought I did." Heartsick, she studied the pair. "I heard that the lady, Joanna, had been taken into custody by the king's commander."

"Loncaster?" Ingrith's newfound friend curled her upper lip with disgust. "Yea, he had the woman, but he was ordered to release her into her betrothed's protection . . . until the Witan rules, that is." Ingrith's expression must have belied her wonder that the woman knew so much, because she added, "My husband, Ealdorman Ormley, is the Witan member from Sussex." She pointed to a portly gentleman in the middle, who was apparently heading this particular meeting.

"Is she talking about the man who ruined you?" Rafn asked from her other side. His voice was rife with fury.

"I am not ruined, but, yea, it appears John belongs to someone else now. Mayhap he always did." She had heard that smitten women could not see the true nature of their men. How could she have thought she was the exception?

"Well, at least you will not have to offer yourself in exchange for the fair Joanna's freedom."

It would appear that even Rafn, who was madly in love with her sister, was impressed with Joanna's *fair* beauty.

"But as for the lord of Hawk's Lair, I will kill him for you."

"Nay, you will not. You must promise me, Rafn. You will do nothing to John."

Reluctantly, Rafn promised, though she was not sure she could trust that promise. Vikings took offense when their women were compromised, and to Rafn's mind, Ingrith had been more than compromised.

In John's defense, he had told her over and over that he would never marry her. He'd made her no promises. It was just that she'd sensed he felt as strongly toward her as she did toward him.

Ingrith had no opportunity to dwell on her heart pain anymore. There would be time later . . . a lifetime . . . to lick her wounds. Just then, Archbishop Dunstan began the meeting with a benediction. "We gather here to decide important issues of state. May God grant us the wisdom to act fairly, according to the Church's dictates and those of the law of man. So it was in the time before Adam, so it is today. Amen."

John and Loncaster, who had one arm in a sling, were both called forward to stand before the Witan.

Loncaster spoke first. "King Edgar commissioned me to seek out the boy named Henry who is conceivably his child by the woman Evelyn of Jorvik, a weaver by trade, who died recently."

King Edgar nodded to the Witan members that Loncaster spoke the truth. Thus far, anyway.

"It is my belief that the boy was taken to Rainstead, an orphanage in Jorvik. I directed Lady Ingrith of Stoneheim, who is affiliated with the orphanage, that I would be coming for the boy. But, when I arrived, I found that the orphanage had been abandoned, and its inhabitants scattered throughout the kingdom. After much searching, I located Lady Ingrith at Hawk's Lair, where I believe that she and the boy were being harbored, contrary to my king's wishes."

"Do you take exception to Commander Loncaster's statement of the facts?" Lord Ravenshire asked his stepson.

"'Tis true, except there are many pertinent facts missing. When Commander Loncaster told Lady Ingrith that he would be coming for the boy, he implied that the boy's life was in danger, possibly at his hands. Lady Ingrith and those running the orphanage at Rainstead had reason to flee. If there were any doubt about that fact, consider the things that Loncaster did subsequently. He burned the orphanage to the ground. He set fire to the flower fields and beehives at Hawk's Lair. He made threats to Lady Ingrith. He raped and held hostage Joanna of Jorvik whose only crime was a former relationship with me. Her home was nigh razed and the kiln she needs for her pottery business was destroyed."

"You have no proof that I was responsible for any of those things," Loncaster contended.

John indicated with a motion of his head that Joanna was proof enough.

"I say that the whore came to me willingly. Her word means naught." Loncaster smirked at Joanna.

Two guards held John back from attacking Loncaster bodily.

"He insults an innocent woman."

Not to mention his betrothed, Ingrith thought.

"What is the woman's relationship to you?" Archbishop Dunstan asked.

"Which woman?" a red-faced John replied.

"Have a caution, Lord Gravely," Dunstan said. "You are in bad odor with this council. You would do well to be cooperative."

"He told me that he was betrothed to Lady Ingrith, a Norse princess," Loncaster inserted.

"And he told me that he was betrothed to that lady," Queen Elfrida said from her seat in a side chair, just off the dais. She was pointing to Joanna.

"My relationship to either of those women is no one's business except mine," John contended.

"I beg to differ," Dunstan said icily. "Bigamy is a church offense."

Lord Ravenshire put his face in his hands, then addressed the other council members, "My stepson, John of Hawk's Lair, is not a bigamist and has no intention of becoming one. The issue here is the king's son, if that is what he is. I have a proposal. Give me guardianship of the boy. I will introduce him to the king, and I will protect him from all other outside dangers."

Ingrith had to admire Lord Ravenshire's diplomatic skill. He had not exactly said that the boy would be in danger from the king himself.

The king, Queen Elfrida, Loncaster, and various others began speaking at once.

"Silence!" shouted Ealdorman Ormley, stand-

ing with hands upraised. "We will conduct this
meeting with decorum. Now, Lord Gravely, let me
ask you this: Where is the woman who started all
this? Lady Ingrith? Why is she not here to speak
on her own behalf?"

Chills ran up Ingrith's spine.

Rafn squeezed her arm in caution.

"Lady Ingrith is—" John started to say.

"Here," she finished for him. She stepped forward, and Rafn and Ubbi came with her, refusing
to leave her side. Bless them!

One emotion after another rippled across John's
face. First, shock. Then, anger. Then, hurt, as his
eyes fixed on the arm Rafn had placed protec-
tively over her shoulders. To her knowledge, John
had never met Rafn. He must think Rafn was
her lover. *Good*, she thought. *Mayhap I can retain a
smidgeon of pride.*

"I would like to speak to Lady Ingrith in private before she is questioned by the council," John
said.

"Request denied," Dunstan declared, although
he should not speak for the entire Witan. "Who
are *they*?" he asked then, waving a hand to indicate Ubbi and Rafn.

"My name is Rafn . . . Rafn the Ruthless," Rafn
said before she could answer. "I represent King
Thorvald of Stoneheim, Princess Ingrith's father."

His credentials seemed to impress the council,
and his looks impressed some of the women in

the room—including Queen Elfrida—who sighed their appreciation. To Ingrith's prideful relief, Rafn did not mention that he was married to her sister Vana, widow of the Earl of Havenshire.

John's face was red now, with fury or embarrassment, she wasn't sure. But he was staring at the arm that still rested familiarly on her shoulder.

"And I am Ubbi, Princess Ingrith's guard."

A snicker passed through the chamber.

"It was never my intention to keep the boy from his rightful sire," she began, "but to protect him from those who would want to harm him."

"And who would that be?" King Edgar inquired icily.

"No one in particular, although Commander Loncaster did tell me that he would kill the boy himself if ordered to do so."

"Liar!" Loncaster shouted and would have grabbed for her if Rafn hadn't stepped in front of her. John had also been coming to her aid. Their eyes connected for a moment, hers no doubt with yearning, his with question, as if asking, "How could you?"

"Since Loncaster is head of *my* Jorvik garrison, are you implying that I would want the child dead?" King Edgar was not happy with her, that was clear.

"I have no idea to whom Loncaster pledges liege, or if it changes with circumstances."

"You bitch!" Loncaster yelled. "I never said or

did anything that would indicate that I am other than the king's man."

"Are you saying that the king condoned the burning of an orphanage and a nobleman's fields, or the rape of an innocent woman?" Ingrith asked Loncaster.

"I . . . I . . ." Loncaster sputtered.

"Where is the boy?" Ealdorman Ormley asked.

"Hawk's Lair," John answered.

"Uh," she said. "Not anymore."

John's hands fisted at his sides and his mouth thinned with disfavor.

"He is in our protection," Rafn said for her. "We will turn him over to Lord Ravenshire's guardianship, if the council so approves." Rafn looked to her, and she nodded her agreement.

The king, queen, and several Witan members wanted the boy delivered directly to the king at Winchester, but in the end, Lord Ravenshire's proposal was accepted. After a quick consultation with Ingrith, Lord Ravenshire, who directed them to call him Eirik, promised to accompany the boy for a visit to Winchester within a sennight. Loncaster gave Ingrith a glance that promised retribution.

After the Witan concluded its business, folks began to leave the chamber, heading toward the great hall, where a meal was about to be served. John approached her then.

"Ingrith, I would speak with you in private."

Rafn, who had been in low conversation with

Eirik, put his hand on her shoulder. "You do not need to speak with the miscreant if you do not want to."

"Miscreant!" John looked at her. "What have you been telling this Viking . . . miscreant?"

Before the two men could come to blows, she stepped between them. "You can leave me, Rafn. And you, too, Ubbi. I will meet you at the stables. I have no wish to dine at the king's table."

When they left, John took her by the arm and led her to a small anteroom.

At first he just stared, taking her measure.

She had dressed for the occasion as well, wearing a scoop-necked scarlet gown in the Saxon style of baudekin silk embroidered on the edges with gold thread in a Nordic design. Her hair was adorned with a string of crystal beads intertwined with the braids atop her head. Ruby ornaments dangled from her ears.

"'Twould appear that Loncaster will escape punishment for all his misdeeds," she remarked quietly while inside she was howling. *I have missed you so much. Have you missed me at all?*

"He will pay, starting with a loss of his position as Jorvik garrison commander. Dunstan has assured us of that."

She nodded. "Thank you for all your missives assuring us at Hawk's Lair of your safety and the outcome of your search for Loncaster."

He ignored her sarcasm and instead went on

his own attack. "Why . . . *why* did you disobey my orders to stay at Hawk's Lair?"

Why is he harping on such unimportant details? "Orders? Dost mean the order that I go about 'women's work' and leave the important decisions to you men?"

"I ne'er said that."

"You did."

He flushed, but did not apologize. "I intended to write—"

"Intended? 'Tis a comfort that you *intended*."

He frowned at her interruption, "—but there was naught to report."

"How about whether you were dead or alive? Or that you had found Loncaster?" *Or that you missed me.* "You had no right to give me orders, John. Not then, and certainly not now."

"What does that mean?"

She shrugged. "Where is Joanna?" *And why have you betrayed me with her?*

"Packing."

It occurred to her then that all of Joanna's clothing would have been destroyed by Loncaster. So, her lovely gown and jeweled combs must have been purchased by her lover. Ingrith wrung her hands nervously. "Packing for where?"

He shifted uncomfortably, then raised his chin defiantly. "I'm taking her to Hawk's Lair until her home and pottery equipment can be repaired. 'Tis the least I can do for her."

Hawk's Lair. Well, that destroyed any hope that Ingrith might have still been holding on to. *'Tis over then. No hope for me.*

"You had no trust in me at all, did you? You left Hawk's Lair with the boy, exposing both of you to danger, because you did not consider me capable."

Still, the brute was laying the blame on her. "That is not true. By the runes! I just wanted to help."

"You unman me with your brand of help. Men protect women. Women accept protection. Some even cherish it. 'Tis the way of the world . . . except that willfull independent world you live in."

"Mayhap if you had behooved yourself to share your plans for Henry's guardianship with me, I would have been more trusting, but, nay, you had to be so *manly.*"

"Now what?" he asked. "Will you be coming back to Hawk's Lair?" There was an odd, vulnerable expression on his face that he quickly masked.

"Why would I do that?" *Ask me to come with you,* she cried inwardly. "You will have your mistress to slake your brutish urges."

"You did not consider them so brutish at one time, as I recall."

She flushed with embarrassment. *How can he bring that up now? Has he not hurt me enough?*

"Why do you continue to missay me, Ingrith? I have told you that Joanna is not my mistress."

"Really? Your betrothed then?"

"Would it matter to you if she was?"

More than I can say. "My opinion matters not since you have told me more than once that I have no permanent place in your life. I wish you joy of each other." *Hah! I wish them no such thing. I wish them bad mating. I wish him bad honey. I wish her warts. I wish—*

"So, it is marriage or nothing?"

She hesitated. "Yea, 'tis."

"By the by, what is Rafn to you?"

That question came at her out of nowhere. Was he jealous? She hoped so. "Suffice it to say, my father considers him good son-by-marriage material."

He winced. "And I would not be?"

She sighed. "I am thankful for all you did for me and the children, who will be sent for, incidentally, once Rainstead is rebuilt. Truly, we imposed on you, and you were gracious in offering us hospitality and protection."

"I do not want your thanks. Why are you crying?"

She swiped at her eyes. "I get emotional when saying good-byes."

"And is this good-bye?"

"Apparently so." Still she waited for him to ask her to stay, that he wanted her in his life for more than a bed romp. He said naught.

Just then Rafn appeared at the door. "Ingrith, we must leave soon if we are to arrive in Jorvik by Friday."

Even then, she might have told John of her despair, that she would go to Hawk's Lair or anywhere else with him, if he truly wanted her. But Joanna appeared at Rafn's side, smiling shyly at John.

Ingrith nodded her acceptance then and would have given John a fare-thee-well hug of parting, except she feared she would fall apart if she touched him. Instead, she said, "Once again, John, thank you for all you have done."

His face was frozen into a mask of anger.

As she walked away, he accused her, "You told me you loved me."

She hesitated only a second before telling him, "And you did not, you loathsome lout. There is the crux of the problem."

On those telling words, she left.

CHAPTER EIGHTEEN

$\mathcal{C}$

They wouldn't even let him wallow in peace . . .

John left Winchester in a rage later that day. In fact, after several hours of ignoring any attempts at conversation, he left Joanna and Hamr behind to move at a slower pace with his troops, and he rode ahead, alone. As he would be for the remainder of his days.

He was being overly maudlin, he knew. After all, he'd gotten along fine before Ingrith. But, blessed Lord, is that how he would be regarding events from now on? Before Ingrith and After Ingrith.

It didn't help matters that the instant he entered his Hawk's Lair keep, Bolthor asked, "Where's Ingrith?"

The worst was when Katherine confronted him. "Well, I hear you let her get away. You get the prize for lackwit of the year."

"I did not *let* her get away. She went of her own accord . . . with a man, I might add. A Viking lover."

"You are sorely mistaken if you believe that. The woman is nigh barmy in love with you."

"Barmy she may be, but not over me."

"You should go after her then."

"You should mind your own business."

"Testy, are we? Love does that to a man betimes."

He growled his opinion of her opinion and stomped off to drown his sorrows in a tun of his mother's best mead, which he was still doing when Hamr and Joanna arrived later that day.

Joanna came to him later that night in his bedchamber.

"M'lord?" She stepped tentatively into the room, closing the door behind her. She wore only a thin sleep rail.

"What," he asked, as if her attire did not say it all.

"I would ease your pain."

He did not need this aggravation now, and wasn't it telling that he regarded an offer of sex as an aggravation? He could not even use drunkenness as an excuse. Despite the vast amount of mead he'd imbibed, he was stone-cold sober. "What pain?" he asked, then could have bitten his hasty tongue.

"Your heartpain, m'lord." She stood beside the bed now, whilst he lay on his back, an arm over his forehead.

"Heartpain?" He snorted with disgust. And,

really, how could he swive a woman who m'lorded him right and left? He would feel as if he were taking advantage of a servant, which Joanna was not. "I am not in the mood, Joanna," he said.

"You do not have to love me, or offer marriage . . . that was foolish of me to presume . . . I mean . . ."

"Joanna, you are welcome to stay here as long as necessary whilst your home is being rebuilt, but you owe me nothing for that. I am the one who owes you for the pain you have suffered."

"That is not why I came to you."

"I know." He sighed, and as gently as he could, rebuffed her advances. "Mayhap another night. Just not tonight."

Nodding, she silently left the room. But he did not take his ease on her in the days to come, either. Now he not only had insanity in his blood, but he was becoming a eunuch, as well, he thought with disgust.

Days ago, he'd made it clear to Joanna that she would not be his wife or bedmate now or in the future. So, he was not surprised when he found her and Hamr in the bed furs together. They apologized profusely, but he waved a hand for them to proceed with what they'd been doing before his interruption. He could not care.

Now it was the night before Bolthor and Katherine were to finally end their lengthy visit to Hawk's Lair and return to their home. Hamr would be taking Joanna back to Jorvik the next day, too, since her home and trading stall had been restored.

Before he sat down for the bland evening meal, Joanna kissed him on the cheek and grinned. " 'Tis true then. The mighty hawk has fallen."

He would have argued with her . . . to save his pride, if naught else, but what was the point?

"You should go after her," Joanna advised, echoing Katherine's advice. Not unexpected since the two of them had become best friends.

"She has someone else now," he told Joanna. "The man she was with at Winchester."

Joanna frowned. "That does not make sense. I saw the way she looked at you. I would wager my best pot that Ingrith loves you."

"You misread her looks, but thank you none-theless."

He was pitiful, and everyone must think so, because Bolthor soon summed John up with re-markable insight.

The saddest words in the human mind
The ones that destroy peace of mind
Are not "I am so sorry,"
Or "I do not love you anymore."
Not "There is no more ale,"
Or "You are too old to swive."
Nay, the saddest words are:
"What if . . ."

What if you had never spoken those harsh words?
What if you had grabbed life by the ballocks?
What if you'd taken a chance?
What if you'd returned that woman's love?
What if you'd married and had sweet babes?
What if you'd realized afore it was too late . . .
That life had handed you a gift.
What if . . . what if . . . what if?

After everyone had left the following morning, John girded himself with resolve. He had to straighten himself out and regain his life. So, with a head-splitting alehead, he made for his honey shed, where he would resume his studies.

That was not to be, however, because no sooner had he thinned the encaustum, sharpened a quill, and pulled out his journal than one of his *housecarls* came to announce visitors.

At first, his heart lifted. Mayhap Ingrith had come back, after all.

Not so. It was his mother and stepfather.

They had come to rescue him.

From himself.

Secrets have a way of coming back to haunt you . . .
Lady Eadyth of Ravenshire, once mistress of Hawk's Lair, looked at her son and could have wept.

John had taken her and Eirik to a small solar off the great hall, which was lightened by the summer sun through several unshuttered windows. The windows had no glass, an expensive commodity her son had not yet indulged in, though he surely had the coin to do so. But that was an issue for her to discuss with him at a later time. For now, she was alarmed by his appearance.

He had shaved his head at some point, and the scalp was now covered by a rough brush of bristly hairs. He had lost weight, and his cheekbones stuck out with gauntness. Eirik had told her about John's shaved head after the Witan meeting, but hearing and seeing were two different things.

Also, by the way he blinked against the light and cringed, she suspected he suffered from the alehead, possibly a days'-long alehead. And he was a man who rarely overindulged.

"You look like hell." Though his comment was frank, Eirik clearly cared about his stepson.

"Thank you for that unwelcome observation. Did you come here to bedevil me, or did you come here to bedevil me?" he inquired ungraciously.

"What is wrong with you, John?" she asked, the hairs standing out all over her body in warning. Something was definitely awry with her precious son. He might be thirty and one, but he would always be her firstborn and only son.

She could see that he was about to tell them that nothing was the matter, but instead, he slunk down in his chair and waited until a maid served them cups of the new batch of mead she'd brought with her—the last thing John needed—along with a tray of oatcakes, of which he could use a dozen or more.

When he sipped at his mead and did not take even one nibble of food, she shook her head with disgust. "I heard you were betrothed."

"Did you? Did you also hear that I was unengaged? Or that I was engaged to two women at one time? Or did your beloved husband with the loose tongue neglect to tell you that bit of gossip?"

"Pfff!" Eirik said.

"I know you too well, John. You are hurting." She took one of his hands in both of hers. "What happened?"

"I have made a mess of my life, if you must know." He bit his bottom lip, as if regretting his hasty admission. John had ever been a quiet boy, and then man, keeping his emotions in check.

"You seemed happy, or leastways content, the last time I saw you, three months ago. What happened since then?"

"Ingrith," he answered succinctly. "I must be still drunk," he muttered under his breath, "or else my tongue has taken on a life of its own."

"Ingrith," she repeated, pondering all the hidden meanings in that one word. "Do you love her?"

He shrugged. "It matters not. She has another man now."

"She does?" Eirik appeared puzzled. "How

would you know that, hibernating here at Hawk's Lair like a bloody hermit?"

John cast his stepfather a glower. "You were there. You saw her with her new lover."

"New lover?" Eadyth homed in on that one word. *New* implied that there had been a previous lover, which could only mean . . .

"John! Did you take Ingrith's virtue? A royal princess, for the love of Mary!"

"I did not take anything. She gave."

She tsk-ed at him over that moot point. "King Thorvald would not see the difference."

"Whoa! Back up here," Eirik said with a frown of puzzlement still furrowing his forehead. "What man did we see Ingrith with?"

"The Viking clodpole who accompanied her to the Witan meeting," John explained.

"Ubbi?" Eirik appeared puzzled.

"Of course not. The *big* clodpole."

"Rafn?" Eirik let out a hoot of laughter. "Rafn is Ingrith's brother-by-marriage, her happily married brother-by-marriage."

John's face brightened for a moment when he finally comprehended what his stepfather had said. Then he turned sullen. "Why would she lie to me?"

"Did she actually say that Rafn was her lover?"

John put a closed fist to his mouth, then admitted, "Not exactly. Now that I think on it, when I asked Ingrith about Rafn, there was a definite tic by her eye."

"Huh?" Eirik and his mother both frowned with confusion.

"When she lies or is hiding something, she gets a tic by her eye, just like Emma used to do."

"Ah!" Eirik said.

"How does she feel about you?" his mother asked.

He shrugged. "She told me she loved me, but that was before I left for Winchester. At our last meeting, she called me a loathsome lout."

Eadyth and her husband burst out laughing.

"Have you two been dipping in the mead?"

"Your mother called me a loathsome lout all the time. That's how I knew she was besotted with me," Eirik explained.

Eadyth slapped at Eirik's arm. How she loved the man! Even after all these years.

"You two are demented," John observed. "If you're going to start kissing, I'm going back to my honey shed."

"Well, that settles it. Since you have compromised Ingrith, you must offer marriage. You shame her good name by doing anything less," Eadyth pronounced. To say that she was happy with this situation was a vast understatement. Eadyth sensed that Ingrith was the key to John's future happiness, and she would do everything in her power to make it happen. Even attempt to guilt him into action.

He shook his head. "That's the problem, just as

it was whilst Ingrith was here at Hawk's Lair. I cannot in good faith offer marriage to her, or any woman."

"Whyever not?"

"You know," he said, "and I really wish we would change the subject. Wouldst like to come and examine my beehives, mother?"

"Nay, I do not want to examine your beehives, you lackwit."

"By the by, thank you for the rosebushes you sent to replenish those I've lost."

"I've never sent you rosebushes," she said.

"Every couple days, more rosebushes arrive." He tilted his head in question. "I wonder who—"

"Do not change the subject, my son. Why can't you marry?"

"Because I carry insanity in my blood, and I would not risk passing it on to any children I might have."

"Huh?" Eirik said.

"Where did you get such a foolish notion?" she asked. "If you carry insanity in your blood, then I must . . . oh, my God!" She turned to Eirik. "He thinks he got it from his father."

She and Eirik exchanged speaking glances. Then his mother rose to her feet, kissed him on the top of his head, and whispered in his ear, "Everything will be made aright now." Then she left the room, telling him she wanted to check out the crates of bees she'd brought with her.

"We need to talk," Eirik said, pulling his chair closer to John's so that they were almost knee to knee. "Your father, Steven of Gravely, was my brother."

Mommy Dearest had nothing on Daddy Dearest . . .

John could not believe his ears.

"I did not know that Steven was my half brother until he died. I killed him myself, John, and for that I will always be sorry."

"I do not understand."

"Like you, I considered Steven a monster. The things he did *were* monstrous. He wanted me to kill him, John. He wanted to die, and it was only as he died that he revealed our relationship to me."

"I do not blame you for killing him, brother or not."

"Whatever gave you the idea that you carried insanity in your blood? I ne'er told you that, and I know your mother did not, either."

"That is the point. No one ever discussed my father, but I overheard plenty. Mostly from servants or the *housecarls*. From the time I could walk, I have been hearing tales of my father's perfidies. Did he really kill your friend Selik's first wife and carry his infant son's head around on a pike?"

"He did. And much, much worse. After all, he raped your mother, that you *were* told. But he was not born insane. He became insane."

"You can defend him?"

"Not defend him. Understand him."

"He was insane. I am his son. The logical conclusion is that any child I breed might be insane,
as well."

Eirik shook his head. "The chances of that are
minimal. Let me explain. Steven's mother had a
brief relationship with my father, one night only.
She went back to her husband, who never forgave
her for her sin, even after she gave him a second
son. He hated Steven, although he acknowledged
him as his son to avoid scandal. Steven's father
died when he was young, and he was put under
the care of a sadistic sodomite who beat him
and brutalized him repeatedly. Ofttimes Steven
accepted this horrendous abuse to protect his
younger brother Elwinus from similar punish-
ments. I have heard of children and even adults
who feel as if their minds split in two in order to
survive abuse of that magnitude."

"You are saying that my father was born as
sane as the next man?"

"I believe so. You really need to go talk with
your Uncle Elwinus, who is a cloistered monk at
St. Paul's Monastery at Jarrow. He could tell you of
those early years."

John nodded, stunned by all he had been told. If
this were true, it meant he could marry. He could
have children. But he could not think on that now.
"And you were the one to end his life?"

"Indirectly. I had a sword pressed horizontally

against your father's throat when he taunted me about our being brothers, pointing out the resemblance betwixt us, which I had not noticed afore then. You look like him, John. He was a handsome man." Eirik coughed to clear his throat of some strong emotion. "In any case, he told me that his father never wanted him, and after his mother and then father died, he was left at a young age in the care of the most evil man in all Britain—Gerald, the Gravely castellan. His brother Elwinus was a mere babe. I always wondered what would have happened if my father had rescued him. As it was, I do not think my father knew of his paternity." Eirik inhaled and exhaled, overcome with some strong emotion. "To this day, I recall your father's last moments. They are imbedded in my brain forever. We were at his castle at Gravely . . ."

Eirik pulled his sword from its scabbard and a dagger from his belt. When he flicked the drape aside, Gravely jumped out at him brandishing a battle-axe. His blue eyes were wide and crazed. Froth dribbled from the edges of his mouth.

"At last!" Steven screamed, and having the advantage of surprise, swung the axe over his head toward Eirik's face. Eirik swerved but not before the blade swiped a chunk of flesh out of his shoulder almost to the bone. With a curse, Eirik ignored the pain and parried his next thrust, managing to wound Steven in the upper abdomen.

Despite the illness that had ravaged Steven's once fine body, he was still a strong warrior, capable of holding his own against Eirik's expert skill, at least in the beginning. Back and forth, they parried and thrust. Steven dropped the axe and picked up a sword with nary a blink. But then the ravages of his illness began to take their toll, and Gravely's endurance faltered. He grew careless and clumsy.

And Eirik lost the taste for the kill. Oh, he would destroy his evil enemy. He had to, if for no other reason than to stop his senseless assaults on any who crossed his path. But the man was clearly insane. His eyes were unnaturally wide and glazed with a berserk lust for blood. His mouth hung slack and trembling, like an aged man. Mayhap he had always been mad, but hid it under a calm exterior.

How can I feel pity for this man who has hurt me so?

Because you know he must have suffered greatly to have reached this sorry state, he answered himself.

With a mighty thrust, Eirik shoved him against the wall and held his sword horizontally against Steven's throat. "'Tis over, Gravely," he snarled. "Finally, your evil will end."

Steven cackled madly. "Yea, but will you be able to live with my death, *brother*?"

A cold chill ran over Eirik. The room rang with an ominous silence. He should have known that, even facing death, Steven would have found a way to leave destruction in his wake.

"Eirik, do not listen to him," his brother Tykir called out from behind him. "Just kill the bastard."

Gravely laughed again, not even trying to break free any longer. "Have you never thought on the resemblance betwixt us, Eirik? Black hair. Blue eyes. Same height. You share my blood, *brother*. And you know it."

"It cannot be so," Eirik said, shaking his head in denial.

"Your father planted his seed in my mother the one time she was able to escape her husband, the notorious Earl of Gravely, the man most people thought was my true father. She returned to Gravely when she learned she was breeding."

Eirik shook his head from side to side, denying Steven's claims. He still held the sword blade against his enemy's throat.

Steven just continued with his incredible story, "My 'father' never wanted me, and after my mother and then he died, I was left at age ten in the care of the most evil man in all Britain— Gerald, the Gravely castellan. And my brother Elwinus barely out of swaddling cloths. Oh,

Lord," he moaned, and his eyes rolled back in his head at some memory so painful even he could not bear to think on it.

Then, Steven seemed to calm himself. He looked Eirik levelly in the eyes, momentarily sane, and whispered brokenly, "Brother . . ." At the same time, he jerked his head forward, deliberately cutting his own throat. Blood spurted everywhere, but still a horrified Eirik held Steven upright by the upper arms.

And Eirik could not see for the tears that misted his eyes for his most hated enemy.

Eirik was unable to speak as his eyes filled with tears. Then he grabbed hold of John and hugged him tightly. "You must forgive your father. I have."

When they broke the embrace, John tried to joke, "So, what do I call you now? Eirik, or Stepfather, or Uncle?"

"What would please me most," Eirik said, "would be your calling me Father."

Forgive, yes; forget, never . . .

"How can you forgive him?" John asked his mother as they walked the scorched rose fields.

"It happened so long ago. And, besides, without that happening, I would have never had you. My son, you are worth a thousandfold more pain."

Which prompted a hug from him.

They strolled in silence then until he noticed something. Going down on his haunches, he dug with his bare hands around a mound. Green growth was coming up. He did the same over and over. It was amazing. More of the rosebushes would come back than he'd expected. It was a miracle to him that so many had survived.

"It's an omen," his mother said, tears brimming in her eyes.

"Of what?" he scoffed gently.

"New beginnings."

"You are referring to Ingrith?"

"That, too. With a little care, the roses might be better than before."

"Better for the pain, is that what you are saying?"

"Mayhap." She smiled at him and ran a caressing hand over his stubbly head. "Mayhap your hair will even come back in curly."

"God forbid!"

By the time his mother and Eirik left the next day, John was feeling much more hopeful.

"Just make sure I am there for the wedding," his mother said.

"I have to find the bride first," he replied. And that proved to be more true than he realized at the time.

Then the other shoe dropped . . .

Ingrith had never been so miserable in all her

life, and not just because her father had invited yet more prospective husbands to Stoneheim for her to view.

"There you are," her sister Drifa said, coming into the large sleep bower they shared. She was carrying a huge armload of roses, which caused Ingrith to burst into tears. Drifa, her only unmarried sister, had a passion for flowers, just as Ingrith had a passion for cooking . . . and a certain man. The tears just kept coming.

"Oh, Ingrith! What is it?"

"The roses," she wailed. "They remind me of . . . oh, never mind."

"Is this related to those rose cuttings you keep sending back to Britain?"

"Yea, 'tis. I owe a favor to someone who"—she shrugged—"likes roses."

"If I were a warrior woman, like Tyra, I would go carve out the heart of the man who has hurt you so."

"He has no heart."

"And exactly who did you say he was?"

Ingrith blinked away her remaining tears and tried to smile at Drifa's lame attempt at discovering the name of the mysterious man who had sent her home to the Norselands in perpetual crying fits.

"Listen, sister, you can't hide up here forever. Father invited a half dozen men here for us to meet. You're not leaving me down there alone like chum over a longboat to lure the fishes."

She smiled at the comparison . . . an apt description. "What are all the roses for?"

"I want to dry them and make potpourri sachets to sell at market. Here, smell them. Isn't the smell spectacular?"

Drifa shoved the bouquet under Ingrith's nose. The scent was overpowering. Nauseating, in fact. Ingrith shoved the flowers aside and ran for the chamber pot, where she proceeded to empty her stomach. Just as she had done every morning for the past two sennights.

Drifa was sitting on the side of the bed waiting after she rinsed out her mouth and dabbed her lips dry with a small linen cloth. "Well?"

Ingrith sat down next to her. "I am increasing." So much for John's "spilling his seed outside the body." And, really, he must have very virile seed because they'd made love the real way only a handful of times.

"You're breeding? Hell and Valhalla! That's wonderful!"

"It is?" She looked to Drifa to see if she was serious.

She was.

"It *is* wonderful, isn't it?" How had she not realized that before? She, who had thought never to bear a child, would be having her very own little one to love. And the baby would be part of the man she still loved, despite his faithless soul.

"There will be problems with you-know-who," Drifa pointed out.

"Father," Ingrith guessed.

"Your reputation, as well."

"Where I will live is another consideration."

"Perchance you can marry the father." Another attempt by Drifa to discover John's identity.

Ingrith shook her head sadly. "He won't marry me. He told me so. Numerous times."

"The lout! We should kill him like we did Vana's first husband. Mayhap if he knew about the baby—"

Ingrith shook her head more vigorously. "Nay, he can never know." She could only imagine John's horror at her bringing a possibly insanity-tainted child into this world. For some reason, she had no fear of that happening. But if it did, she would love any problem out of the child.

"Is he married?"

"Nay. Leastways he wasn't last time I saw him, but he might be by now."

"Then I do not see why—"

"I am not telling him, and that is final."

"We have to make plans then."

"We?"

"You do not think I will let you go through this alone? Tsk-tsk-tsk! How far along are you?"

"Only two months or so, I think."

"And how long afore your pregnancy will show?"

"Pfff! I have no idea. Some women do not show

until the fifth month. With a Norse apron, much can be hidden."

"Just to be sure, we should leave here no later than two months from now."

"Leave here?"

"Ingrith! You cannot imagine that Father would allow you to bring an illegitimate child into the world. He would have you wed to the first two-legged being with a phallus afore you could blink."

"We could go to Breanne's or Tyra's, but, nay, I do not want to return to Saxon lands, where he would find out."

"So, *he* is a Saxon?"

She ignored the question as she pondered where they could go. "We need to go somewhere that no one knows me, at least until after the babe is born. Then I can come up with some tale of having met and married a man who died suddenly. That way Father will have to accept me and my child without forcing me into a marriage I do not want."

"Whew! It is going to be difficult to accomplish all that. But we both have wealth enough of our own to establish residence . . . somewhere."

"Like you said, we have two months to work out the details. Promise me, Drifa, promise me that you will tell no one of this. Not even Vana."

Drifa lifted her chin with affront.

"Well, I best go down to the kitchen and see how the dinner preparations are going. Besides, I have a craving for leftover boar with horseradish sauce. Or peaches."

"First, we should present ourselves at the hall and see what dolts Father has to parade afore us this time, lest he send guardsmen to carry us down like he did last time."

As they walked side by side down the corridor, Drifa remarked, "I saw one of the men in passing whilst I was gathering the roses. A Viking warrior from Iceland. He was quite attractive."

"Oh?" That was a surprise. The older she and Drifa got and the more desperate her father became, the less likely the array of men paraded before them were to be prime examples of Norse manhood.

"He has one leg."

Ah! Not such a surprise then. "How does he walk?"

"With a wooden leg."

"A peg-leg Viking?"

They both burst out laughing.

And that was a good thing. Ingrith had found that humor could cure many ills, or leastways make life more bearable.

CHAPTER NINETEEN

❧

*H*ope blooms . . .

John arrived at the Monastery of St. Paul at Jarrow a sennight after talking with his mother and stepfather.

Although his uncle Elwinus was a cloistered monk, he'd been given permission to speak with John today. As it was, the silence rule only applied to part of the day, and even then they were permitted to use a form of sign language.

He was escorted from the priory outside to a back area of the enclave, where a tonsured monk was on his knees clipping . . . oh, Good Lord! . . . rosebushes.

Hearing his approach, Elwinus stood and dusted his hands on a cassock made of brown homespun material with a rope belt. A far cry from the wealth he could enjoy as one of the heirs to the Gravely estates.

"Uncle Elwinus?" he said.

"John!" There was shock on the man's face, and

not just because they had a similar lack of hair on their heads. "You look just like your father."

That was not a compliment in John's mind.

"I understand you have many questions about your father. Come, let us sit over here, and Father Cyril will bring us cups of mead."

He decided to jump in headfirst. "I have lived my life under the belief that my father was insane, and that I conceivably carried that trait in my blood."

Elwinus shook his head. "Your father was an angel in his early years. Without him protecting me, God only knows whether I would have lost my mind, too. You see, I was there. I saw the things Steven suffered, and it was horrendous."

"His father, you mean?"

"Our father was a bitter, sometimes vicious man who took out his unhappiness on Steven at times. I was his natural son, and he did not like me much, either. But it was after father died that the horror began. We were left in the care of the Gravely castellan, Gerald. Satan's disciple, for a certainty. Steven was only ten. I was much younger, but I saw . . . oh, my heavens, what I saw! Most people did not know this, but Steven's back was covered with whip scars. His arms had been broken more than once, and his ribs cracked repeatedly."

"Why would someone want to punish a child so?"

"Because at first Steven resisted . . . That was before his mind split. That is the only way I can describe the change in him."

"My stepfather said the same thing."

Elwinus nodded. "There is more." By the expression on the monk's face, John suspected the worst was to come.

John could not imagine anything worse.

"Gerald sodomized Steven. Repeatedly. And then he passed him around to friends of his with similar tastes."

"What happened to Gerald?"

"Steven killed him when he was fifteen. Probably some of the other abusive men as well."

"You condone the murders?"

"Of course not. But I understand why he did it. The damage done to him was irreparable by then. He could not go back to the innocent boy he had been five years before."

"And so you think my fears are unfounded about never having children."

"Oh, John, the best thing you could do is fill Gravely with lots of happy children to erase the past."

The image of that possibility filled his head, but John had lived for so long under the misconceptions about his possibly inherited insanity that he found it hard to be hopeful. But it was seeping slowly into his consciousness.

Ingrith. He could go for Ingrith now. He could ask her to marry him.

He only hoped it wasn't too late.

A welcome wagon it was not . . .

Three sennights later, and John was still searching for Ingrith.

Even though the remaining orphans at Hawk's Lair had been sent back, Ingrith had not returned to the orphanage in Jorvik to help in its rebuilding, as he'd assumed. A logical assumption. Unfortunately, too much assuming and not enough logic.

While in Jorvik, he stopped to visit with Joanna, to see how she was progressing. Turns out she had a nicer home and merchant stall than before, and a new kiln had been installed. Even more amazing, Archbishop Dunstan had ordered Loncaster to pay for these repairs. He was not surprised to find Hamr there with her. For how long, he did not know, since Hamr had been informed that his outlaw status had been removed, but the Viking looked very self-satisfied. It was strange the twists and turns of fate, he thought.

"Mayhap she has decided to become a nun," Hamr offered.

He offered a famous Anglo-Saxon word in return.

"Nay, I have not seen Lady Ingrith, not since the

Witan meeting at Winchester," Joanna told him. "Mayhap she went to visit with one of her sisters. Two of them live in Northumbria, I believe."

And so he'd wasted another two sennights going first to Larkspur in far northern Northumbria, where Ingrith's sister Breanne lived with her husband, Caedmon, and then to Hawkshire, where her sister Tyra, an Amazon of a woman— *a warrior, for the saints' sake!*—lived with her husband, Adam the Healer. Now John dabbled in the healing arts with his honey experiments, but Adam was a true man of medicine. Highly skilled and trained. But John had to say, regarding Ingrith's sisters . . . they had warped senses of humor, if you asked him, laughing when he told them he was searching for their wild sister.

"Wild?" Breanne remarked. "Ingrith is the most sensible, tame person I know. All she wants is to be left alone in peace in her kitchen to cook."

He'd merely raised his eyebrows at that misconception.

But Caedmon revealed to him in an aside, "All of King Thorvald's princesses are wild, in my experience."

"Good wild or bad wild?" he had been foolish enough to ask.

"How can you ask?"

Then there was Adam, who was unable to stop laughing at him. "I knew it, I knew that one day you would be trapped in some woman's wily net."

"Ingrith ne'er set out to trap me." *More like I tried to trap her.* "Else, why would she have run from me?"

"Run from you?" Tyra rose to her full height, which was almost as tall as he and Adam. The woman had muscles where women were not supposed to have muscles. "I will lop off your private parts if you have shamed my sister."

"I am the one who is shamed, running hither and yon after her like a besotted calf."

That remark satisfied Tyra and caused Adam to burst out in another bout of laughter.

He even stopped at Ravenshire to report to his mother and Eirik on the visit he'd made to his Uncle Elwinus.

Finally, the consensus was that Ingrith must have gone home to the Norselands, which disturbed John more than he could say. Ingrith had told him on more than one occasion that she would not go back to Stoneheim, where her father was obsessed with offering her prospective husbands. She'd better not have accepted one of them.

"Go after her," his mother advised when he was about to leave the following day.

"I'm trying, I'm trying," he replied with a long sigh.

It took him another sennight to find a longship

going to the Norselands, and it was a decrepit ship he traveled on, too. Plus, he soon learned why many Vikings went berserk after sampling the ship's fare. Lutefisk and smelly *gammelost*.

By the time he got to Stoneheim, he was not in a good mood. And his mood got worse when he saw his two-man welcoming entourage. Ubbi and Rafn.

Ubbi kicked him in the shin. Whilst John contemplated picking up the little troll by the scruff of his neck, Rafn punched him in the gut, catching him off balance afore he could defend himself, knocking him to the ground. Then, Rafn helped him to his feet and said the oddest thing:

"It took you long enough to get here, Saxon."

Beware of rogues with an agenda . . .

Ingrith was three and a half months pregnant, and still she and Drifa were the only ones who knew of her condition, thank the gods, largely due to voluminous Viking aprons and only a tiny bump low on her belly.

They had narrowed their prospective home-to-be to Norsemandy, where many Vikings were settled. Drifa had contacted a friend of a friend . . . a fellow flower expert, who had agreed to have them stay with her family at their vineyard until they located a home of their own. Everything was handled slowly and secretively.

So, while Ingrith knew she was not in the market for a husband, her father did not. The well-intended old man continued to bring forth potential mates for both her and Drifa.

She was in the kitchen experimenting on a new dried elderberry relish while Drifa sat at a nearby table breaking off lavender and rosemary sprigs to freshen the rushes throughout the keep. Vana sauntered in with a mischievous grin and plopped down in a chair. Plopped being an apt description since she was more than eight months pregnant. Ingrith could not imagine being that big herself one day.

"What now?" Drifa asked.

"Father has expanded his husband search."

"How so?" Ingrith asked, although she really could not care less.

"He's added a Saxon to the mix."

"Really? I ne'er thought Father would accept aught but a Norseman," Drifa said.

Lot of good that did Ingrith, since she did not have a particular Saxon offering for her. Nor would she want him to. Not now.

"Father asked that you make the dinner extra special tonight."

"Hmpfh!" Ingrith snorted. "All my meals are special."

After Vana waddled off, Drifa came up and gave her a hug. "It will only be two more sennights."

"I feel bad making you give up so much for me."

"Hah! Dost think I want to stay here alone with Father whilst you are gone? He would double his efforts to find me a husband. Besides, I yearn to see all the new flowers in Norsemandy. I have ne'er been there. Have you?"

She shook her head.

It was late before Ingrith entered the great hall that night, having spent extra time on the meal preparations and then bathing and dressing. She seemed to move in slower motion these days. So, dinner was already in progress when she arrived. She stopped here and there to talk with men and women she'd known for years as she made her way toward the dais, where her father, Rafn, and three strange men rose with respect. Except one of them was not strange.

It was John.

She faltered on the step and almost fell. What was he doing here? And why had no one informed her of the identity of the Saxon "suitor"?

But John wasn't a suitor for her hand. He must be here for some other reason. Oh, my gods! Could it be Henry?

She waited for the introductions. Geirfinn, a Danish warrior of noble birth, though a fifth son . . . in other words, landless. He was not so bad, although she did not like the perpetual smirk on his face, as if he were doing her and Drifa a great favor by his presence. The other was a short . . .

very short . . . a Viking from the Isle of Man, Atzer by name, widower with eight . . . EIGHT! . . . children under the age of fourteen. Then there was John.

"You know John of Hawk's Lair, Lord Gravely, do you not, daughter?" her father asked her.

She nodded, her eyes held by John's, which carried some message she was unable to decipher. He was thinner than before, and his hair had grown in somewhat, though still very short. But he looked good. Very good. Clean shaven and wearing a fine black wool tunic embroidered with red and silver thread over beaten hide *braies* and half-boots, all accented by a priceless gold-etched belt. On his finger was a heavy gold ring in the shape of a hawk.

Tears welled in her eyes—she could not help herself. He was a loathsome, faithless, selfish lout, but he was here, and she had missed him so much.

Drifa began passing the ornate bejeweled welcome cup around, accompanied by the usual grandiose toasts by her father, Rafn, and anyone else who wished to make a fool of themselves. It was a Viking custom called *sumbel*. Each recipient of the cup was expected to make a toast, or a boast, or sing a song, or recite a saga. By the time the meal was over, everyone would be half *drukkinn*, and they would have toasted everything from good friends to good crops to good ships to luck in battle. Once one of her father's hersirs had even made a toast to good swiving.

But all this toasting gave Ingrith a moment to collect herself and not nigh swoon at the Saxon scoundrel's feet.

John stared at Ingrith, taking her in with a deep sigh. Whilst he had been living in agony these months since she'd left, she glowed with good health and apparent happiness. And she was entertaining prospective husbands. He would wring the neck of either of those louts if they dared to touch her.

But why was she weeping? Hopefully, not because she wished him gone.

John took both of her hands in his, despite propriety, and garnered frowning glowers from her father and the two other "suitors," whom he intended to send on their way forthwith.

Ever since John had arrived, Rafn kept chuckling, and Ubbi had shadowed him like an irksome puppy. He'd been here at Stoneheim nigh on five hours, and no one would let him meet with Ingrith. Until now.

The keep was a maze of additions put up in a haphazard manner over the years, thanks to Ingrith's sister Breanne, who fancied herself a builder, of all things. He'd gotten himself lost twice when trying to find Ingrith on his own, and there seemed to be a conspiracy amongst servants to hide her whereabouts. Well, he had her now, and he was not letting her go. He was done cooling his heels amongst these Norse dunderheads.

"Ingrith, you have no idea how much trouble I have gone to in order to find you." The wrong thing to say, he realized immediately. "I mean, I have been searching for you for many sennights."

"Why? Is it Henry? Oh, please, don't tell me he is harmed."

He frowned. "Nay. Why would it be Henry? The boy is living with my mother and stepfather, happily, I might add. He has met the king, who accepts him in his own neglectful way."

"There is no longer any danger to the boy?"

"Not from the king."

"Then why are you here?"

He was not happy by half at her rudeness. Best they pass that welcome cup this way so that the wench could welcome him properly. "You are the reason I am here."

She made a very unattractive snorting sound. "I thought you would have been married by now. *Are* you married?"

"Huh? Who would I have married?"

"Joanna."

He waved a hand dismissively. "She is back in Jorvik . . . with Hamr, if you must know."

"Your mistress rejects you and you think you can come sniffing after me?"

"What?"

She slapped him on the chest and stomped away. When he started to follow her, she turned and snapped, "Stay away from me."

"Not a bloody chance in hell!"

She headed toward the end of the dais, where a smirking Viking knight, Geirfinn, whom he'd met earlier, was watching the bounce of her breasts as she walked toward him. John bristled. No one else should be noticing the bounce of her breasts, which, by the by, he could tell even with the shroud of an apron were fuller. In fact, she seemed a little fuller all over, including her bouncing rump. Not that he minded. In fact, if she were in a more receptive mood, he would tease her about her wag-tailing him.

The smirking knight made room for her by shoving the short Viking Atzer into an adjoining chair. He'd also met Atzer earlier. A widower, he was forty if he was a day and he had eight children at home looking for a mother. Well, he had news for Atzer. It wasn't going to be Ingrith.

"Move over another chair," John demanded and slid into Azter's chair on Ingrith's other side. It didn't matter to him that every other person had to move down a seat to make room. It also didn't matter to him that he was creating a scene to the amusement of the two hundred or so warriors and ladies who filled the hall.

"I told you to go away," she said, turning her back on him as she began to make conversation with the smirking Norseman. If she only knew why Geirfinn had that perpetual smirk on his face. He fashioned himself a prize and that he was lowering himself to wed such an aged maiden as herself, and didn't mind boasting to one and all about his generosity. "Go. Away!"

She thought she could ignore him, did she?

"I didn't travel on a leaky longboat eating stinky *gammelost* to be ignored by you, witch," he muttered under his breath.

She still ignored him.

"Have you gained weight, Ingrith?" he asked amiably, figuring he could lure her into a deeper conversation once he got her talking.

Atzer slapped his thigh and said, "Even I know enough not to mention a woman's weight."

Ingrith turned slowly to glare at him. "Are you saying I am fat?"

"Of course not. You are perfect. Besides, a man likes a bit of flesh to hold on to in certain situations." He smiled at her.

"Could you possibly be more stupid?"

"I just gave you a compliment."

Atzer and Geirfinn both guffawed at his apparent stupidity.

"Ingrith, you know that I think you are beautiful. You are more beautiful now than you were before. Call me clumsy in expressing myself, but do not call me stupid."

"Stupid!" she repeated.

Ingrith's sister Drifa walked up the steps of the dais with the huge welcome cup then. "Will you partake of the *minna*?" she asked from behind them. "The memorial toasts?" It appeared that he and the two Viking dolts were expected to give toasts.

Atzer went first. He went on and on expounding on all the gods to bless this land and this family and its warriors in their battles against the miscreant Saxons, ending with a toast to Freyja, the goddess of fertility, thanking her for all the children he already had and those yet to come. He glanced pointedly at Ingrith on that ending.

She pretended not to have noticed.

Then Geirfinn stood and preened before speaking. His toast was pretty much a praise poem to himself and all his manly feats, which included a suspiciously high number of Saxon kills.

Did everyone forget he was a Saxon?

At the end, Geirfinn raised his cup to Ingrith, and he winked at her.

John would have liked to poke the cockscomb in the eye with one of his gaudy mantle brooches. What man needed three brooches at one time, anyway?

Drifa put a hand on his shoulder then, and handed him the cup. She was a petite woman, part Arab would be his guess, by the slant of her eyes and hue of her skin.

If these folks thought he was going to blather on about this and that, he had news for them. He stood and said, "Here's a toast to women with

wag-tail arses and an enthusiasm for bedsport."
Then he plopped back down to his chair and took
a long swig of the strong ale.

Everyone was laughing and commenting on
his lewd jest.

Who was jesting? Not him.

Except King Thorvald who was frowning as he
called out to Rafn, "Is he talking about one of my
daughters?"

"Nay," Rafn replied, casting him a glance that
said John owed him. "He was referring to lusty
Saxon wenches."

"Oh," the king said and smiled at him.

Ingrith merely remarked, "Crude oaf," and
turned away from him again.

Drifa took the cup from him, then paused.
"Lord Hawk, welcome to Stoneheim. We met at
my sister Tyra's wedding years back."

"Yea, I remember you, Drifa. You decorated
Adam's house with so many flowers we all
smelled like perfume," he teased.

She grinned. "So, are you the person getting all
the rosebushes?"

"Drifa!" Ingrith said, apparently listening to
their conversation, while she'd been pretending
to be absorbed in something Geirfinn was saying.

At the same time, John said, "Ingrith!" and
grabbed for her hand on the table, though she
tried to tug it away. " 'Twas you who sent me all
those bushes and cuttings? I thought it was my

mother." He kissed the knuckles of the fisted hand, just before she yanked it away.

"I only did it because I felt guilty over the damage, not because I care about you."

He smiled nonetheless. She cared, all right.

"You sent rosebushes to this Saxon?" Geirfinn asked. "How . . . unique!"

" 'Twas just a gesture of thanks," she explained primly.

God, but she looked like a sex goddess when she did her prim posture.

John leaned in front of Ingrith to address Geirfinn. "Eleven thanks, in all."

Disconcerted, Geirfinn said, "My mother likes roses. You would have much in common with her, Ingrith, although roses do not grow well in our region of Iceland. Too cold."

" 'Tis a pity. Ingrith could not live without roses," John said.

"I could, too," she protested.

"I am the one who cannot live without flowers," Drifa remarked.

Atzer tapped Drifa's shoulder and said, "We have lots of flowers on the Isle of Man."

"How nice!" Drifa said, then winked at John before ambling over to speak with Rafn.

John put a hand on Ingrith's thigh, up high.

She was too shocked, at first, to protest.

"I have missed you, Ingrith."

"You had Joanna."

He rolled his eyes. "Ingrith, I am going to have a bronze plaque made and planted in our rose garden. It will say, 'Joanna is not John's mistress.' If you must know details, I have not had sex with Joanna in more than a year."

Her jaw dropped, but the only retort she could come up with was, "*We* don't have a rose garden."

"*We* will," he said.

She seemed to have forgotten his hand on her thigh, which worked to his advantage. By now, he had the hem rucked up to her knees, and her leg and knee bared to his touch.

She blinked at him as she realized that his fingers were creeping under the cloth, higher and higher. Letting out a little squeak of dismay, she shoved his hand away, but not before he flicked his fingertips at her woman-fleece. That would teach her to ignore him.

"You are a wicked man," she said.

"I know."

"Have you no shame?"

"Apparently not."

"What are you two talking about?" Geirfinn wanted to know.

"Nothing," he and Ingrith said at the same time.

By now, food was being served, and he had to smile at the vast array of dishes. Even more varieties and quantities than she'd prepared at Hawk's Lair. "I see you are in your glory here, cooking to your heart's content. I did not realize there were eight ways to cook beets."

"Are you criticizing me?"

"Hardly! I cannot wait to have you back in my kitchen."

She eyed him narrowly. "You want me back in your kitchen?"

"And in my bed."

"Your arrogance passes all bounds." She stood and said, "I am going to leave. I need air. You are not to follow me. I mean it. I will cut off your randy cock if you do."

He laughed, which was not the reaction she was looking for.

"Did she really say 'randy cock'?" Atzer asked.

"Yea. Isn't she wonderful?"

"I would not want my wife using that kind of language in front of my children," Atzer said.

"Good thing she will not be your wife."

Now that she was gone, he sat back and sipped at a cup of ale. By the cross, it was good to be back word-sparring with Ingrith. "Well, that went well," he said to himself.

"Are you crazy?" Rafn asked.

"Crazy in love," he replied, with no embarrassment at all.

CHAPTER TWENTY

Some men bang their heads against a wall, others bang their . . .

Ingrith was tired, more tired than usual from her pregnancy. It was wearisome, evading John.

He kept trying to get her alone, kept saying he had things to tell her, but she knew what he really wanted. He wanted to swive her, and if he did, there was a strong possibility he would notice her little belly. What would he do about her breeding a child with potentially insane blood? Would he run in horror? Or would he attempt to force her to end the pregnancy through some herbal remedy? Perchance he even knew of some abortive method that involved honey.

She grinned at that last thought and therefore wasn't paying attention as she hurried up a back stairway to a third-floor addition Breanne had put on several years ago for servants and overflow guests.

John, coming down, caught her against his chest

and lifted her off her feet, walking her enfolded in his embrace into a small alcove. "At last!" he said, his mouth swooping down on hers. No soft, enticing kiss was this, but a hungry, demanding kiss that took no prisoners. And a bit of punishment, as well, for all the grief she had been giving him, no doubt,

She should protest. She should shove him away. Instead, she was kissing him back, her fingers threading through his short hair, her breasts brushing against his chest.

"Heartling," he whispered against her open mouth. "My heartling." Then he angled his kiss in another direction, showing her with lips and tongue and teeth that he did miss her, as he'd kept trying to tell her. As she had missed him.

His hands were everywhere. Her hands were everywhere. Reacquainting themselves with each other in all the ways of lovers throughout time. She loved him, she loved him, she loved him. How would she ever live without him? How would she ever live without this?

"Put you legs around my waist," he whispered in her ear, cupping her buttocks.

Startled, she realized that he had raised her *gunna* and dropped his *braies*. As he lifted her by the buttocks, she did indeed wrap her legs around his hips, compliant wench that she'd become. Hah! More like a melting mass of instant arousal.

"Coming home, sweetling." He held her eyes as

he eased inside her tight sheath. As always, she welcomed him with tight constrictions of pleasure. "Being inside you feels like coming home. Tell me you feel the same."

She nodded, unable to deny the powerful emotions swirling around them. What this man did to her! Was it a spell? Was he a wizard? Or the devil, more like.

Bracing her shoulders against the wall, he began to thrust inside her. Slowly. Too slowly. She tried to hasten the pace, but he shook his head, forcing her to match his agonizing rhythm. As she began to peak under his hawk eyes, she lowered her gaze, shy to be acting so wanton. "Do not hide from me, sweetling. You are mine. And I am yours."

She began to weep.

"Shhhh!" he said, kissing away the tears.

When he reared his neck, the tendons in his neck visible with his attempt to control his passion, he thrust deep into her and held. "Marry me, Ingrith."

So shocked was she was by his question and their fierce peaking together that she did not realize that he'd failed to spill his seed outside her body. This was precisely what he'd predicted would happen if they stayed together. They would get careless, and she would get pregnant. Little did he know, it had already happened.

With a cry she shoved away from him and ran up the steps, slamming and locking the door of a small bedchamber at the top. Almost immediately, he was knocking at the door, "Ingrith, what is amiss? Let me in. I am sorry to have rushed things with you. I could not help myself. You are too tempting a morsel."

She could hear murmuring outside the door then. It sounded like Drifa talking to John. "I'm going, Ingrith, but we need to talk. We really need to talk."

"Let me in, Ingrith. He's gone," Drifa said.

Ingrith almost fell into her sister's arms. "Oh, Drifa! What am I going to do? We had sex and he didn't pull out."

Drifa stared at her, wide-eyed. "Are you worried about getting pregnant?"

Ingrith realized how foolish she must seem, and they both burst out laughing.

"We cannot wait for two sennights, Drifa. We must leave sooner."

"Oh, Ingrith! I think . . . I think you must tell John. He seems like a good man. I do not think he would react badly."

Now that John was here, Ingrith explained everything to Drifa about him.

"He asked me to marry me," she revealed.

"He did? See? You should talk with him."

She shook her head. "Just the opposite. He has convinced himself that we can have a marriage under certain conditions, and already we have broken one of those conditions."

"He told you all this? You mated with him, then had a conversation about the conditions under which he would marry you? Blessed Valkyries! You left the garden only a half hour ago. I thought sex took longer than that."

Ingrith smiled despite her dismay. "Nay, we did not have a lengthy discussion. I just know."

"You are not making sense."

"I love him, Drifa, and I cannot bear to hurt him by presenting him with a child that he would be watching every moment for signs of insanity."

"I understand, but I still think you may be acting in haste."

"John is an honorable man. He would do the right thing, but I would be condemning him to the misery he has avoided all his life. Truly, it would be best for me and for John that I leave."

"Methinks he will be heartbroken over your leaving."

"Mayhap, but there would be far greater heartbreak if I bore him a child who carried certain traits."

"Could you be underestimating him, dearling?"

"He is a wonderful man, Drifa, but he has suffered so. I cannot in good conscience give him more pain."

"If your baby . . . your child . . . proves to be, well, normal, will you tell him then?"

She shook her head. "John is perfectly normal

himself, but there is always the chance that could change . . . or so he thinks."

"I can't imagine loving a man that much . . . more than yourself, really."

She shrugged. "In any case, we need to leave as soon as possible. I will break things off with John for good before that. I do not want him following me."

"Don't worry. Things will work out fine."

Somehow, deep down, Ingrith doubted that.

The cat was out of the bag . . .

Ingrith was up to something. Not only were she and Drifa whispering together every time he saw her, but that tic was going wild beside her eye. And, God forbid that he should approach her! When he did, she shot off like a skittish cat.

Was it only last night that he'd asked her to marry him, causing her to bolt as if he'd suggested something despicable? He must have been demented to think that she would be pleased by his proposal.

Not that he was giving up.

First stop next morning was a visit with King Thorvald.

"I intend to marry your daughter Ingrith," he announced right off.

The king, who was a majestic old bull with his flowing white hair and still massive body, cast him a patronizing gaze. "Were you asking for my permission or telling me?"

John had been pacing about the king's chamber, but he stopped, caught off guard. "I would like your permission to wed your daughter, but if you refuse my suit, I will marry her anyhow."

"Why?"

"Why?" he repeated back.

"Have you become a parrot now, boy? Why do you want to marry Ingrith? You are a high-placed Saxon nobleman. You could have practically any woman you wanted."

"I want Ingrith."

"Why?"

"We suit."

"Pfff! I hope you didn't tell her that when you proposed. You did propose, didn't you? Otherwise, you would not be storming around here like someone set fire to your tail."

"I do not appreciate your finding mirth in my dilemma."

"It *is* mirthsome. I hope you were not looking to me for advice. For ten years and more I have been trying to marry the girl off, although she does cook the best meals. I do not suppose you would live here once you wed? Nay, I did not think so."

John reached up to tear at his own hair, forgetting that he did not have much.

"By the by, is that the new hairstyle in Saxon land?"

He cast a cutting glower at the king.

Thorvald grinned. "*Did* you propose?"

"I did."

"And?"

"She said nay."

Thorvald shook his head at John's hopelessness. "You are not the first. She said nay to at least three dozen men. And some of them were more than desirable, especially in the early years. Would have made great alliances." He sighed deeply. "Why, I recall this one Varangian guardsman. He was so good-looking that I could have fallen in love with him myself. Then there was—"

"I am different," he interrupted.

Thorvald raised his bushy white eyebrows.

"She loves me." Which was sort of the truth. She had loved him before he'd made a mess of things.

"She told you so?"

He nodded. Again, not quite an untruth.

"That is something. Why are you telling me this? If all the advantage is in your corner, why not persuade her to marry you?"

"I'm trying."

"I can tell you are not a Viking. A Viking would take matters into his own hands. He would carry the maid off and make her his and worry about her affections later."

"Oh, that is very civilized!"

"And who said man-woman matters are civilized? I have been married four times, you know. Did I tell you about the time I had a hole drilled in my head? You should try it some time. I swear it made my cock get bigger, or leastways it—"

John walked away in the middle of the conversation.

He had the misfortune of running into Geirfinn then, who had the misfortune to make a remark about Ingrith's breasts compensating for her advanced age. Geirfinn hotfooted himself to the king right afterward, protesting the fist John had levied at his nose, which John had, hopefully, broken.

Ubbi walked up and kicked him in the shin.

"What was that for?"

"Making my mistress cry. All the time. She ne'er cried afore she met you."

Instead of being distressed by that news, he grew hopeful. She must care if she cried. Then, he turned about-face and chastised himself, *What kind of half-arsed illogic is that? Even if I have no insanity traits in my body, she will drive me crazy.*

"Would you like my advice?" Rafn asked, leaning lazily against a doorjamb as he munched on an apple. Loudly. John's shattered nerves heard every crisp chew.

He wanted to tell Rafn to shove his advice and the apple somewhere unpleasant, but he was getting desperate. "Spill your vast array of woman knowledge, oh, Viking God of Love."

Rafn grinned. Of all the Norsemen he had met,

Rafn enjoyed John's discomfort the most. "You need to get Ingrith alone—"

He waved a hand. "Dost think I haven't tried? Methinks she must have cat blood. She scoots away afore I can grab her."

"—preferably before she escapes on that longship she and Drifa have arranged."

John froze.

"'Tis waiting for them at the wharf as we speak."

"What? You maggot-eating son of troll! Why didn't you tell me this earlier?"

"You had not suffered enough yet."

He punched Rafn, too, except the Viking ducked at the last minute, and his fist only grazed his chin. Without another word, John stormed out of the keep and walked angrily toward the wharf where there were dozens of longships. *Think, John, think.* There was no sign of Ingrith or her sister. And there was activity around a number of the longboats. Surely Ingrith wouldn't leave without telling him. What the hell was wrong with her? Just then, he saw someone he recognized. Ubbi. And he was coming off the gangplank of a small longboat.

He stalked up and grabbed the little man by the front of his tunic. "Tell me where she is, or I swear you will be swimming in the fjord with all the fishes."

"I cannot swim," Ubbi said.

"Good."

Ubbi motioned with a jerk of his head toward a far longship.

"Where are they going?"

"I doan know. Norsemandy, mebbe."

"When are they leaving?"

"I doan know. Later t'day, mebbe."

"Is she on board now?"

Ubbi shook his head.

John dropped the little man, too angry to even say thank you for his information. He should just forget about Ingrith. He should save a little pride and go back to Hawk's Lair. But he was beyond furious now. What was Ingrith's game? Was she deliberately making a fool of him? He didn't understand any of it.

One thing was certain, though. Ingrith Sigrundottir was going to regret ever entering the Hawk's Lair.

Trust goes two ways, you know . . .

Ingrith was in her bedchamber packing another chest with clothing when the door swung open. John entered, without knocking.

She and Drifa both glanced up with surprise, then exchanged glances of question. What should she do now?

"You," John said with ice in his voice, pointing at Drifa, "Out! I would speak with Ingrith alone."

"You cannot order my sister—" Ingrith started to say.

But Drifa, the traitor, was already at the open doorway. "I will be down in the kitchen gathering—"

John slammed the door on her sister before she'd even finished speaking. How rude! Even ruder . . . how dare he lock her bedchamber door?

Leaning back, arms folded over his chest, he surveyed her and the room. "Going somewhere, Ingrith?"

"Yea. Drifa and I decided to visit a friend."

"Where?"

"Uh."

"Do not lie to me, Ingrith. Your tic is giving you away."

She put a hand to her eye and willed the tic to stop.

"You were going away without saying good-bye to me? Without giving me the chance to talk?"

"I was going to talk to you."

"When?"

"In a little while."

"When the deed was almost done."

She hesitated, then nodded.

"Why?"

"Why what?"

He growled. "Why won't you marry me?"

" 'Tis for the best."

"Do you love me?"

Oh, that was unfair. She refused to answer.

"You told me that you loved me. Is your love so

fair weathered that it cannot last through a few minor problems?"

"Minor problems!"

He shrugged. "Serious problems, then. But you gave me no leeway to work things out."

"You had all the leeway you wanted until you went for Joanna."

Ingrith had to sit down on the bed. She was starting to feel weak. Unfortunately, John chose to sit next to her.

Taking her hand in his, he asked once again, "Will you marry me, Ingrith?"

She shook her head, fighting the tears that were already leaking from her eyes. He wiped them away with the pad of his thumb. "I cannot, John, and you know why. You were the one who said that if we wed, even if we practiced the safe method of sex . . . you know, the spilling outside the body business . . . that eventually, the way we go at each other, we would get careless. We already have, if you have not already realized what happened yesterday on the stairs."

"I know. I knew when it happened."

"What?"

Before she could realize what he was about, he lifted her onto his lap and then leaned back against the headboard with his legs extended. Now, she half sat, half laid atop him.

"Tell me where you were going, sweetling," he urged.

"How can I answer when you are touching me?" she griped.

He had been caressing her back and kissing the top of her hair, which he had already unplaited and finger combed over her shoulders.

"Sorry. I cannot help myself. You are too tempting."

"Not so tempting pretty soon," she murmured.

"What?"

"John, you have to stop this."

"Touching you? I cannot stop."

"Nay, not touching me. I mean, yea, you must stop that. But you must stop pursuing me."

"Why?"

"Why? Why? Why? You are not going to let this go, are you?"

He shook his head and tried to kiss her, but she ducked her head.

"This is bloody hell why," she snapped, taking his palm and laying it across her belly.

He looked confused. "You cannot marry me because you have eaten a few too many of your own honey oatcakes?"

"Aaarrgh! I am pregnant, you idiot."

She could almost see the wheels turning in his head as he slowly assimilated what she'd said.

"Let me see if I understand. You are pregnant with my child. I'm guessing three months along."

"Three and a half."

He made that growling noise again. "You were harrying off on dangerous seas in a longboat for bloody damn Norsemandy."

"The seas are not dangerous this time of the year. Usually."

Growling again. "You have been avoiding me like I am a leper."

"With good reason."

"Reason be damned."

"You don't have to swear."

"Damn, damn, damn! All of which points to the fact you ne'er intended to tell me. Do I have this right?"

She nodded hesitantly. It sounded halfbrained when he related it like that.

Suddenly he shoved her off his lap, almost dumping her on the floor. Stomping about the room, he muttered to himself, occasionally shooting her a cutting glare.

"It all comes back to trust again with you, doesn't it, Ingrith?"

"That is so unfair. You told me yourself that we could never marry because eventually, if we continued having sex like rabbits, you would forget to withdraw. And that is exactly what happened yesterday. Can you not see, I was protecting you."

"So, you did it all for love of me?"

Tears were streaming down her face now, but he appeared untouched by her pain. She nodded.

"I know how difficult it is for you to accept passing on your possibly tainted blood to a child. I wanted to spare you."

"Instead, you would be the one always on the alert for signs in our child."

She homed in with pleasure on the way he said "our" child. "I would not care. Honestly. Mayhap it is naive of me, but I believe I could love the madness out of him . . . or her."

"And you do not think I could do the same?"

"Well . . . you said . . . I mean . . ." She was flustered and not sure how to answer.

"Things change, Ingrith," he said tiredly. "People change. You should have given me a chance to decide for myself. I kept telling you, ever since I got here, that there were things I needed to discuss with you." An idea seemed to come unbidden to him. "You thought I would force you to abort my child. Oh, God! You did, didn't you? What kind of monster do you think I am?"

She tried to rise from the bed, but her knees were shaky, and she sat back on the edge. Her head hurt, and she felt weary to the soul. "I need to lie down," she said.

Immediately solicitous, he helped her into the bed and covered her with a light blanket. "Are you all right? Do I need to get a midwife or one of your sisters?"

She shook her head. "I just get tired easily."

"And stress does not help," he said ruefully.

She nodded. "What do we do now?"

"We get married. Sooner than I planned."

"Oh, John! I hate that I am trapping you like this."

"Ingrith, you forget. I asked you to marry me afore I knew about the babe."

He was at the door, about to leave, when what she wanted . . . what she needed . . . was for him to crawl into the small bed with her and hold her. Just hold her.

Instead, he pointed a finger at her and snarled, "Do not think of leaving Stoneheim, let alone this bedchamber. I will chase you to the ends of the earth."

She gulped, the tears coming fast and furious again.

"And do not delude your foolish self that I am angry over the baby. I am angry over your lack of trust in me. I am angry that your love is so shallow. I am angry that I was a hairsbreadth away from losing all that is important to me. I am just bloody damn angry."

On those words, he left her alone and miserable. And tired. So very tired.

CHAPTER TWENTY-ONE

☆

A man can only be pushed so far . . .

John was so worked up he had to let out steam. So, he let himself be talked into swordplay exercises with Rafn, who was half a head taller and several stones heavier than he was. But anger fueled him, and he nigh beat the Viking to the ground.

"So, wouldst like to unburden yourself, Saxon?" Rafn asked as they relaxed over a cup of ale.

"Ingrith is pregnant."

"Congratulations." Rafn didn't seem surprised, though he must be.

"And she had no intention of telling me."

"Uh-oh!"

"I do not understand women."

"Really? I imagine your Christian Adam said the same thing to the snake in the Garden of Eden afore eating the forbidden apple. A wise man once told me there are two ways to understand a woman, and neither of them works."

"I am going to be a father," he said with a wide grin.

"Yea, you are," Rafn said, clapping him across the shoulders.

"I ne'er thought I would be, or could be," he said, and explained all that had happened with his father and with Ingrith.

"Seems to me that you and Ingrith just need to talk."

"Which is what I've been trying to do since I got here."

Rafn nodded.

"She says that she didn't tell me because she loves me."

"Typical woman illogic," Rafn opined. "Wait 'til she is farther in her pregnancy and waddles around like a duck the size of a warhorse, then asks if her rump is too big. Bit of advice: Do not answer."

"*What* did you say?" Vana had come up behind them and stood with her hands on her wide hips afore slapping Rafn over the head with a dusting cloth.

He grabbed for her and forced her to sit on his lap. "Good news, Vana. Ingrith is pregnant."

"Rafn!" John and Vana both said at the same time, he because he did not want the news to spread in this fashion, and Vana because she was surprised.

"Oh, I cannot wait to plan the wedding. There will be a wedding, won't there?" She narrowed her eyes at John in an adorable threatening fashion, like a puppy threatening a boar.

"There will definitely be a wedding. Soon."

"Not too soon," Vana said. "There is much to be planned. Guests to invite. Food, drink, games, gifts."

"Uh, I was thinking we could just stand before a priest, or whoever Ingrith would want to administer the vows. No big fuss!"

Rafn just laughed while Vana glared at him.

"A wedding. Whose wedding?" King Thorvald asked in passing.

John put his face in his hands. He was not ready for this. He wanted to nurture his hurt and anger a bit longer.

"Ingrith is pregnant," Vana announced.

The old king's face went florid. "You got my little girl with child, you spineless Saxon cur. We should beat him to a pulp, Rafn."

"He already tried to beat *me* to a pulp," Rafn said with a grin, rubbing at his sore chin.

"When is the wedding?" Thorvald asked, sitting down next to John on the bench, way too close.

"As soon as possible," he said.

"Not for at least a month," Vana said.

"Is she willing?" the king wanted to know.

"Not very."

"Does not matter." The king laughed, raising a hand to a passing maid to give him a cup of ale.

"Seems you took my advice to handle your courtship in the Viking manner."

Seems he did, though he had not known it at the time.

"Take the maid, seduce her later," Thorvald explained to Ragn and Vana, the former amused, the latter not amused.

"The maid declines."

They all looked up to see Ingrith standing in the doorway, glaring at each of them in turn.

"Now, daughter—" King Thorvald began.

She raised a hand. "I am not going to be rushed into marriage."

"Rushed?" the king roared. "You are almost thirty and one years old. More like dragging your feet, if you ask me. I am thinking 'tis time for a rip-roaring Viking style wedding here at Stoneheim. Enough ale to sink a longboat. Dancing. Singing. Wrestling. Horse racing. Head butting."

"Don't forget *lygisogur*," Rafn offered unhelpfully. To John he explained, "Lying stories. We Norsemen do like to tell tall sagas."

"How soon can your mother and stepfather get here?" King Thorvald asked John. "We must sit down and negotiate the marriage terms. Ingrith may be long in the tooth, but she still carries a vast dowry. Best you be thinking about your *morgen gifu*, as well. The morning-gift you provide for Ingrith is not just to show how well pleased you are with her performance. 'Tis part of the marriage settlements."

"Whatever you say," John agreed.

Ingrith glared at him.

"What? You want me to disagree with your father?" John said.

"I want you to go away."

"Nay, you do not, Ingrith. You love me."

Ingrith let out a hiss of displeasure. "You should discuss these things with me first."

John studied her closely. Her rest had apparently rejuvenated her. The old snapping Ingrith was back. Good. He relished a good fight, especially in his present mood. He had had more than enough of the games she'd been playing, making a fool of him. From the time she'd first arrived at Hawk's Lair with the orphans in tow, she had been attempting to control their relationship. Thought she could lead him about like a bull with a ring in its nose. Well, he had news for her. This bull was breaking loose.

"Dost finally want to talk, Ingrith?" he asked. The menace in his voice should have forewarned her. Standing, he walked over, picked her up by the waist, and tossed her over his shoulder. "Then let us go talk."

As he stomped off to find a private room, with Ingrith screeching and kicking, he heard Thorvald say, "Are you sure he's not a Viking?

Sometimes a man's just gotta be a man . . .

"Put me down, you big oaf."

Ingrith slapped and kicked and called him names she'd never spoken aloud before. To no avail. He would not release her until they had reached his guest bedchamber and then he only let her drop to her feet, keeping a hold on her around her waist.

She shoved away and walked to the other side of the small room. He used that opportunity to close and lock the door.

"All right, so you want to talk," she said. "Talk."

"I've changed my mind. We will talk later."

She tilted her head to the side.

"Take off your garments, Ingrith. I would see my bride's new body."

She gasped at his order. "I am not your bride yet. Mayhap I will never be. And, nay, I will not take off my garments."

"You either take them off, or I tear them off. Your choice."

"Here," she said, raising her gown to show a pair of linen small clothes. "You may see my belly."

He laughed. "How generous of you! Take off the damn clothes. All of them."

She thought about balking, but knew when the battle was lost. Removing her apron and *gunna*, she turned away from him to lower the thigh-high small breeches she'd taken to wearing since her pregnancy. Her nether parts got cool here in the North, and, though it probably made no sense, she felt as if she was keeping her baby warm.

When she was done, he said, "Turn." His voice was raspy, as if he were overcome with emotion.

She did.

As he circled her, he talked, "My mother and stepfather came to Hawk's Lair. I learned things about my father I ne'er knew."

Despite her embarrassment at being naked and examined thoroughly, she was curious. "About his insanity?"

"'Twould seem that the insanity was not inbred." He was lifting her breasts from underneath, as if weighing the difference in them. Then he sank to his knees in front of her, touching her belly with reverence. "I would not have known you were pregnant from this alone, Ingrith. 'Tis just a small bump." He glanced up at her and smiled . . . a smile so enticing she almost swooned. "Our baby."

He kissed her stomach and then tongue-kissed her down lower. Just a fleeting flick of his tongue, but enough that her legs folded and she joined him on her knees.

"Tell me more about your father," she said to keep herself from melting into a puddle of arousal.

"He was tortured mercilessly since he was a small child. Unspeakable things were done to him. I know this because I went to visit my uncle Elwinus, a monk, who told me of the early years."

Even as he talked, he was kissing her shoulders, the tops of her breasts, her fingertips.

"Stop it," she demanded. "How can you talk and do *that* at the same time? I cannot concentrate."

He chuckled and rose to his feet, taking her with him.

Once he'd laid her on the bed and settled himself on his side leaning over her, he continued, "So, 'twould seem that I can wed and have children after all."

Unable to wait for more prolonged foresport, he was already sliding into her when he made that statement.

"Oh. Oh. Oh." She made puffing sounds trying to delay her peaking. "Say that again."

"We can wed and have children." He pressed hot kisses against her mouth and moved ever so slowly in and out of her spasming channel. "I love the way you do that, heartling."

"Do what?" she gasped out. He was touching her breasts, breathing into her ear, and plunging into her in such a way that each downstroke touched a throbbing ache in her slick folds.

"Fist me in welcome."

She realized then what he had told her. Important news. And not about the fisting. She slapped his shoulder. "Why did you not tell me as soon as you got here?"

"As if you would let me!" He laughed against her neck, and she felt the ripples all through her body, down to his cock that rippled inside of her. A laugh tup, she decided. She liked it.

"Will you marry me, Ingrith?" he asked as his strokes became shorter and harder.

"Do I have a choice?" She had peaked twice already and could feel another approaching.

"None whatsoever." He smiled at her.

"Have I told you what your smile does to me?"

"Tell me again."

When his excitement grew to such a pitch that she could feel it even inside her body, he slammed into her one last time, declaring, "I love you, Ingrith." And he spilled his seed where it was meant to be.

Later, as she stroked his back and kissed his neck, she said, "I love you, too, John. Forever."

"What would you like for a *morgen gifu*, heartling?" he asked, after they'd made love a second time. "I figure we have already had our morning after, several times, and I am well pleased."

"I know exactly what I want," she said, raising herself to lean over him, pressing her fingertips to his kiss-swollen lips, "and it is not jewels or land. Not even precious spices."

He arched his brows at her. "What shall I give you, then?"

"A rose garden."

Time goes slow when you're not having fun . . .

It took four more sennights before they could exchange vows, to Ingrith's chagrin because of her growing bump and to John's chagrin because he'd been forbidden to tup Ingrith until after the wedding ceremony under threat of having a special body part lopped off. And, of course, it had to be on a Friday, or Frigg's Day, as if it mattered what day of the week it was!

"I will look like a ship's prow by then," Ingrith complained to him in one of the rare moments they'd managed to be alone.

"It will only be a few more days," he said, "and a person could hardly tell you are breeding."

"Liar!" she said, punching him in the arm. "I am almost four and a half months pregnant, you idiot."

"Wear a big apron," he advised.

She gave him one of her looks that told him what he could do with his advice.

"By the by, here is the first of my *arrha* gifts to you." He took her right hand and slipped the heavy gold band with the embossed hawk onto the third finger. "After the wedding ceremony, you move this to your left hand. That will be a sign of your coming obedience to me."

"Hah!" she said, "I will keep this beautiful ring, but let us just say that instead of obedience I will give you good counsel. Besides, I have a gift for you, too." She opened a fabric-wrapped bundle she'd been carrying and handed him a soft leather half-boot."

"One boot?" He raised his brows at her.

"Yea, I will slap you over the head with it during the wedding ceremony as a sign of *my* authority.

Then on our wedding night I will put the other shoe on my side of the bed as a sign of *my* authority." She grinned at him.

"Hah!" He grinned, too. "Let us agree that neither will have authority over the other." *Except in certain matters where I demand to be in charge.*

She nodded hesitantly, not sure he was serious.

But they were wasting time when they could be having near-sex, something he'd become proficient at these past sennights. He pulled her down beside him on a bench facing a back garden . . . a magnificent garden, thanks to Drifa's talent with plants. She'd already dug up dozens of rosebushes for him to take back to Northumbria once they got through this bloody wedding. "All those plants Drifa dug up for me will be dead afore I manage to get back home," he griped.

"'Tis your fault it is taking so long," Ingrith said.

"How so?" he asked and at the same time lifted her up to straddle his lap.

"Ooh, I do not know about this," she said on a groan, even as she wiggled her rump to get more comfortable.

"I do," he said, then changed the subject, not wanting to talk about whether they should or should not be enjoying a bit of sexsport, *bit* being the key word. "I had to agree to wait until my mother and stepfather could come, if that is what you refer to. My mother would never forgive me if I got married without her. Then they decided to stop off at the monastery for Father Elwinus. Wasn't it nice of him to get a special dispensation to come to Norselands to administer the rites?"

"Very nice," she said, but he wasn't sure if she was remarking on Father Elwinus or the fact that he'd bared his cock and rucked up her *gunna* so that he was riding her moist folds. Not inside; he'd made a promise, after all. You could say it was a non-tup. And Ingrith . . . by the saints! . . . With a talent only she could pull off, she kept talking while he was channel thrusting. "And your stepsisters and their husbands. Do not forget them."

"Do not be so fussy, Ingrith. Your sisters and their husbands came, too. And every bloody Viking in the Norselands is here, as well. Aaaah, that is the way. Twist from side to side. Just like that. Bloody hell! Where did you learn that?"

"Vikings do love a feast. Father expects five hundred in all," she said, ignoring what he was doing down below and blathering on about wedding preparations.

"Well, I am not going to wear that red tunic my mother made for me. I will tell you that right now."

"You have to. It matches the trim on my wedding garments."

"There are roses on the tunic, Ingrith. Gold embroidered roses! Men do not wear flowers."

"Would you rather it were bees?"

"Hell, nay!"

"Roses, then. Please," she begged.

"What will you do for me if I agree?"

"How about this?" And the witch did something with the muscles between her legs that had him peaking instantly. Not that she wasn't matching him in peaking. They were both panting and moaning their ecstasy within seconds.

"Well?" she asked when their breathing returned to normal and her head rested on his shoulders. She still straddled his lap.

"If you do that another time or five, I would wear anything you asked, even a *gunna*."

She laughed and kissed his neck.

"What was that?" he asked, straightening to glance downward.

"What?"

"Your belly moved."

"Oh, that! I think that was little Ingrith."

"Or little John."

She put a hand over his hand on her stomach, and they stared at each other with wonder. Whoever would have thought the two of them would reach this point?

"Have I told you lately that I adore you?" he asked, his voice thick with emotion.

"Not nearly enough," she said, swiping at the tears that rimmed her eyes. She did a lot of that lately due to the pregnancy, that and piss a lot. He'd learned not to remark about either. "Did I tell you that, if it's a boy, Father wants to gift him a longship?"

"And if it's a girl . . ."

"A longship, too. I insisted on equal treatment."

He laughed. God, how he enjoyed his soon-to-be bride. "Let us go finalize this wedding afore they keep adding more festivities and inviting more people," he said, helping her off his lap, then standing. "At this rate we'll be here 'til Christmas, and I want our child to be born at Hawk's Lair."

CHAPTER TWENTY-TWO

✧

*They were party animals before party animals were
invented . . .*

John had never seen anything like it in all his
thirty-one years. He'd attended many a wild feast
in the past, but this wedding of his to a Norse
princess boggled the senses.

Good thing it was a balmy autumn day, because
he didn't know what they would have done with
the five hundred or more guests standing about the
fields normally used for military exercises. Today,
there was an enormous tent with an unusual trel-
lis, which had been built by Ingrith's sister Breanne
and decorated profusely with roses by Drifa.

Standing behind him were his witnesses . . .
an ungodly number. Eirik, Hamr, Rafn, Bolthor,
his two brothers-by-marriage, his Uncle Tykir.
Not to be surpassed were Ingrith's witnesses. Her
four sisters, including Vana, holding week-old
baby Baldr, his mother, his Aunt Alinor, and Bolthor's wife, Katherine. Hamr had wanted to bring

Joanna, but fortunately had the good sense not to do so in the end.

They'd already been wed according to Christian rites by his uncle, Father Elwinus, early that morning, but now would come the elaborate Norse wedding ceremony. When he'd asked the monk if he objected to their exchanging vows in both religions, Elwinus had shrugged. "As long as there are no pagan blood sacrifices."

Well, there would definitely be no sacrifices per se, but a huge number of animals had already been sacrificed for the feast to come. Twelve boars, ten red deer, fifty chickens, twenty rabbits, and enough fish to fill a fjord. Even a black bear had given its life for the benefit of their wedding. Ingrith had been in kitchen heaven for days now, supervising all the various dishes.

But wait, everyone was turning around. Ingrith had left the castle and was now heading toward them on her father's arm. And what a beautiful sight she was!

A lump formed in his throat, and he could scarce breathe.

Mine, he thought, and his heart truly overflowed with the joy of that knowledge.

She wore a gauzy white linen *gunna*, ankle length in front and trailing in pleats behind. The rounded neck and wrists had crimson silk bands embroidered with gold-thread roses. Over that was the traditional Norse apron, except this one was a sumptuous crimson, edged with white bands with gold roses. On her head was an enormous headdress made of woven straw, silver mesh, ribands, and lace. Her golden hair was loose today, but would be worn up in future, except in her husband's bed. He liked the idea of that.

The crimson of Ingrith's garments matched his crimson tunic . . . and, yea, he had agreed to wear it, and it was crimson, not mere red, he'd been corrected repeatedly. It, too, was edged with bands of embroidered roses. Who ever heard of a man wearing flowers? But no one would listen to his protests, except Rafn, who couldn't stop smirking. Oh, well, John did want to please Ingrith. At least his slim breeches and boots were black, and the only other adornments were a gold-linked belt.

As they got closer, he smiled at Ingrith, and she smiled back, nervously. Hah! She should put a hand to his thumping heart.

He linked his fingers with hers, and they both turned to face her father, who would act as lawspeaker and a minister of sorts today. The old man looked magnificent in royal blue with enough jewels adorning his beard and side braids to sink a ship.

King Thorvald raised his arms high and said, "Hear ye, gods and One-God, friends and family. Come join us today in witness to the wedding of John of Hawk's Lair, Lord Gravely, and Princess Ingrith of Stoneheim."

On a table in front of them was a goblet of red wine, a bowl of barley seeds, an amber-studded knife, a silver cord, a hammer similar to that of Thor's *Mjollnir*, and a round stone the size of a fist. John had rehearsed his part in the ceremony to come.

First, John took the cup in hand and took a sip of the heady brew, stating in his own revised version of the Norse rite, "From this nectar may Ingrith and I be filled with wisdom from the heavenly well of knowledge so that we may deal well with each other in the future."

He placed the cup at her lips so she would drink from the same spot. After drinking, she said, "From this nectar may we be filled with the wisdom of the gods and may John recognize that betimes I have the greater knowledge."

The crowd laughed. Her father frowned. And John pinched her buttock.

After that, the king took a handful of the seeds and tossed some on her shoulders, some on his, and the rest over his shoulder, praying, "Freyja, goddess of fertility, bless this union with sons and prosperity."

"Fertility!" John murmured. "I don't think that will be a problem."

And she murmured with chagrin, "How about daughters?"

Her father murmured, "Both of you, shut your teeth, lest I tell you otherwise."

Ingrith gifted John with a new sword then, on

the tip of which was a gold wedding band. He gave his sword to her as well, in keeping for their firstborn son.

John took her hand then so that both of their wrists were exposed upward. The king took the knife and speedily made a shallow slit in both their wrists, which he bound together, wrist to wrist, with the silver cord.

At the king's nod, John began to repeat his vows, "As my blood melds with yours today, Ingrith, so too shall my seed." Under his breath, he whispered for her ears only, "Methinks my seed has already done enough melding, don't you?"

She squeezed his hand hard and whispered, "Behave."

He continued with his vow, "With this mingling of our blood, I pledge thee my troth . . ."

It was her turn to repeat the vow, and she did so with a clear voice. "With this mingling of our blood, I pledge thee my troth."

"From the beginning of time to the end of time . . ."

"From the beginning of time to the end of time . . . ," she repeated.

". . . let it be known that I, John of Hawk's Lair, give my heart to thee, Ingrith of Stoneheim."

And she said, " . . . let it be known that I, Ingrith of Stoneheim, give my heart to thee, John of Hawk's Lair."

John took the hammer then and lifted it high, bringing it down to crush the stone. "Like Thor, the god of thunder and his mighty hammer *Mjoll-nir*, I will protect my wife from all peril. Her foe will be my foe. She is now under my shield."

"And he's under mine, too," Ingrith quickly added, although it wasn't part of the rites as told to John earlier.

"It is done!" the king yelled, and a loud cheer resounded through the crowd.

John kissed Ingrith then. Hungrily. And he didn't care who was watching.

"You are mine," he said.

"And you are mine," she said back.

Now, came the good part. The feasting. But first the *brudh hlaup*, or bride running. Ingrith had already lifted the hem of her gown and was running toward the keep. He soon caught up and overtook her and laid his sword at the threshold. If she stepped over the sword, it would indicate that she accepted her new status as his wife. He leaned against the doorjamb, arms folded over his chest, ankles crossed, grinning at her lazily.

Would she balk, or would she yield?

She pretended to hesitate, then jumped over into his arms. He twirled her around with happiness, burying his face in her scented neck. The headdress fell to the floor, but they could not care. They were joined now. One. Forever.

"I love you," he said, drawing back to look at her.

"I love you, too," she said, tears of happiness running down her cheeks.

Much later after innumerable toasts, good food and drink, dancing, and music, Bolthor stood. He of course had a poem to celebrate the festivities. At first, he had wanted to write a *mansongr*, a special kind of love poem, but John and Ingrith had both objected. Instead, they got his ode to their particular wedding.

Once was a Saxon lad
Thought he was a bit mad.
Came a Viking miss
Soon learned what was amiss.

He fought, he did rail,
He drank too much ale.
But alas and alack
He eventually did crack.

Because who can deny
That when it comes to a woman's thigh
And a Viking one at that
A Saxon man's good intentions go splat.

The moral of this saga is:
When a Viking woman wants a man,
He is hers.
But more important,
What she does not know is that
He intended to have her all along.

On a blustery winter day in Northumbria, almost four months later, a baby was born at Hawk's Lair, following a ten-hour labor. It was a black-haired, blue-eyed girling, as her father had predicted. He wept when he first held the baby in his arms, warm from Ingrith's womb.

They named her Rose.

READER LETTER

❦

Dear Reader:

Hey, four princesses down and one more to go! What did you think of Ingrith's story? And how about John of Hawk's Lair? His story was a long time coming.

I've said before and will repeat . . . you've gotta love a Viking. And I especially do because I have Viking in my blood, all the way back to my many-times-removed great-grandfather, Rolf the Ganger, first duke of Normandy (Norsemandy), in the tenth century.

My own grandfather was named Magnus.

I hope you were not put off by the birth-control issue in this book. Believe me, men were trying to prevent conception way back before the time of Christ. Heck, cavemen might even have tried it. I know this is true because I was sitting at a writers' conference one time when the woman next to me asked what I was writing. Flippantly, I told her that my book was about a modern woman going back in time to help Viking women make homemade condoms. This very conservative-looking woman just looked at me and said, "Oh? And have you been to the condom museum?" Turns out she was the curator of an honest-to-God condom museum in Canada. Later, she sent me posters of the history of birth control and condoms. My son who opened that particular mail tube was amused, telling me, "My mother won't let me listen to heavy metal music, and yet she has heavy rubber posters!"

Keep in mind that *The Viking Takes a Knight* is a sequel of sorts to a loosely linked series (stand-alone books that can be read out of order). Most recently, there was *Viking in Love*, Breanne's story. But before that there were *The Reluctant Viking*, *The Outlaw Viking*, *The Tarnished Lady*, *The Bewitched Viking*, *The Blue Viking*, *My Fair Viking* (Tyra's story), and *A Tale of Two Vikings*. These books should be back in print soon, if they are not already available.

Please visit my website at www.sandrahill.net for news of old and upcoming books, genealogy charts, videos, freebies, and other good stuff. I'd love to know your views of my books and what you'd like to see next.

As always, I wish you smiles in your reading.

Sandra Hill

GLOSSARY

Arrha—a series of gifts given by the bridegroom to the
     bride; money or valuable things given to seal any
     contract.
Asgard—home of the gods.
Braies—slim pants worn by men.
Brudh gumarind—the bridegroom's ride.
Brudh hlaup—the bride running.
Brynja—chain-mail shirt.
Burh (or burgh)—fortresses or fortified towns built
     in strategic locations throughout Britain, first
     ordered by King Alfred, circa a.d. 871. Eventually
     they became known as towns. The name burh
     became burgh, then bury, then borough. So, any
     modern town with that suffix usually means it was
     an original fortified town dating back a thousand
     years.
Castellan—one who oversees a castle in the absence of
     the castle's lord.
Companaticum—"that which goes with bread," which
     usually meant whatever was in the stockpot of thick
     broth always simmering in the huge kitchen caul-
     dron. Usually with chunks of meat. Unfortunately,
     not cleaned out for long periods of time.
Coppergate—a busy, prosperous section of tenth-century

York (known then as Jorvik or Eoforic) where merchants and craftsmen set up their stalls for trading.

Drukkin (or drukkinn)—drunk, in Old Norse.

Ealdorman—a royal official who presided over shire courts and carried out royal commands within his domain. Comparable to later earls.

Ell—a measure, usually of cloth, equaling 45 inches.

Encaustum—tenth-century type of ink made by crushing the galls from an oak tree (boil-like pimples on the bark) which contain an acid. Mixed with vinegar or rainwater, the substance was thickened with gum arabic. Iron salts added color to the ink.

Hectares (of land)—equal to about two and a half acres.

Hide—a primitive measure of land, equaling the normal holding that would support a peasant and his family, roughly 120 arable acres.

Hird—permanent troops.

Housecarl—part of the permanent troops assigned to a king or nobleman.

Jorvik—Viking word for Viking-Age York, known by the Saxons and Romans as Eoforic.

Lygisogur—lying stories.

Mancus/es (of gold)—equal to six shillings.

Mansongr—maiden song or love poem.

Minna—an Old Norse term meaning literally "memory," but came to be used to indicate a "memorial cup or toast."

Morgen gifu—the morning gift given by a bridegroom the day after the wedding to show that he was well pleased. In fact, the bride price consisted of three parts: the mundr and morgen gifu given by the groom or his family and the heiman flygia given by the bride's family to the groom.

Norsemandy—tenth-century name for Normandy.

Northumbria—one of the Anglo-Saxon kingdoms, bordered by the English kingdoms to the south and in the north and northwest by the Scots, Cumbrians, and Strathclyde Welsh.

Odal rights—laws of heredity.

Sennight—one week.

Skyrr (or skyr)—soft cheese similar to cottage cheese.

Sulung—area that could be kept under cultivation by a single plough team of eight oxen, equal to two hides.

Sumbel—a Viking practice of passing around a drinking cup at a feast whereby each recipient was expected to make a toast or a boast, sing a song, or recite a story.

Thrall—slave.

Valhalla—Odin's hall, where Viking warriors who die in battle spend eternity.

Valkyries—female warriors.

Wattle and daub—early method of building.

Wergild (or wergeld)—a man's worth.

Witan, or witenagemot—the king's council of advisors, precursor to the English Parliament.

Can't get enough of *USA Today* and *New York Times* bestselling author Sandra Hill?
Turn the page for glimpses of her amazing books. From cowboys to Vikings, Navy SEALs to Southern bad boys, every one of Sandra's books has her unique blend of passion, creativity, and unparalleled wit.

Welcome to the World of Sandra Hill!

The Viking Takes a Knight

For John of Hawk's Lair, the unexpected appearance of a beautiful woman at his door is always welcome. Yet the arrival of this alluring Viking woman, Ingrith Sigrundottir—with her enchanting smile and inviting curves—is different . . . for she comes accompanied by a herd of unruly orphans. And Ingrith needs more than the legendary knight's hospitality; she needs protection. For among her charges is a small boy with a claim to the throne—a dangerous distinction when murderous King Edgar is out hunting for Viking blood.

A man of passion, John will keep them safe— but in exchange, he wants something very dear indeed: Ingrith's heart, to be taken with the very first meeting of their lips . . .

Viking in Love

❧

Caedmon of Larkspur was the most loathsome lout
Breanne had ever encountered. When she
arrived at his castle with her sisters, they were
greeted by an estate gone wild, while Caedmon
laid abed after a night of ale. But Breanne must
endure, as they are desperately in need of protection . . . and he is quite handsome.

After nine long months in the king's service, all
Caedmon wanted was peace, not five Viking princesses running about his keep. And the fiery red-
head who burst into his chamber was the worst of
them all. He should kick her out, but he has a far
better plan for Breanne of Stoneheim—one that
will leave her a Viking in lust.

The Reluctant Viking

☙

The self-motivation tape was supposed to help Ruby Jordan solve her problems, not create new ones. Instead, she was lulled into an era of hard-bodied warriors and fair maidens. But the world ten centuries in the past didn't prove to be all mead and mirth. Even as Ruby tried to update medieval times, she had to deal with a Norseman whose view of women was stuck in the Dark Ages. And what was worse, brawny Thork had her husband's face, habits, and desire to avoid Ruby. Determined not to lose the same man twice, Ruby planned a bold seduction that would conquer the reluctant Viking—and make him an eager captive of her love.

The Outlaw Viking

❧

As tall and striking as the Valkyries of legend, Dr. Rain Jordan was proud of her Norse ancestors despite their warlike ways. But she can't believe it when she finds herself on a nightmarish battlefield, forced to save the barbarian of her dreams.

He was a wild-eyed warrior whose deadly sword could slay a dozen Saxons with a single swing, yet Selik couldn't control the saucy wench from the future. If Selik wasn't careful, the stunning siren was sure to capture his heart and make a warrior of love out of **The Outlaw Viking**.

The Tarnished Lady

Banished from polite society, Lady Eadyth of Hawk's Lair spent her days hidden under a voluminous veil, tending her bees. But when her lands are threatened, Lady Eadyth sought a husband to offer her the protection of his name.

Notorious for loving—and leaving—the most beautiful damsels in the land, Eirik of Ravenshire was England's most virile bachelor. Yet when the mysterious lady offered him a vow of chaste matrimony in exchange for revenge against his most hated enemy, Eirik couldn't refuse. But the lusty knight's plans went awry when he succumbed to the sweet sting of the tarnished lady's love.

The Bewitched Viking

Even fierce Norse warriors have bad days. 'Twas enough to drive a sane Viking mad, the things Tykir Thorksson was forced to do—capturing a red-headed virago, putting up with the flock of sheep that follows her everywhere, chasing off her bumbling brothers. But what could a man expect from the sorceress who had put a kink in the King of Norway's most precious body part? If that wasn't bad enough, Tykir was beginning to realize he wasn't at all immune to the enchantment of brash red hair and freckles. Perhaps he could reverse the spell and hold her captive, not with his mighty sword, but with a Viking man's greatest magic: a wink and smile.

The Blue Viking

✧

*F*or Rurik the Viking, life has not been worth living since he left Maire of the Moors. Oh, it's not that he misses her fiery red tresses or kissable lips. Nay, it's the embarrassing blue zigzag tattoo she put on his face after their one wild night of loving. For a fierce warrior who prides himself on his immense height, his expertise in bedsport, and his well-toned muscles, this blue streak is the last straw. In the end, he'll bring the witch to heel, or die trying. Mayhap he'll even beg her to wed . . . so long as she can promise he'll no longer be . . . **The Blue Viking**.

The Viking's Captive

(originally titled MY FAIR VIKING)

☙

yra, Warrior Princess. She is too tall, too loud, too fierce to be a good catch. But her ailing father has decreed that her four younger sisters—delicate, mild-mannered, and beautiful—cannot be wed 'til Tyra consents to take a husband. And then a journey to save her father's life brings Tyra face to face with Adam the Healer. A god in human form, he's tall, muscled, perfectly proportioned. Too bad Adam refuses to fall in with her plans—so what's a lady to do but truss him up, toss him over her shoulder, and sail off into the sunset to live happily ever after.

A Tale of Two Vikings

⸙

*T*oste *and Vagn Ivarsson are identical Viking twins*, about to face Valhalla together, following a tragic battle, or maybe something even more tragic: being separated for the first time in their thirty and one years. Alas, even the bravest Viking must eventually leave his best buddy behind and do battle with that most fearsome of all opponents—the love of his life. And what if that love was Helga the Homely, or Lady Esme, the world's oldest novice nun?

A Tale of Two Vikings will give you twice the tears, twice the sizzle, and twice the laughter . . . and make you wish for your very own Viking.

The Last Viking

✥

*H*e was six feet, four inches of pure, unadulterated male. He wore nothing but a leather tunic, and he was standing in Professor Meredith Foster's living room. The medieval historian told herself he was part of a practical joke, but with his wide gold belt, ancient language, and callused hands, the brawny stranger seemed so . . . authentic. And as he helped her fulfill her grandfather's dream of re-creating a Viking ship, he awakened her to dreams of her own. Until she wondered if the hand of fate had thrust her into the loving arms of . . . **The Last Viking**.

Truly, Madly Viking

ᛦ

A Viking named Joe? Jorund Ericsson is a tenth-century Viking warrior who lands in a modern mental hospital. Maggie McBride is the lucky psychologist who gets to "treat" the gorgeous Norseman, whom she mistakenly calls Joe.

You've heard of *One Flew Over the Cuckoo's Nest*. But how about *A Viking Flew Over the Cuckoo's Nest*? The question is: Who's the cuckoo in this nest? And why is everyone laughing?

The Very Virile Viking

⊗

Magnus Ericsson is a simple man. He loves the smell of fresh-turned dirt after springtime plowing. He loves the feel of a soft woman under him in the bed furs. He loves the heft of a good sword in his fighting arm.

But, Holy Thor, what he does not relish is the bothersome brood of children he's been saddled with. Or the mysterious happenstance that strands him in a strange new land—the kingdom of *Holly Wood*. Here is a place where the folks think he is an *act-whore* (whatever that is), and the woman of his dreams—a winemaker of all things—fails to accept that he is her soul mate . . . a man of exceptional talents, not to mention . . . **A Very Virile Viking.**

Wet & Wild

ॐ

What do you get when you cross a Viking with a Navy SEAL? A warrior with the fierce instincts of the past and the rigorous training of America's most elite fighting corps? A totally buff hero-in-the-making who hasn't had a woman in roughly a thousand years? A dyed-in-the-wool romantic with a hopeless crush? Whatever you get, women everywhere can't wait to meet him, and his story is guaranteed to be . . . **Wet & Wild**.

Hot & Heavy

In and out, that's the goal as Lt. Ian MacLean prepares for his special ops mission. He leads a team of highly trained Navy SEALs, the toughest, buffest fighting men in the world and he has nothing to lose. Madrene comes from a time a thousand years before he was born, and she has no idea she's landed in the future. After tying him up, the beautiful shrew gives him a tonguelashing that makes a drill sergeant sound like a kindergarten teacher. Then she lets him know she has her own special way of dealing with overconfident males, and things get . . . **Hot & Heavy**.

Frankly, My Dear . . .

&

*L*ost in the Bayou . . . Selene had three great passions: men, food, and *Gone with the Wind*. But the glamorous model always found herself starving—for both nourishment and affection. Weary of the petty world of high fashion, she headed to New Orleans for one last job before she began a new life. Little did she know that her new life would include a brand-new time—about 150 years ago! Selene can't get her fill of the food—or an alarmingly handsome man. Dark and brooding, James Baptiste was the only lover she gave a damn about. And with God as her witness, she vowed never to go without the man she loved again.

Sweeter Savage Love

ॐ

The stroke of surprisingly gentle hands, the flash of fathomless blue eyes, the scorch of white-hot kisses . . . Once again, Dr. Harriet Ginoza was swept away into rapturous fantasy. The modern psychologist knew the object of her desire was all she should despise, yet time after time, she lost herself in visions of a dangerously hand-some rogue straight out of a historical romance. Harriet never believed that her dream lover would cause her any trouble, but then a twist of fate cast her back to the Old South and she met him in the flesh. To her disappointment, Etienne Baptiste refused to fulfill any of her secret wishes. If Harriet had any hope of making her amorous dreams become passionate reality, she'd have to seduce this charmer with a sweeter savage love than she'd imagined possible . . . and savor every minute of it.

The Love Potion

☘

Fame and fortune are surely only a swallow away when Dr. Sylvie Fontaine discovers a chemical formula guaranteed to attract the opposite sex. Though her own love life is purely hypothetical, the shy chemist's professional future is assured . . . as soon as she can find a human guinea pig. But bad boy Lucien LeDeux—best known as the Swamp Lawyer—is more than she can handle even before he accidentally swallowed a love potion disguised in a jelly bean. When the dust settles, Luc and Sylvie have the answers to some burning questions—can a man die of testosterone overload? Can a straight-laced female lose every single one of her inhibitions?—and they learn that old-fashioned romance is still the best catalyst for love.

Love Me Tender

⊗

*O*nce upon a time, in a magic kingdom, there lived a handsome prince. Prince Charming, he was called by one and all. And to this land came a gentle princess. You could say she was Cinderella . . . Wall Street Cinderella. Okay, if you're going to be a stickler for accuracy, in this fairy tale the kingdom is Manhattan. But there's magic in the Big Apple, isn't there? And maybe he can be Prince Not-So-Charming at times, and "gentle" isn't the first word that comes to mind when thinking of this princess. But they're looking for happily ever after just the same—and they're going to get it.

Desperado

☙

Mistaken for a notorious bandit and his infamously scandalous mistress, L.A. lawyer Rafe Santiago and Major Helen Prescott found themselves on the wrong side of the law. In a time and place where rules had no meaning, Helen found Rafe's hard, bronzed body strangely comforting, and his piercing blue eyes left her all too willing to share his bedroll. His teasing remarks made her feel all woman, and she was ready to throw caution to the wind if she could spend every night in the arms of her very own . . . **Desperado.**

THE BLACK COBRA QUARTET
from *USA Today* bestselling author

STEPHANIE LAURENS

The Untamed Bride
978-0-06-179514-5

He is a man who has faced peril without flinching, determined to fight for king and country. She is a bold, beautiful woman with a scandalous past, destined to become an untamed bride.

The Elusive Bride
978-0-06-179515-2

He's focused on his mission, then sees a lady he never dreamed he'd see again—with an assassin on her heels. She secretly followed him, unaware her path is deadly— or that she'll join him to battle a treacherous foe.

The Brazen Bride
978-0-06-179517-6

Shipwrecked, wounded, he risks all to pursue his mission— only to discover a partner as daring and brazen as he. Fiery, tempestuous, a queen in her own realm, she rescues a warrior—only to find her heart under siege.

and coming soon

The Reckless Bride
978-0-06-179519-0

At Avon Books, we know your passion for romance—once you finish one of our novels, you find yourself wanting more.

May we tempt you with . . .

- **Excerpts** from our upcoming releases.
- **Entertaining extras,** including authors' personal photo albums and book lists.
- Behind-the-scenes **scoop** on your favorite characters and series.
- **Sweepstakes** for the chance to win free books, romantic getaways, and other fun prizes.
- **Writing tips** from our authors and editors.
- **Blog** with our authors and find out why they love to write romance.
- **Exclusive content** that's not contained within the pages of our novels.

Join us at
www.avonbooks.com

An Imprint of HarperCollinsPublishers
www.avonromance.com